ABANDONED

A SECOND CHANCE ROMANCE MYSTERY

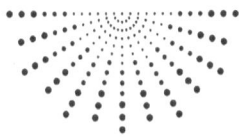

LYZ KELLEY

Belvitri
Services

A SPECIAL GIFT JUST FOR YOU.

I have a present for you…

…your very own ebook exclusive when you sign up for my newsletter.

Newsletter Sign Up:
https://geni.us/LyzKelleyFreeBook

CHAPTER ONE

*L*ife didn't ever go as planned. Ashley Bryant understood that better than most.

She never expected to bury her mother when she was only twenty-five years old. She never expected to be forced to liquidate her childhood home and mom's antique store. She never expected to have no one to guide or help her make decisions. She absolutely never expected to feel so lost and broken, shattered like her grandmother's delicate china and her mother's prized bird figurine, both now scattered across the floor.

Ashley knelt to pick up the precious broken wing and jerked back from the burn of sliced flesh. The sharp porcelain edge had cut deep into her finger, and blood flowed, spreading across her palm and mingling with the shattered porcelain on the floor. She sucked on the wound, soothing the stinging flesh.

Ashley scanned the front room of Time Capsule, her mother's antique store, looking for a way to stop the bleeding. *Ah, there it is.* The little red and white tin First Aid box sat on top of the curio cabinet, its corner peeking out from behind boxes filled with silver spoons, forks, and knives, out of reach.

Figures.

She gently placed the little wing on the table. A soul-aching melancholy seeped into her heart just as the store's front door cowbell clanked.

Go away. I've got so much to do, and the clock's ticking.

She groaned under her breath, only now remembering she should have removed the 'special event' sign from the day before. Peering around the tarnished, circa-eighteenth-century tea service, she inspected the customer.

Massive, broad shoulders and long, lean legs filled the front doorframe. She observed him while he pushed sunglasses to the top of his closely shaved head, his size and sheer masculine presence contrasting with the store's delicate china and lace. A contrast intensified by the way the black motorcycle jacket hugged his shoulders and the faded jeans hung low on his hips, making it clear there was nothing delicate about this man.

Ashley straightened her legs to stand. "I'm sorry, the store's no longer open. The closing sale ended yesterday."

He pointed a thumb over his shoulder. "I guess that means the 'apartment for rent' sign out front is no longer valid either."

She glanced toward the sun-faded sign that should have come down months ago, but was, in fact, still propped between the tattered Steiff bear and the Lionel train set.

No one had ever paid attention to the darn thing. She'd placed the sign in the window, hoping to add more income to her and her mother's joint and almost empty bank account.

After paying the remaining medical and cremation bills, Ashley could almost hear the pennies clinking against the edge of the bank account jar. Unfortunately, her mom's enormous medical debt had long since chipped away at the collection of antiques, collectables, and personal household items. Everything she or her mom owned that wasn't glued or bolted down was for sale. At least she'd managed to sell several items on eBay to get cash to cover the water heater going kaput. No matter what she sold, the money was never enough to cover expenses, and she refused to ask her father for a nickel.

Her frustration escalated, tightening the muscles in her neck. "My apologies. I should have removed the sign," she said, mostly because she'd just listed the apartment furniture, and was hoping someone would come by to make her an offer. Plus, she didn't have time to deal with another drop in an already overflowing must-do bucket. "There's a ski resort up the road. You should be able to find some lodging there."

He took a step closer and pocketed his keys. His gaze drifted over the quickly bundled hair piled on top of her head, to her favorite sweater, to her frayed jeans, and then settled on her hand. He pointed. "You need help with that?"

She studied the swelling red skin. After years of dealing with her mom's infected bedsores and catheters and daily injections, she could stomach a little blood.

"I'll see to it in a minute," she managed, proud of the fact she didn't swoon for lack of breakfast or his amazingly good looks. "Thanks for the offer."

He scanned the room at a leisurely pace, in no hurry to leave.

"Shopping for something? There are some Harley Davidson items over there in that glass cabinet, if you're interested. I don't figure you for a tea set kind of guy."

"No. Not a tea drinker. Why did you assume I was a Harley guy?"

"Steel-toed boots. Leather jacket. Just a guess."

"Gotcha."

"Why Elkridge, if you don't mind my asking?"

Until recently, nothing much ever happened in Elkridge. Occasionally, some kid would steal beer from the mini-mart, or the sheriff would drive a local home for being drunk or disorderly, or a moose might decide to walk down Main Street. Lately, there'd been some robberies, and nine months ago, the former sheriff was killed. A poacher, people assumed. Truth was, no one really knew for sure. People were scared, and a stranger showing up in Elkridge created questions. Questions like what had attracted him to the out-of-the-way town.

"Seemed a good place to start," he said with a bit of aloofness. "A buddy of mine recommended I stop here. He said the café had good food. The coffee's good. That much I know."

"If you come back through, you should plan to stop for lunch. Ted cooks up some good grub, and Jenna's pies are the best in the area."

He turned and leaned his beautifully muscled rump against the oak checkout counter. "You're making me hungry."

His smoky gaze and intense scrutiny made her feel a bit awkward.

Wishing she'd at least showered that morning, she fought hard not to tuck a flyaway hair behind her ear. His build and the farmer's tan beneath his open shirt collar said outdoor type, but the tan still seemed a bit odd since winter had come early. The way he filled the entryway indicated he was no stranger to physical labor.

His elegant face appeared chiseled from a block of aged oak. No emotion, no insight into what he was thinking. But his brown eyes spoke of sadness. She recognized the emotion, and could see the hurt, and wondered the cause. The softness conveyed he'd seen way too much in his short life. It was the sadness that drew her attention. That emotion she understood. The common awareness spread a soothing balm over her stretched nerves.

A kindred soul, maybe?

"You might also try Jenna's cinnamon rolls. They're really good," she added, volunteering the free advertising for her friends. She looked out the window, but didn't see anyone waiting. "Is your buddy with you?"

The way he pulled his ear when asked a personal question gave her the impression he didn't like to talk about himself much. She understood not wanting people messing in one's business. Although in a town as small as Elkridge, there wasn't much a person could keep secret.

Mr. Gorgeous, clearly uncomfortable with her small-town interrogation, shifted, crossed his arms, and gave her another once-over. "Nope. Just me. I thought I'd stick around until the holidays."

Holidays. New Year's. Only twenty-nine days away.

She didn't want to leave Elkridge, but she had only a handful of weeks before the bank foreclosed on her mother's house, January 1st, and put a padlock on the door and her life. Since she had no job and no place to live, being locked out of her home caused a brain-numbing panic. The crushing bleakness made her feel small and hesitant—even sad.

She loved Elkridge. Her hometown was nestled in a Colorado Rocky Mountain valley where the sky was blue three hundred days a year. The crisp, clean air smelled of fresh wild flowers and evergreens. The locals would say Elkridge had the tastiest rainbow trout and the best cross-country ski trails around. But it wasn't a tourist destination. It wasn't even a destination, and that most likely was the reason her parents' home had been on the market for close to seven months with no takers. Last week, she'd given the collector her father's contact information. He could deal with the belligerent calls and nastygrams.

The bank wouldn't listen to her pleas for more time, and delaying the inevitable wouldn't make a difference. She didn't have two coin wrappers to rub together. That gut-wrenching feeling sneaked in again and made her nauseous.

"If you're still in the area, there's a Christmas Bazaar here in a couple weeks. People come from all over to attend, and the town decorates a tree and we sing carols in the square. It makes everything festive," she said, trying to muster at least a semblance of cheer.

"Good to know."

And maybe I can show you around. Her chest tightened. *Geez.* Three years without sex made a woman desperate for human touch. But a one-night stand wouldn't solve her problems. Sure, she didn't want to be alone for the holidays. The truth was she didn't want to be alone, period.

Loneliness could wait, though. Right now she had to concentrate on the basics—food and shelter—and for both of those, she needed to stick to the plan. No distractions.

Mr. Sexy was certainly a distraction.

"If you keep going up the highway, there are some historical sites which have nice photo opportunities," she added.

His eyes darkened and sparkled like a newly polished stone. "It sure is pretty here."

The way he studied her, he was talking about her, not the mountain ridges looming over the valley walls.

"Yes, it is," she said, echoing his meaning.

A DROP of her blood dripped onto the floor, and Chase scanned her for signs of shock.

"Before I go, I'd like to check your hand. From here it doesn't look good," Gunnery Sergeant Chase Daniels offered.

"Really, it's not necessary."

Her chin lifted with a stubborn little attitude, the spunky kind of attitude he liked. Then her expression glazed. She had the same bewildered look Jimmy had after he'd taken three bullets and had no idea he was about to go down. Jimmy, the lucky bastard, had somehow managed to talk his way out of a death-sentence.

Her attention locked on her hand and she started to sway.

He hustled around the large, weathered oak table and wrapped his arm around her waist, which startled a wide-eyed peep from her. He guided her to the nearest stack of boxes and helped her sit. "Put your head between your knees," he instructed in a calm, no-nonsense tone. "Stay with me and let me take a look."

Her pulse pounded against his thumb. "That slice is deep. Where's your first aid kit?"

"On the cabinet."

She pointed at a little tin box, and then

propped her head against her uninjured hand and gave him a monumental view of her top assets. He shouldn't have looked, but he'd been in a desert, sucking sand for eleven months. Looking wasn't just an option; it was a requirement.

He gently pressed a clean red bandana into her hand. "Keep the pressure on. I'll be back in a minute."

Extending his arm, he plucked the box from the cabinet and returned to her side, his first aid training kicking in. When he balanced her wrist on his thigh, the blood made him pause and think of his best friend, Bobby—the twenty-one gun salute, the choked back tears, the white marble stone markers. He fisted his fingers to steady his hands, and took a deep breath before grabbing an alcohol swab.

It's just a cut. Relax. Breathe. It's just a cut. Not fatal.

When he wiped the pad across the cut, she hissed.

"Sorry, but I want to make sure this cut is

clean. Focus on your breathing."

Focused and sober. That's what he needed to stay.

Drowning his sorrows in a bottle wasn't an option, women were out as well...until he walked into this small store just off the main street. The town sat several miles off the major interstate highway, about thirty miles west of Denver. He knew Colorado was beautiful from the pictures Bobby had shown him, but he didn't know it contained this kind of beauty.

She certainly was the prettiest sight he'd seen on four continents. Her little white sweater hugged tight around every curve. When she leaned over, thong underwear peeked out from the back of her jeans and gave him a wink. The same body-hugging jeans with holes in each kneecap gave him a peek-a-boo glimpse of her creamy white skin. Only a bit of makeup covered her natural beauty, and he liked how she looked a little bit rumpled, like she'd just popped out of bed.

He applied first aid cream and a bandage and assessed her condition. *Good to go.*

She reminded him of a jar of peanut butter, a rare treat after being in the field for three months. The unexpected excitement. The craving for something he couldn't get enough of. She made his mouth water, and he wondered when she'd last seen a man who wasn't from her zip code. His heart rate accelerated, revving into overdrive.

Easy, Tiger. You've been out of commission way too long. Don't make an ass of yourself.

"You should go easy on that hand for a while," he said while shoving bandages and ointment back into the first aid kit...which was surprisingly up-to-date, considering the box looked like it had been around since World War II.

"I'm so embarrassed. I don't usually get light-headed. I shouldn't have skipped breakfast. I usually eat breakfast. Breakfast starts the day off right..." He liked the way her cheeks tinged red. "I'm babbling. Aren't I? I'll be quiet now."

"It's okay. Talking will take your mind off the cut."

She nibbled on her lower lip while assessing his handiwork. "You've done this a time or two."

"Maybe once or twice."

A contentment he hadn't felt in weeks, if not months, worked its way into his heart. The sensation felt foreign. Even made him feel a bit guilty. After all, he was the one still alive, walking around, taking vacation. Regret flooded back in. It should have been him on that road in Afghanistan, not Bobby.

All he wanted to do was find a hole somewhere and disappear, but first he would honor his friend.

He was bag-ass tired, and if he didn't find some food and a soft, horizontal place to lie down, he just might fall down. It had taken sixty-two hours to get in-country, followed by two straight days of release medical exams and paperwork, followed by a military funeral.

Hazel-green eyes studied him like he

might study the horizon, watching and assessing any movement or sound. Her expression changed from curious to serious, then closed off completely. The closed-for-business signal meant he'd best be hitting the road while he still had some daylight left. Checking his watch and considering the longitude, he calculated he had another three, maybe four hours before the sun went down.

"I'd better go." He stood and took a step back. "You might want to check that bandage in a bit. I'd also suggest taking a pain reliever if you have something. And consider getting stitches. You were bleeding pretty good."

"No stitches."

There was the stubbornness he liked.

She tried to stand, but her legs were still wobbly, and his arm went around her waist automatically. When her good hand touched his chest, the heat from her fingers penetrated his cotton shirt. The heat felt several degrees past just-being-friendly.

He didn't move. He didn't react. But he wanted to. He really, really wanted to.

The woman bracing herself on his chest was a long way from the ones who frequented off-base bars, he reminded himself. Those women were after one thing —a good time and a hard ride. And this wasn't that kind of woman. She was the long-term kind. And he couldn't do long-term.

Leaving would be a good idea.

Instead, there he stood, breathing in her soft, feminine scent, feeling every finger press into his chest, and doing nothing to correct the situation.

"I, um..." She licked those sensual lips, but couldn't quite get out the rest of her sentence.

"Yep, got it." He took a step around the table toward the door, creating some distance. "Before I head out, I need to fill my truck with gas. Could you point me in the direction of the nearest station?" he asked, to help change the awkward back into a just-passing-through kind of thing.

She brushed past him and opened the door to point down the street. "Take a left out of the parking lot, and just before you get to the first light, you'll see Hank's on your right."

He sure liked the way her face contained a riddle he'd like to solve. She was scared, in control, and about to lose it, all at the same time. He liked the intrigue, and the way her nicely built frame measured to about chin height. She gave him something to think about other than his aching back, hip, and knees from too many parachute jumps and long patrols. Or how losing Bobby had carved out a big, empty hole in his chest.

"Thanks for your time, ma'am."

Before he was halfway through the door, she whispered, "Military. Should have known."

She said the word 'military' like he'd just eaten the last piece of pie. He turned back. "Is there a problem?"

He was temporarily off duty, and shouldn't have allowed her statement to affect him the way it did. But after allowing the government to use his body as a target, day in and day out, for months on end, he couldn't quite let the statement go. He shouldn't care, but he did. Cared too much, in fact.

She looked through the store window at what he called 'the grumpy old man,' Bobby's old gunmetal gray Ford pickup—with the Marine insignia displayed proudly in the window.

"Yours?" she asked with judgment in her tone, a tone he didn't like.

"Borrowed. But the insignia still applies."

She stared at him for a long, silent moment. He'd experienced all sorts of ridicule from foreigners. The last thing he expected was to be hit with it from a U.S. citizen.

Just walk away, Bobby's voice urged in his head.

Bobby had always been his better. Not a

better soldier, but a better person. He could laugh more easily, find the positive in situations, or just get along. On the other hand, Chase wasn't a people person. He had tried to change, to be more like Bobby, but he never could get it quite right. He turned, zipped his jacket, and retrieved the keys from his pocket. Before he could unlock the door, rapid footsteps made him turn.

His in-zone awareness hadn't had time to mellow, and his brain was still on high alert. Obviously so was his body because every muscle dropped into a defensive posture. Good thing she stopped a foot short. He took a deep breath and stepped back into an at-ease stance.

Gone was the conspicuous bitterness narrowing her eyes moments earlier.

"My father's a Marine. He always told me he could spot a Marine a mile away. I just didn't put the pieces together until you called me ma'am. My comment wasn't meant as an insult. I should thank you."

"For?" He hated the worn-out 'thank you

for your service' phrase. It felt fake, too easy. He braced for the same insincere statement to tumble out of her all-too-cute mouth.

"For making sacrifices." Her unshielded gaze turned honest. "For living with visions of things no person should have to witness. For enabling me to walk down the street and feel safe."

Surprise tightened his gut and then twisted. The sentiment somehow bridged the gap between them.

"You're welcome. And thank your dad for his sacrifices."

She opened her mouth to say more, but he couldn't handle any more, so he opened the truck door, got in, and started the engine.

The only thing he could do was choke back the pain, give her a nod of acknowledgment, and be on his way because her words had sunk in deep.

Things no person should have to see.

Like seeing your best friend in chunks.

CHAPTER TWO

*A*shley watched the soldier's truck rumble down the street. A strange stillness and sense of loneliness gave her a chill.

For the last three years, she'd had a purpose—taking care of her mom. Now alone, she felt stuck, even abandoned, and attributed the feeling to the gorgeous man who was moving on. Then something else took shape inside her, something resembling guilt.

Maybe she should have given the traveling soldier a place to stay.

The guy smelled delicious, like Oreo cookies, an odd smell for a man who didn't have a teaspoon of fat on his lean frame. Anyway, the thought of offering him milk to dunk his cookies had crossed her mind, but the suggestion would just complicate things. She had enough to do in the next five weeks. Adding one more plate to an already-teetering stack of dishes seemed reckless.

She retrieved a bottle of pain reliever from under the front counter, but a couple of pills wouldn't help the type of pain she wanted to dull. Moving to the back kitchen for a glass of water, she realized she'd never asked the guy's name. She could hear her mother winding up for another lecture. This time, she allowed the familiar encouraging yet demoralizing words to circle. *I'm sorry, honey. I should have better prepared you. Taught you how to be independent. To make decisions. To make something of your life. To take risks. We don't have much time.* The spiel flowed so easily when any little thing went wrong or when she needed to make a decision. She wasn't a total loser. After all, she'd raised enough money to keep a roof over her mother's head for the last eight months.

Seeing her grandmother's shattered china strewn across the hardwood floor again engulfed her in deep sadness. While sweeping the fragments into the dustbin, she remembered handwashing every dish, saucer, and cup for special holidays since the age of eight. She'd hated being forced to sell the set, but the dishes could have paid either a back mortgage payment or the first month's deposit on an apartment.

What a waste.

Disappointment and hunger made her stomach rumble. A brisk walk and some food might do her good. At least they'd give her something else to think about besides her miserable situation and growing list of things to be done. The problem was, her compass was broken, and she hadn't a clue what to do first or which direction to go. Her mom had always, always, *always* made those decisions for her.

You have a plan. Money. Shelter. Food. Stick with the plan.

She exhaled the rising panic and snatched her keys off the hook under the counter, shrugged on her coat, then pulled the 'special event' sign down and locked the door. Stepping off the plank porch, she inhaled, letting the crisp mountain air calm the frantic must-dos careening through her mind. The sun was out, but the air had a nip she hadn't felt when she walked Oreo-man out.

This time of day, Elkridge was in full swing. The semi-weekly delivery truck from Denver had arrived at The Tool Shed, and Mr. Mason was busy unloading hardware and lumber supplies. A single car rumbled down the street. She raised her hand to give Lizzy Cranston a wave, knowing the old biddy would only give her a crusty grimace, but she greeted the town's grump anyway, hoping one day to get a smile.

One day. Time was running out. Denver

might be her only option if she couldn't find a job and apartment fast.

Entering the local hangout, she nodded instead of waving to Doc Brennan and Doc Handle and a few other regulars, hoping they wouldn't notice her hand. She couldn't afford stitches, and she wouldn't accept charity. The doctors had done so much for her mom. Ten bucks a month for the rest of her life wouldn't begin to repay the debt.

The restaurant buzzed with talk about Jack Clairemont wanting to bring in a big developer to build a park to attract tourists. Some residents were for it, many against it, but the arguments had gone round and round the same hitching post for the past several months.

Few things in the small town ever changed, and Jenna's glad-to-see-you greeting was one of the welcome daily routines. Ashley took her regular spot at the counter while Jenna served her a steaming cup of the best brewed coffee this side of the Continental Divide.

"So what happened?" Jenna lifted a quizzical brow.

Ashley raised her hand, displaying the bandage. "It's nothing. I cut it on a broken piece of porcelain."

Jenna acknowledged the bandage across her finger. "Not that, silly. I want to know what happened with the hunk of man sitting at the end of the counter."

Ashley leaned in to peer down the counter, her gaze connecting with Mr. Oreo's. She sighed. He still looked drop-dead yummy, sitting with his elbow propped on the counter, a steaming cup of coffee tilting toward his lips. Those kissable lips that had already crossed her mind a time or two since he left her shop.

Mentally, she shook her head like a dog shaking off water. She had to stop. Now. She didn't have time for this kind of nonsense. But oh, that tempting mouth looked more delicious than Jenna's chocolate éclairs.

Her eyes narrowed into a suspicious line. "Did you send him over to the shop?"

"Of course I did. He came in looking for a place to stay. You're wandering around in that big old house by yourself and have three or four beds he can kick those expensive boots under. You could get a few weeks' rent…and possibly a bonus, if you know what I mean," Jenna suggested with a blink, blink, blink and a wide grin.

She understood perfectly what her friend meant by *bonus*, but that store wasn't open for business. "A stranger? At the house? With the break-ins we've been having? I don't think so."

"Why? Maggie gave him her patented once-over and said he checked out. You know Maggie. That woman can smell a bad fish in the next county."

"Tell me about it. If I ever decide to jump into the dating market, Maggie will be my first stop, since my nice-guy radar sucks."

Three years ago, Ashley had been set to marry her college boyfriend. Todd had professed his love the night before her mom called asking for assistance and pleading for her to come home. He dumped her the next morning. His excuse? He just couldn't go more than a week without sex, and her absence would cramp his style.

She hated men.

No. That wasn't true. She only disliked the ones who'd ripped her heart out and then pulverized it. Her father was living proof males weren't dependable. Even though she still wanted to love him, her dad wasn't someone she could count on. Especially when the going got tough. And that hurt.

She unzipped her coat. "Just because I've known every eligible guy in this town since kindergarten—and there isn't one I'd consider dating—doesn't mean I need to jump the first out-of-towner who walks through the door."

"No, but being alone on the Ridge isn't a good idea, either. I think he's cute. What happened?"

He happened. *The gods granted him mortal status and allowed him to stroll in and knock the air out of my lungs.* Jenna's waiting eyes, plus a few other pairs, studied her. The conversations around them stalled, waiting for her reply.

"Nothing happened," she asserted. "I told him the room wasn't available. It hasn't been cleaned in weeks. Plus, I've got to get Mom's inventory sold and boxed before the bank liquidators take everything."

"Excuses. A little dust never hurt anyone, and maybe he can help cart those boxes for you. I thought you supported the military." Jenna not-so-subtly looked over her shoulder at the man who'd now recognized her and was staring back. "I bet he looks awesome in his dress blues."

How had Jenna already figured out what Ashley had missed until that 'yes, ma'am' thing? His short-cropped hair, ramrod-straight posture, and controlled movements, combined with the way he sized up a situation and made a decision, should have tipped her off immediately. She surreptitiously peeked around the bodies between them. Sure enough, he had U.S.

Marine stamped on his forehead in big, bold, invisible letters. He had to be on leave and looking for a place to pass the holidays. Harold Talbott, the Valu-Stop Grocery Store owner, had already managed to get his mitts on him. Poor grunt. If the guy wasn't rescued, and fast, he might have to listen to the twelve years of Air Force battle history Harold could rattle off without pausing for breath.

"So you think the guy's safe?" Ashley asked, still assessing him.

"Heavens, no. Are you kidding me? He's as dangerous as they come." Jenna studied him for a second. "See? He keeps looking at you like a woman on a diet looks at my cupcakes, not sure if he should indulge or not. I think if you gave him a reason, he might be tempted to lick you to death."

Patricia and Margaret Bainbridge, sitting at a nearby table, snickered and turned fifty shades of pink. Ashley gave Jenna a good-natured smirk and pushed back from the counter before her mom's beyond-the-grave, last-minute advice rewound and started again. She wanted to straighten her hair or jeans, but couldn't very well do it with all of Elkridge watching.

"Hey, Harold." She wrapped her arm around the older man's shoulders. "Claudia sent me to remind you of your honey-do list," she said, knowing the man always had a list of his wife's to-dos.

Overgrown gray eyebrows hiked up in response. "For forty-two years, that woman's had a list a mile long. Never can quite get one thing crossed off before she puts another three things on." He folded his napkin in perfect squares and placed it back on the counter. "By the way, I talked to Claudia. She thinks you ought to use our old camper. It's a big ol' thing. Too cold to sleep in this time of year, but with some planning, you might be able to store some stuff until you find something more permanent."

"That'd be great, but I need to find a place to stay first. I wouldn't have enough spare cash to pay you rent."

"Who said anything about rent? Maybe we could trade. I've got a honey-do list that keeps on growing."

Jenna slid a to-go box overflowing with a slice of banana cream pie across the counter. "Take this with you, Harold. It will make you feel better."

Harold stood and placed his hand on the Marine's shoulder. "Watch out for these women. They'll have you back there doing dishes before you know it."

"These women. Really?" Jenna reached for the dessert box, but missed, since Harold scooped it up, gave her an I'm-faster smirk, and headed toward the door.

Jenna winked at Ashley before grabbing the coffee pot and sashaying to the nearest booth to refill empty cups.

Ashley removed her coat, draped it over the stool next to the Marine, and hopped on. She moved Harold's empty water glass aside to stall for time.

She studied his handsome jawline while he gave her a speculative, intense once-over and then took a bite out of his BLT. The way he sat with his arms surrounding his plate, like any second someone might steal his food, seemed familiar. Her father's similar eating habit made her uneasy, but the allure of the man made her stay in the seat next to him anyway.

"I'm embarrassed. You came to my rescue, and I didn't even ask your name," she said in the middle of him shoving a bundle of fries in his mouth. Watching him lick salt from his fingers did something to her, especially her lower parts. A feeling she craved, but didn't want. "Sorry. Not a great time to ask a question."

He swallowed, leaned sideways and lowered his voice. "I didn't know you asked a question."

The hot breath brushing her cheek and the humor dancing across his face made her mind go blank. His lips twitched, then a slow-blooming smile spread like a wildfire, heating her innards as it went. "Chase Daniels at your service, ma'am."

His strong, deep voice rolled over her the way water cascaded over river rock. But because he was a military man, her caution sign lit up. Her heart had been burned to a crisp a long time ago by her military dad, and she felt the need to heed the warning. There wasn't much left to salvage. That didn't mean she didn't respect the Corps. She might not walk around waving the red, white, and blue, but she hung a flag every Memorial Day, the Fourth, and Veteran's Day, and every day in between.

She locked her brave in place, pushed back her shoulders, and said, "Ashley, Ashley Bryant." Picking up a spoon, she rolled it over and over in her hand before meeting his assessing gaze. "This town generally supports the military. I didn't quite do my part. Not exactly small-town hospitality, is it? If you're not picky, I think I may have something I can offer you."

His facial expression flared hot. She blushed, imagining what he'd assumed she might be offering.

"It's a room. There's a small studio over the store. I'm warning you in advance, it's not in great condition, and that's why I hesitated. But it's a place to lay your head. If you don't mind some dust, I might be able to fix you up. It's got a kitchenette, shower, and a toilet that works. It's yours until you find something better, or I sell the furniture. I would still recommend heading up the hill, though. I'm sure you'd find better accommodations there."

"Much appreciated. It's been a long couple of days, and a place to lay my head is all I need."

The tired Marine Corps mask seemed too familiar. His unreadable, exhausted face and lack of enthusiasm might have given another woman pause, but she'd seen her dad's empty expression often enough to know not to take it personally.

A sense of responsibility settled in her gut like a ten-ton rock. As Jenna had pointed out, several bedrooms sat empty at the main house, but the way he made her blush and tingle…and every once in a while forget to breathe…created too great a temptation. She didn't need the distraction, even if Maggie had given the thumbs-up.

The crumbs on his plate and his napkin refolded beside it in a perfect rectangle jolted her back to awareness. "Are you finished eating?"

"I am, but don't let me stop you."

As if on cue, Jenna plopped a bowl of homemade chicken noodle soup and a fresh slice of bread in front of her, disappearing before Ashley could get a thank-you out.

He gave her a crooked grin. "Is she a mind reader or something?"

"Jenna's always been like that, anticipating your needs even before you need something. Maggie, the café owner, recognized her gifts and, just like that, gave her a place to stay and made room for her in the kitchen."

And apparently she thinks you're solid, too.

His look went straight to her lips and stayed there, caressing each corner gently, softly before his gaze shifted and lifted to hers.

"I might have to sample the sweets sometime."

She got his meaning and instantly focused on her soup spoon circling in the broth, forcing herself to concentrate on making sure each rotation had the same diameter. With each passing second, she became more mesmerized by the rising steam. Blowing to cool the liquid, she allowed the heat rising in her body to also cool.

He's a Marine. He won't stay. Don't go there. Just be friendly.

Ashley tentatively tested the hot soup with the tip of her tongue, then sipped from her spoon. "So are you stationed in California or North Carolina?"

"Carolina."

"Second Battalion. Are you attached to a special unit?"

The guy had a way of sitting very still, showing a person only what he wanted them to see. His eyes held open the only door to what he was thinking because his body language certainly wasn't saying a thing. "If I'd known I was going to be put through an inquisition, I might have brought my military record."

"Sorry, just a small-town habit. We tend to know everything about everyone here, so when a new person shows up, people get interested. It's not personal or anything. You shouldn't take offense."

"None taken."

His words were even, precise, not demanding, just confident. Confident in a way she wanted to be but never managed. He was attractive, but she couldn't allow this guy to awaken her hormones. She'd sworn an oath never to get involved with a uniform. At college in San Diego, it had been easy. Precision-pressed jackets were everywhere, easy to spot, and easy to avoid. But she never expected to find one in disguise, straddling a stool in her little town.

"Then let me guess." She tore off a bite of

bread and studied his face. He looked older than she was, maybe thirty. "A tour in Kuwait, maybe Japan, Kabul, a couple in Iraq and Afghanistan."

"Impressive. You a military buff?"

She spread a pat of butter on her bread and watched it melt, just like her willpower. Putting the knife down, she sneaked another peek at his biceps. Nice. "Military buff? Not really. Like I said, my dad's a Marine. My mom framed a map when I was little and we tracked his deployments with colored pushpins. In school, I liked history, so I just kept it going until I went to college. Haven't kept up with it since then. I know it sounds a bit odd."

His brow lifted, but he said nothing.

She shrugged. "You're also not from a small town. I can tell. Folks around here have a gift for gossip and tend to anticipate."

"Anticipate?"

Jenna stopped to fill Chase's cup and deliver a chocolate chip cookie before disappearing again.

"Yep, anticipate."

He watched Jenna retreat, his eyes wide, eyebrows lifted. "Now I get it."

Elkridge was almost as predictable as a sunrise. Gossip spread faster than a flood, and before a person would stop it, the whole town would be drenched with information that might or might not be true. It drove her crazy the way people got into each other's business. It just wasn't right.

But then there was the good side. The caring side. If people learned a family might need help, there'd be a line outside the door full of people offering pies, advice, services, or anything else they might think useful.

She downed her soup while the silence eased in. With her good hand, she fumbled around in her pocket for a twenty-dollar bill.

"Ready to go?" She slid the bill under her plate, hoping the ten dollars in her dresser at home would pay for groceries until next week.

He retrieved the twenty and tried to give it back. "Let me pay for this."

"I got it. You'll find military money is no good in this town. Just the way it is."

His warm fingers encircled her wrist and placed the money in her hand. "I insist."

Obviously, he'd gotten used to giving orders and having people obey, but she wasn't someone he could boss around. She turned to put the twenty back on the counter and got Maggie's evil eye.

"Put that money in your pocket this instant, missy." Maggie pointed a stiff finger. "You too, Marine."

"Maggie, I know you've always been there for me, but you can't keep feeding this whole town for free." Ashley's chin jutted forward to emphasize her point.

"Didn't your momma teach you not to argue with your elders?"

Ashley sighed while embarrassed heat ran up her face. "Fine. But next week I'm going to come and help you can your jellies for the Bazaar. You need help, so don't give me that elder crap."

Confidence. Didn't her mother tell her she had to grow some?

The prior habit of unquestioning compliance was her mother's doing. She'd always required immediate acquiescence. During the last couple of years, her mother had identified her mistake. Compliance had led to an inability to make decisions. Ashley had never quite figured out what her mom wanted her to be or do, forcing a life of indecision.

She'd spent the two-day drive home from the University of San Diego carefully crafting an excuse to return to school. But when she saw nursing home patients stuck in wheelchairs with pureed food dried on their gowns, her resolve had crumbled and she'd complied. She couldn't leave her mother in such a disgusting place. Giving up three years of her life and dealing with bedpans 24/7 had been the result.

Chase gave her a long, hard, assessing look. "Ma'am, are you ready to go?"

A shiver brushed up her spine. "If you

don't mind, that 'ma'am' thing's gotta go. Hearing it reminds me of my grandmother. Call me Ashley, or Ash."

Saying nothing, he lifted her coat and held it open for her. She tilted her head, not knowing what to think of the old-fashioned gesture. Gathering the sleeve ends of her wool sweater into the palms of her hands, she pushed into the coat sleeves, accepting his courtesy. Before she could thank him, he'd circled the tables and headed for the door.

The view couldn't have been more spectacular. His upper body formed a nice V shape, ending at a perfectly compact rear. And there couldn't be another pair of muscular legs in Colorado filling out jeans the way his did.

"Don't let him intimidate you. Go jump him," Jenna whispered with a spark in her eye.

"That's all I need—to be a target of town gossip."

"Forget about the old biddies squawking.

Nobody pays attention, anyway. He's interested. I can tell by the way he looks at you. You're interested as well. And don't tell me you're not."

Chase Daniels was a whole lot of man—more man than she knew how to handle. The moody guy shared his thoughts only when it suited him, preferring to observe and watch. She assumed he didn't play much, settled more on the serious side, and she got the feeling he was swift to make decisions. Unlike her.

The idea of him scared her. Intrigued her.

He turned. Her eyes locked to his.

She noted his rigid stance and took a fortifying breath. This guy would test her and bring her close to the edge. An edge she hadn't been close to for a long time—a dangerous, uncomfortable, exciting place. A place she wanted to explore, but a heavy dose of caution and reality kept her desires in check.

She lifted the collar of her coat up around her ears and took a step forward.

"Let's see if I can find you some clean sheets."

CHASE WATCHED Ashley sprint up the wooden staircase snuggled against the side of the antique shop.

"Be careful with the railing. It's loose," she said, placing her key in the lock and using her shoulder to open the door.

The way Ashley's jeans fit across her perfectly formed butt reminded Chase of a bullet fitting tight and precisely into a rifle chamber. His eyes were definitely on lock, and she was fully loaded. He bet each one of her individual body parts would fit perfectly into the palms of his hands, one right after the other.

The other guys in his unit gave him crap about liking women who had just enough. Of course, he would look at any female who wanted to show off her equipment, but he preferred the all-natural type, and Ashley was organically pure.

She covered her eyes with her hands and then slid them down her cheeks. "I'm sorry. I didn't know how bad it was up here."

He checked the ceiling. No leaks. Good sign. The flowery wallpaper was a bit much, but the solidly built bed with no footboard would allow him to stretch out, so no problem there. If the sheets weren't clean, he could always use the poncho liner he'd found behind the seat in the pickup. Drawers and closets were redundant, since he'd lived out of a rucksack for so long. A few boxes scattered across the room needed stacking, but that would be easy enough to do. He'd spent plenty of days and nights in places where even the bomb-sniffing dogs couldn't get comfortable. Being able to find a place to sleep without first digging a trench was a bonus.

Ashley had turned pale, most likely from embarrassment.

"It'll do. I don't need much," he assured her, but she marched to the bed and began lifting boxes. "Hold on there. You don't want to open that cut."

Chase took the heavy box from her hands and placed it by the far wall, then turned and grabbed the second box she'd picked up. Gritting his teeth in irritation, he considered picking her up and setting her outside the door to get her to stop. However, pissing her off might lead to sleeping in a truck, which wasn't ideal in winter.

She leaned over again, and he got distracted. Her feminine hips reminded him he'd been without a woman for way too long. He needed to stay focused on the task at hand. For the next ten minutes, they danced with boxes until she finally ran out of things to move.

She scanned the room and pointed at a door. "Through there's the bathroom. The other door leads to the kitchenette on the main floor. You'll also find a washer and dryer, but I'll warn you, they haven't been used in a while. There's vinegar in the cupboard if you want to run a cleaning cycle first." She studied him for a second. "Towels. You need some towels."

Reaching into a wall closet, she removed a burgundy bath sheet, hand towel, and washcloth. He couldn't remember the last time he'd used a washcloth, but didn't want to interrupt her fussing. And about the vinegar, why bother? He'd lived in the same clothes for days. A washer got dirt out. No fuss needed.

She opened the bathroom door to check the water pressure in the sink and shower. It impressed him how she went out of her way to make sure he had everything he needed. There were some in this world who'd rather run a person over than stop and help. One thing for sure, the woman sure tried hard.

"Ashley?" He took a step toward her. Leaned his arm on the bathroom doorframe. "Please stop. The room is fine. It's a palace compared to my last bunk."

Distracted, she blinked, then her amazing

hazel eyes remained steady. She wrestled with something, he could see it in her eyes. But then she shifted and ducked under his arm, retreating to the apartment door.

"I'm assuming you'll be tired after traveling, so I won't disturb you too early. I've got things to do in the store tomorrow, but I shouldn't be here until after ten." She retrieved a key ring from her pocket, removed a key tied with a pink ribbon, and tossed it to him.

"How much do I owe you?"

"Your money doesn't work here," she explained with more patience than he had. "There's coffee and tea at the bottom of the stairs in the kitchen. Help yourself. The store's locked, so no one should bother you. Get some rest. You look like a tank ran over you."

The concern in her eyes, he liked. There wasn't any pity, or sorrow, or buck-it-up Marine, only a consideration for his well-being.

He took a couple of steps to place the key

on the table beside the door, and she took off like a scared rabbit. She fled down the stairs to the parking lot, where she dove into a VW Bug that had no business being driven on a civilian road, and disappeared around the corner.

When he sat on the bed, dust particles filled the air and a musty smell permeated the room. He eyed the floor, figuring it might be a safer place for the night. At least the room sheltered him from the brewing snowstorm. He'd do something about the bed tomorrow.

Tomorrow. Sometimes there were no tomorrows.

If it weren't for Bobby, he'd be on a beach in North Carolina or in a cabin somewhere. Losing his best friend, the guy everyone admired and respected, cut deep. He would have traded his life for Bobby's in a second.

He'd chosen to accompany Bobby home, to tell his parents and sister about their heroic son and brother. Yesterday at Ft. Logan Cemetery, the prepared summary stuck in his chest. What did you tell a mother who'd lost a son? He touched the tender left pectoral where he'd hired a tattoo artist to give him a permanent reminder of Bobby's initials and the date of death. Bobby's mom had been so strong—even in her grief—offering him a place to stay, but claustrophobia had crept in, and he couldn't do it. He needed to keep moving.

Seeing Bobby's parents' and sister's grief for those few hours had been more than he could bear. With a promise to visit their home for Christmas, he'd borrowed Bobby's old truck and started driving with no destination in mind. When he recognized the name of Elkridge on the map, he turned off the highway, remembering Bobby's description of the small town. On tour, Bobby had talked nonstop about the people and places of his youth, making every story or individual come alive.

Elkridge might be the place Chase could find a sense of peace and a place to rest that didn't activate memories from the past. No loud noises. No crowded spaces. No malls, big chain grocery stores, sporting events, any venue with a large number of people. Space. He needed space to get his head clear. Figure out the next steps.

His commander's last words came to him. *You need to decide.*

Thirty-three days to decide what to do with his life: military or civilian.

He inhaled deeply, considering his options.

Either just might kill him.

CHAPTER THREE

Stopping in the café just after nine the next morning, Ashley received a minute-by-minute update on Chase's activities, whether she wanted one or not. He'd gone for a pre-dawn run, then arrived at the café just when Jenna pulled the first batch of cinnamon rolls out of the oven. After a hearty pancake breakfast, he'd been seen puttering around Ashley's store, fussing with the side door, then the railing.

Maggie stopped halfway through the counter coffee run. "Please encourage that gorgeous man of yours to come over when he's done with your place. I've got plenty of fixing needed here. Besides, he's easy on the eyes."

Her man? Since when did Chase Daniels become hers? Someday she wouldn't mind becoming part of a 'we,' as in two people building a life together. But becoming a 'we' with a Marine just wouldn't happen. No way. No how.

Her parents somehow managed to remain married for twenty-seven years, but not many of those years were happy. For some reason, they'd chosen to live apart. Because of that decision, her father would be gone months at a time, missing almost every important event in Ashley's life, and when he did come home, he wasn't really there.

"You sound like my mom. Just to make it clear," she raised her voice a little just in case the gossipmongers were listening in, "I'm not Chase Daniels' keeper. If you want something done, I suggest you ask him yourself."

"What's got your panties in a wad so early

in the morning?" Maggie gave her a what-for stare before moving on down the counter to shout an order to Ted, the cook.

Jenna picked up her empty breakfast plate. "I've seen you scraping the bottom of the emotional barrel, and I've seen you fired-up mad, but I've never seen you get knotted up over some guy. Granted he's a GQ Joe, but why does he irritate you so much?"

"I didn't ask for his help." *And I don't have the money to pay for the repairs.*

She wasn't a charity case. She didn't need anyone…well, except those times in the early morning hours when she hadn't been able to sleep and found herself singularly and heartbreakingly alone.

Jenna shoved a thermos across the counter. "Even if you told him to stop, I'm not sure he's the kind who would. He seems rather determined. Take some hot coffee to the poor guy. It's starting to snow."

Ashley looked out the window toward her mother's store at the end of the block. The least she could do was take him a decent cup of coffee, and somehow between the café and the store she should be able to find the will to be a tad bit gracious.

"Thanks for the coffee and tasty samples," she said, pushing from the stool and sliding a couple of dollars under the napkin when neither Maggie nor Jenna were looking. "See you tomorrow."

Snowflakes swirled in the air when she exited the café and crossed the street. The dry Colorado air made the snow float and spin like the colorful oak leaves in the fall. The beauty eased the tension in her shoulders. Drawing closer, she watched Chase pluck a nail from a box and pound it into the railing with swift, efficient movements. He wore an old pair of camouflage pants and his steel-toed boots.

A sensation she hadn't felt in years made her draw in cold air to calm her sweltering reaction.

After adding six additional nails, he dropped the hammer into an old toolbox and held out a hand. He studied the sky like a ten-year-old boy, hand stretched out, palm up. She waited for him to stick his tongue out to catch some flakes, but he never did. The childlike wonder on his face drew her interest, but the crunch of gravel under her boot must have given away her presence and spoiled the moment. His moody eyes connected with hers. His melancholy reflected her soul and pulled her forward.

"Good morning," Ashley said, offering him the thermos.

"What's this?"

"You've been busy. Early morning run, breakfast, fixing things. Maggie sent over some coffee, compliments of the café." For some inexplicable reason, she didn't want him to know that the cute, young, single baker sent the coffee. Call it jealousy. Call it self-preservation. Call it whatever, she wouldn't examine it too carefully. "There's not much that goes unnoticed in a town this size. Maggie says she has a job for you. You don't need to be fixing my things."

"You won't let me pay rent...and just

maybe I'm not doing this for you. Maybe I'm doing it for me. The steps aren't safe, and working with my hands keeps my mind occupied."

Distractions. She could understand the need for distractions. Especially since he'd occupied her dreams last night with all-too-graphic and arousing images. At night the visions were bad enough, but during the day the attraction became too real. He hadn't yet shaved, and his early morning shadow had Kris-Kringle-red highlights. Between his light blond hair and red highlights, she imagined a candy cane, all pepperminty and tasty. The fantasy she could handle. The actual man, probably not.

"Does that snowmobile work?" He pointed over his shoulder toward the shed.

"A guy responding to a classified said the sled needed an oil change and a new battery. He only wanted the engine and a few parts. Since it was my mom's, I just couldn't let it go for parts."

"Do you mind if I take a look?"

Looking. Isn't that what she'd been doing? But he meant the snowmobile, not her.

She paused, remembering the old days of racing through the hills above the town, the sun beating down on the glistening snow, the sting of the wind on her cheeks, and the thrill of going fast. She hadn't ridden in years. Coming home had meant 24/7 care. No days off. No girls' night out. And no fun in the sun on the snowmobile that brought back so many pleasurable memories.

"If you're going up in these hills, you'll need a guide. Some of the logging roads and animal trails are dangerous."

People have gotten severely hurt. I wouldn't want an accident on my conscience, Jenna's voice reminded her. *Maggie says he checks out.*

Stop being a chicken, Ashley grumbled to herself. Help the guy out. "Tell you what. If you get the old girl running, I'll take you up the Ridge. I know the area. There are some places with hidden rocks and trees you'll want to avoid."

"I'd appreciate the guidance." He managed a genuine half-smile—the first real effort she'd seen since he arrived—and she felt encouraged.

"May I ask a personal question?" he asked.

Now why did he have to go and spoil the moment by adding the word *personal*?

"Sure," she said, stifling the bubbling apprehension wanting to skip into her thoughts.

He stepped closer. His eyes were keen, way more intelligent than she would have liked. "I can't figure out whether it's me or the military you don't like. Which is it?"

"I don't know you, so it's not you." *There, question answered.* She turned to escape, but he stepped around her so fast, she ran into his chest and had to back up.

"Then it's the military you don't like."

Damn. Either way she answered, she'd be stuck.

He was way too smart to be standing in Elkridge, Colorado. He should be solving the world's hunger problems or creating world peace. She let out a slow, steady breath to stall for time. "The military's a mighty big organization to dislike, don't you think?"

His gaze scanned over her like a general inspecting his troops. "You don't want to answer my question. I get it. I'm pretty private myself, but I would like to know."

Why did he ask for her thoughts? No one asked her opinion. Not her mom. Especially not her dad. Not even the doctors. The sting in her eyes made her pause. Why was she getting emotional over some guy asking what she thought?

No way was she going to be some leaking faucet. It would make her mascara run and she'd look like a zombie. She must be getting her period. Damn hormones making her all emotional.

"It's okay. You don't have to answer." Reaching out, he tucked one of her stray hairs behind her ear, then let the back of his knuckles caress her face.

How did he know she craved human touch?

The last time she'd been hugged or cuddled or kissed had been in San Diego, and before that, she couldn't remember. Touching another human, feeling connected, even for a second, made a difference, a big difference.

For months on end, she'd watched her mother shrivel—the muscles contracting, curling inward, until her soul dried up. Ashley sat for hours reading, or playing music, or trying to find food her mother would eat. She'd missed having a physical connection. Without meaning to, she leaned into his palm and gathered strength from his warm, callused hand.

"You okay?" he asked.

She jerked her head upright. How could she explain? No, she wasn't okay. Her family was virtually gone, and she had only a few weeks to sell everything she could and find an apartment. Otherwise, she'd be homeless. Either way, she'd be alone, with no job, no college degree, plus student loans to pay off. And it scared the crap out of her.

"Sure. Why wouldn't I be fine?"

With a gentleness she hadn't expected, he placed a finger under her chin and lifted her face until their eyes met. "You want to try that again? Maybe the truth this time?"

Her throat tightened. She turned her head, trying to brush him away, but he didn't budge. She was drowning, and he just stood, solid as a boulder, a lifeline.

"I have to go," she said, but in actuality, she wanted to stay. Kiss him. Climb him like the face of a mountain.

She took one step back, then another, and another, out of his reach. Nerves made her knees shake to the point that she braced herself on the side of the building to keep steady. "I have a lot to do today, and standing here isn't getting it done."

And standing here with you all sexy and ready to kiss me, isn't good. It's bad. Very bad. Somebody would see them, and it would be all over town faster than a blink of an eye that Ashley Bryant had let some stranger cop a feel. And here she thought her sexually forward high school days were behind her. She'd worked hard to repair her tarnished reputation.

He just stood there with a glint in his eye, no doubt fully aware that if he moved an inch closer, she would shimmy up his body, wanting his big hands and hot lips doing their magic.

Double crap!

She turned and hauled the car keys out of her pocket, walking faster than she probably should to her mother's beat-up VW Bug.

Through the windshield, she saw him. Standing there. His arms now crossed. A smile like a jack-o-lantern stretched across his face. All bright and shiny.

Holy mother of saints.

She put the key in the ignition and turned it. The engine revved, then sputtered, wheezed, and died. She pumped the gas pedal. *Don't do this today. Please.* Turning the key again, she got the same result. *Come on. Come on. Come on.*

Chase dropped his arms, his happy-smiley dimming. He took a step toward the car. If her mom hadn't sold the Lexus when she moved into the nursing home, Ashley wouldn't find herself humbled and pleading with the stupid hunk of junk. She turned the key again and the car sputtered to life. Throwing the vintage beetle in reverse, she smiled and waved him off, hoping he got the impression the car was okay. On a good day, the odds of the car starting were sixty-forty. In the car's favor.

The jumble of emotion consumed her during the three blocks down the street, until she drove into a parking space in front of the thrift shop, cut the engine, and dropped her forehead to the steering wheel.

She shouldn't have offered to take him to the Ridge. The meadow above her home was her private place, a little piece of paradise, a place to think.

How was she supposed to concentrate

with visions of Chase in his fatigues hammering away at the stair rail? Her whole body sighed with sizzling, lustful anticipation.

Holy moly. She jumped when someone knocked on the driver's side window.

Her heart leapt and crashed into her throat, then settled back down. Just Gwen Keebler, the thrift store owner.

Ashley opened the car door. "Hey, Gwen. I brought you another load of stuff."

"That's what I figured. I came out to help."

Ashley popped open the front trunk. She and Gwen unloaded bags of dresses, purses and shoes, making a few more trips back and forth.

"It's a shame to sell these wonderful things," Gwen said, rounding the counter. "You sure you don't want to keep any of it?"

"What would I do with fancy stuff? I have nowhere to wear it or store it. Plus, with your help, I'm hoping we can make enough for me to afford a place to live."

"I'll see what I can do. I know you don't have a lot of time."

It wasn't surprising everyone in town knew the stopwatch was ticking, and she was racing toward the finish line. Gwen's eyes softened. Today she was wearing a form-fitting charcoal sweater and a pair of trendy jeans that fit perfectly. Her red-highlighted black hair hung down her back, and chandelier earrings dangled to her shoulders. With her high cheekbones and full, pouty lips, she looked like a runway model. She'd arrived in Colorado to work the ski slopes, but finding them too crowded, opted to open a consignment shop in Elkridge instead.

Ashley dropped her chin, not wanting to see the sympathy in Gwen's eyes. "There's still more to go through. I should have another load next week." She set her mother's clothes on the counter. "It's just that I hate going to the house. The creditors keep calling, and every day I expect to get home and find the locks changed. I called the real estate agent again, but he hasn't returned my calls. It's so frustrating. I keep paying a little to every bill collector so I can keep stalling for more time."

"I don't know why your house doesn't sell. It's in a great location."

There was that soft-eyed sympathy again in Gwen's expression. Ashley pulled at a small thread on one of her mother's jackets. "Yeah, if you like living in the middle of nowhere. According to the real estate agent, there are very few house buyers in the market who are looking for and can afford the five-bedroom, three-acre price tag." Ashley pointed at the two-foot-high pile. "There's a designer suit in there, and a dress still with the tags."

"This is cute." Gwen lifted a short beige jacket. "Bummer. It's missing a button."

"I bet my mom has it somewhere. Let me look for it."

Gwen lifted and considered one of her mother's Donna Karan blouses. "I took your suggestion and started selling on eBay. I've been able to get more for some of these pieces, and I hope you don't mind, but I purchased a few for myself."

"I don't mind," she said, even though seeing other people in her mom's stuff might sting a bit. She'd get over the hurt when the money hit her bank account. "eBay's been my savior. However, I'll eventually have to find another way to make money because I can't see eBay being a long-term thing. If I'd had to buy the stuff I'm selling, I'm not sure how much money I'd really be making."

"I read this article about people selling stuff they don't even own. Might be worth a try."

"Maybe."

One step at a time. Money. Shelter. Food. That's all she could wrap her mind around right now.

"Jenna says you've got a new hottie staying at your place."

Hottie? The title fit. "Yep. Military. Needed a place to overnight."

"Maybe you should show him around

town. You haven't had a break in quite a while. Might be fun."

Fun? The word seemed foreign.

"No time. Harold offered to let me use his old camping trailer to store some things, but first I've got to get everything sold that I can. Plus, I want to finish making those teapot chimes for the Bazaar. And, most important, I need to find a place to live, preferably with a Wi-Fi hotspot so I can keep selling stuff I've put aside."

"Yeah, but—"

"No. I need to stay focused."

"If you say so. Jenna told me he was looking to stick around for a few days. I'm thinking you might trade some fun for having boxes packed. Just sayin'."

Ashley's eyes squinted and her mouth dried with frustration. "What's up with you and Jenna? If you think he's so hot, why don't you ask him out?"

"I just might."

Ashley might have made the suggestion,

but Gwen's comment still stung like a wasp protecting its hive.

Maybe she didn't have the time for Mr. Gorgeous, but she didn't want anyone else escorting him around town either. There was something about him. Something strong and reassuring. Something that made her heart beat a bit faster and her mind spin a bit slower.

"I'd better go. Like I said, got a million things to do."

"Let me know if you want help sorting through your mom's things. I'd be happy to help."

Help. She hated asking for more help. This town had given so much, and she still had no idea how to reciprocate. After her mother died, Harold and Claudia had invited her over for dinner and to review her plan. Budgeting, paying bills, and house repairs were all recent revelations. Having a mom who insisted on making all critical decisions and micromanaging Ashley's choices had left her with very little in the way of survival skills.

She had a lot to catch up on. Figuring out her way around the real world scared the crap out of her, but she was trying to transform twenty-plus years' worth of destructive nurturing into a healthy, functioning life. Some days she did okay. Other days, she wanted to drag her favorite teddy bear into the closet, shut herself in, and hide.

Ashley choked back the wad of panic setting in. "I'll let you know if I need help. I appreciate the offer," she managed to say without crumbling or pleading for help. She gave Gwen a hug and made it to the car before the acid in her throat made her gag.

You can do this. Just stick to the plan.

If she ever had kids, she was going to teach them to do, never do for them.

Life skills.

Coping skills.

She had neither.

CHAPTER FOUR

A couple days later, Chase stopped by the hardware store. Studying the six types of two-stroke oil on the hardware shelf, he debated synthetic versus blend versus high performance. Since the old snowmobile had been around a good long while, he eliminated high-performance. She most likely didn't need it.

Now Ashley, on the other hand, could rev her engine at high speed. She'd already proven that. The way she felt against his body sent a fifty-watt jolt straight to his heart and brought him back to life. And with a little bit of encouragement, he bet she just might kiss him.

At least he hoped.

"Need help with something?" a gruff voice asked.

Chase studied the man, who could have been his father's age, if he'd ever had a father. The man looked to be in his late fifties, but the rasp in his voice and the condition of his body indicated he'd likely overindulged in booze and cigarettes at some point in his life.

"Looking to do some maintenance on an old snowmobile," Chase responded.

"Would that be Sally Bryant's old sled?"

He pulled on his ear while considering the question. Ashley's last name happened to be Bryant, and he supposed there weren't too many other Bryants in this town. "S'pose so."

"That gal is mighty finicky."

Yes, she is. But he was thinking more about Ashley than the snowmobile. She was like a spark plug who could run hot or cold.

He grabbed one of the two-stroke bottles

off the shelf. "I think I can manage. Got any spark plugs, possibly some brake oil?"

The man squinted, giving him a thorough once-over like his boot camp drill sergeant. "Saw the insignia on the truck out front." He shoved his hand forward. "Bill Mason. First Marine Division, retired after twenty."

Chase grasped the man's hand and released it. "Chase Daniels. Gunny Sergeant, Second Marine Division, active." *For now.*

"Son, let me show you what I got."

Son. The last time he'd been called 'son' was when he was twelve. He'd gotten caught lopping the heads off Mr. Chester's flowers with a new wire trick that Lester Lewis, a fellow foster kid, devised. The proprietor's voice, however, didn't have quite the same gonna-whup-your-ass tone.

While Chase didn't know Bill Mason, he knew a lot about the man. Where he'd fought. What he saw. The visions that kept him awake most nights. It didn't matter whether the guy was a cook or mechanic or on the front lines, every soldier tasted war long after they'd left the service. Whether the guys came back from the field or in a casket didn't matter. Marines understood Marines. Chase wondered if the man had the same kind of recurring dreams.

Bill stopped at the air filter section just as Chase's cell phone rang. He went to press ignore, until he recognized the number.

"I apologize. I need to take this call."

Bill nodded and gave him privacy. Chase stepped around the end of the aisle.

"Yo. What's up?" he answered.

"Banker, you're an asshole," Jimmy's voice blared from the phone.

"Nothing new there," Chase responded, feeling himself smirk. "You out chasing bones, Fido?" He leaned and placed his hand on the metal shelf.

"No, man. Skirt chasing days are over. Katie and I got engaged over Thanksgiving."

Loneliness crept up and sucker-punched Chase in the throat. He swallowed hard. "Glad to hear it. Congratulations."

Jimmy was the last guy Chase had ever expected to settle down.

That's what three bullets do to a person.

"You steady?" Jimmy suddenly sounded way more serious, and Chase heard his concern.

Steady…as in mentally. Too many guys he'd known had put a gun to their heads, but he wouldn't be one of them, no matter how bad it got. He'd seen firsthand what leaving like that did to people left behind. The unofficial Facebook page was full of memorials, reminiscences from loved ones. He'd even talked a few of the guys off the proverbial ledge.

"Like a rock," he said.

"Good to hear. When are you coming back?"

"Not sure yet."

He considered telling Jimmy about the woman he'd discovered. He'd get a kick out of knowing Chase managed to find a woman in a small town when he couldn't find a suitable one in any of the dozens of places they'd been deployed. But something stopped him.

Chase studied the oversized display of batteries in all shapes and sizes. "You going to be around later? Found an old snowmobile at the place I'm staying. Needs some repairs. Might require some Jimmy Reed expertise."

"Anytime. While I have you on the phone…"

His gut clenched. Shit. No more bad news. He'd had enough for a while, but from hundreds of miles away, and after being off the grid for a few days, he couldn't guess.

"Fido, you got a bone stuck in your mouth. Spit it out, my man," Chase said with a gut twisting cautiousness.

"Banker, I know how you don't like to open that wallet of yours, but I was hoping you'd be the best man at my wedding."

The guys might make fun of him for being a tightwad. Foster care could do that to a man. But, he'd gladly open it for Jimmy. "It would be my honor." The fifth time to stand-up at one of his military brothers' weddings. And, he was even a godfather four times already. He wasn't sure he had the qualifications to be a godfather because he wasn't sure he believed in the Big Guy. Then again, if God was real, Chase certainly didn't want to piss him off, so he hedged his bets. "You're wearing dress blues, right?"

"None other." The pride in his buddy's statement resonated even through the phone.

"I'll be there. Just let me know when and where."

There was a time he didn't think Jimmy would be standing, much less walking. He still hadn't gotten the feeling back in his left leg or right shoulder, but thanks to Katie's physical therapy, he was making progress.

"You won the bet," Jimmy said. "You're the last one, my man. We owe you six hundred bucks."

There had been seven. Bobby, Jimmy, and he were the only ones not married. They had sworn off commitment, but as time went on and life got tough, the others had found someone to share their lives. Several even had kids on the ground or pending. The loneliness emptied Chase's reserves and left him dry.

"Tell the guys to keep their money. A late wedding present from me and Bobby."

"Banker, I know Bobby meant a lot to you, but dude, you gotta quit blaming yourself."

Right. Jimmy had to go there. If Chase hadn't made a comment about his toothache in the vicinity of his commanding officer, Bobby wouldn't have been on that road. He'd lived with the ache for a month and was planning to do something about it stateside, but no, his commander told him to report to medical and get it checked out. When the evac call came in, he knew Bobby had gone on recon that morning in his place. Chase had hopped a ride with the medical crew as security cover, and the crew was first to the scene—God, the destruction. Bodies and trucks and everything, mangled.

"I hear ya." He took an unsteady breath. "Hey, Fido. I need to get going. Send me the date and I'll be there." He ended the call before Jimmy could say anything more.

Shit. He needed to stay busy. Have some fun. Get some rest. Get his head screwed on straight. Target something besides Bobby and bombs.

He looked around till he found the right spark plug, then moved back to the filter aisle and found what he needed there before perusing the tool section. While he ogled the sanders and drills and ratchet sets and other things he'd love, but had nowhere to keep, his phone rang again.

Thinking Fido was calling him back, Chase moved to press the ignore button, but the sound of monks chanting identified the caller. "Pastor Chris." He forced a note of cheer into his voice. "How's your flock?"

A pause. "Are you real? This isn't voice mail? A miracle! It's a miracle!"

Guilt pressed in and made it hard to breathe. "I just got in-country. You know what it's like. Being in the backcountry of Somalia isn't much different from Afghanistan. Phones aren't always accessible. Plus, I've had some things to attend to."

"I heard."

He liked how Pastor Chris was a man of few words. The tall, thin guy didn't look like a man of God. He didn't talk like one, either. During a game of one-on-one, Chase discovered Chris traveled to Ethiopia and Somalia and Kenya a lot. Over a burger and fries, Pastor had filled Chase's fifteen-year-old head with vivid pictures. He talked about the lack of clean water and food, the diseases that ravaged the countryside, the civil unrest, and the genocide. After a while, Chase realized failing algebra wasn't the end of the world.

"You want to talk about your friend?" Pastor Chris asked without judgment or pressure, just kindness, his way of caring for his people.

"No. I think I need to let that one rest for a bit. I do have a question for you, though, about…" *Women? Marriage? Fatherhood?* All of those, and yet none of those topics seemed right.

"About?" The Pastor had more patience in his little finger than most people tallied in total.

He took a deep breath. "About me, I guess. You know my background. My mom's addiction and the losers she brought around. The abuse. The foster care. You and Coach have been the only two stable people in my life. You know?"

"Go on."

"Well, I've been thinking of that 'man' poem, by Kipling. The one called 'If.' I've been thinking a lot about it lately…well, not the poem, more about being a man. You know, marriage, having kids. I don't feel I'm qualified."

"I see. Chase, no one is really qualified. There isn't a handbook for such things. Those who end up being good at it work hard. Sometimes fail. Sometimes succeed. I might be biased, but I think you're more qualified than most. You know what it's like to be hurt by someone you love. And I bet you'd be careful not to hurt anyone else the way you've been hurt."

"Some say drug addiction and physical abuse are hereditary."

"And I say the human spirit can overcome any obstacle. You just have to keep trying. You're a good man, Chase. I'm as proud of you as I would be my own son."

A knot of emotion stuck in Chase's throat. He had to swallow. He had to breathe. "That means a lot. Especially coming from you." For a man who didn't say much, Chris had certainly said a lot.

He didn't want to dwell on the kind words. Words he couldn't quite believe. "How did the animal thing go?"

"Not so good. We took cows, sheep, and three dozen chickens to the village. When you're hungry, the animals look like food, not milk and eggs and wool. Plus, we had to run off poachers. Change isn't easy."

"What you're saying is you just have to keep trying."

A snort of a laugh came through the phone. "That's right. I just have to keep trying."

"A five hundred-dollar check might help replace one of those cows. It's the least I can do."

"Like I said before, Chase, you're a good man. Reach out if you want to talk about your friend."

"I will. Go tend your flock, Pastor. When I get back to Jersey, you owe me a game of basketball."

"Hope to see you soon. And take care, my friend."

"'Bye." Chase ended the call and stood in the small tool aisle, trying to rationalize Pastor's final comment.

A good man. Was he really? Was he a good friend? He hadn't been there for Bobby, and with flashbacks freezing his brain unpredictably, being around him wasn't safe.

Getting out of the Marines meant no job. How could he be a good husband and father?

With the flashbacks, how could he be a good soldier?

He walked to the counter and placed the air filter, oil, spark plug and a pack of gum on the counter. "Sorry about that, Mr. Mason. I needed to take a few calls. Been out of the country for a while."

"Call me Bill." The store owner nodded his understanding. "If you want help, just let me know. I'll be happy to stop by on my way home." He glanced at the register. "That'll be twenty-two dollars even."

Chase reached for his wallet, hesitated to do some calculations in his head, and then studied the computer screen. The twenty percent discount at the bottom caught his attention. He looked at Bill. The guy didn't respond because that's just how the Marine family worked. When a brother needed something, it might appear on his bunk, or in his shaving kit, or on his plate. An understanding passed between them.

"Thanks," he said and handed over some bills.

"You know, Ashley was in here a couple weeks back looking for a mechanic to work on that piece of shit VW Bug she's been driving. Hank, over at the station, broke his hand a couple months ago and hasn't been able to work on cars since. If you ask me, she should shoot the thing rather than try to fix the rusted piece of tin."

Chase agreed. When Ashley had driven off, he noted the car sounded like it should have been spare parts in a wreckage yard. A few minor repairs wouldn't fix it, only keep it going for a bit longer.

He wouldn't mind getting a nut-and-bolt kind of action going with the woman. She intrigued him. She smelled nice, had a great smile when she chose to share it, and an electrical charge vibrated between them any time he got within three feet. That kind of attraction hadn't happened for him in quite a while, if ever. But the one sticking point he couldn't ignore was the fact she didn't like the military.

"I'll keep that in mind if I get the sled working." *And stick around long enough.* "Thanks for the help." He lifted the bag of supplies and gave the retired Marine a nod.

Stepping into the afternoon sun, he felt the odd sensation of bitter cold and bright sunshine and slid his sunglasses into place. At the familiar beep notification on his phone, he swiped a thumb across the screen. Two missed messages. Another call from Coach Jon. And a follow-up call from a buddy who'd left him a message telling him he'd better call him back pronto, or he'd beat him bloody the next time he saw him. *Fat chance.*

Everyone was worried about him. He got that, but what they didn't get was he wanted some time alone. He opened the truck door and slid behind the wheel.

If it hadn't been for Coach Jon and Pastor Chris, he might have ended up in a gang or prison at the rate he'd been racking up juvie violations. Both men had somehow hammered into a stubborn kid's head that he had a choice. A choice about what he wanted out of his life.

Enlisting in the Marines had put food on the table, provided him a built-in support system, and twisted his childhood frustration into a positive blessing—although the frustration part was a massive understatement. Red-hot anger might have been a bit more precise.

He dialed Coach's number from memory, but got no answer. He'd try again later.

Today Pastor Chris had suggested he keep trying. Maybe he'd become a better man, but was he a good enough man to get involved in a relationship?

The sweet image of Ashley warmed his grief-stricken heart.

Maybe.

Then again, as emotionally busted up as he was, maybe he shouldn't go there.

CHAPTER FIVE

Chase blew on his hands, trying to warm his numb fingers while he surveyed the café. Six a.m. on a weekday morning, and the place was packed. Sitting at the counter, Harold Talbott turned and gave him a nod, so he moved in that direction.

"Bring the man a coffee, quick. He looks like he needs defrosting," Harold shouted to Maggie, who was halfway across the room. Harold gave him a thorough inspection. "Looks like you haven't slept in weeks."

Chase cringed, not liking the attention,

and hoped the friendly man didn't guess what kept him from sleeping, or the irrational need to keep a sharp knife under his pillow.

He took the seat next to Harold. "I spent the first part of the night trying to get the space heater to work, and the other part shivering. I'm just not used to the hundred-degree swing between the desert and the mountains. I'll adjust. Always do."

Maggie flipped his cup and poured a cup of java that smelled so good he couldn't wait to taste his morning liquid booster. "Want some breakfast?" A napkin-wrapped silverware set landed in front of him.

"Depends on if I can pay this time."

"You good with a screwdriver?"

His tired brain wondered what pancakes and tools had in common, and then it dawned on him. "I can find my way around a toolbox. You got something needs fixing?"

"I've had a new handle and lock for the back door for about six months. Never have found anyone to replace the broken lock. Think you can manage?"

The soldier in him winced. The small town wasn't a military installation, where security was a matter of routine. Here, people probably left their wallets and keys in their cars as well. Bad shit didn't just happen in big cities and foreign countries. Nowhere was safe. "I should be able to fix a lock."

Slapping a menu in front of him, she pointed. "You help me, and you can order anything on that menu."

"How about you have him install that security system while he's got the toolbox out."

Maggie glanced down the counter toward a guy who looked about Chase's age and was wearing a sheriff's uniform. "Joey, just 'cause you come in here lugging a security system doesn't mean it's going to be my first priority. I don't need some fancy system to tell me what's going on in my place."

"Maggie, you know as well as I do a

security system's like buying insurance. You don't need either until the day you do." The man got up to extend his hand to Chase. "You've probably guessed I'm the town sheriff. My name is Joe. I understand from Harold you're passing through on leave."

"More like finding a quiet place to rest." Chase winced for giving away too much, especially when talking to a man he suspected saw more than just the words spoken.

Joe pulled out his wallet and tossed several bills on the counter.

"Now, Sheriff. What did I tell you about overpaying?" Maggie chastised.

Joe pointed at the bills. "Tell you what... you get that security system installed, and I'll stop leaving a few extra dollars. How's that sound?"

"I'll install that camera, but it won't just be to get you to stop over-tipping." Maggie's hands lifted to her hips. "You need to find the guy who shot your brother so the whole town can rest easier, and you can help your new bride stop worrying so much. What do you think of that idea?"

"Catching a killer takes time, Maggie, but every bit helps. Thank you."

Chase studied the boulder-sized burden on the sheriff's shoulders. The distant look in his eyes created a connection for Chase and a sense of empathy.

"If Maggie will let me, I'll see if I can take care of that security system for her." Chase extended his hand to the sheriff.

The woman behind the counter gave him a direct stare. She was built like a tank, and tall enough that if he'd been standing, she'd have looked him directly in the eye. He hoped she didn't mind the offer, especially when a stack of thick, rich, maple syrup covered pancakes was on the line.

As overbearing as she was, Chase detected a little softness behind the bravado. The way she took care of the townspeople told him she was the type of person who collected stray cats and dogs and gave them a safe place to stay, put food in their empty bellies, and gave them a gruff, but loving scratch behind the ear every day.

She pointed at the menu. "So what'll it be?"

"I'll have a stack of pancakes." He handed the menu back. "Thank you, ma'am."

"Maggie," she said in her no-nonsense way. "Call me Maggie or don't bother me. And after breakfast, see Ted about that lock and that box of electrical stuff." She pointed to the cook, whose face suddenly appeared in the window behind the counter, and then moved along to fill coffee and takeout orders. Chase turned to watch the sheriff's patrol car pull from the café's lot.

Harold leaned into his space. "Don't worry about Maggie. She barks, but she doesn't bite unless she has a good reason. Just a warning, though. If you ever see a baseball bat in her hand, hightail it the other way. She took a bat to Bill Mason's place one night. It wasn't pretty."

Wonder what that's all about. "Got it," he said, before picking up his cup to take a sip so Harold wouldn't see the questions circling. He didn't need to hear the blow-by-blow.

"Any plans for the day besides fixing locks, a snowmobile, and chasing a cute blonde across town?"

Coffee went straight up Chase's nose and burned its way back down his throat. He coughed and sputtered. *What the hell?* Harold gave him a couple of good fist hammers on the back to straighten him out, but it didn't help. He reached for the water and took a much-needed drink, more to stall than clear the coffee still stinging his sinuses. "I beg your pardon?"

"What? If you don't want people to know your business, you shouldn't be standing in the middle of Main Street snuggling up to Ashley Bryant."

Had he just been transported back to the eighties?

Since meeting the woman, every other thought had been about her—her sweet smell, nice curves, and stubborn jaw. She'd disrupted his thoughts every other minute. He needed to screw his head on.

"I wasn't snuggling. I don't snuggle." He could feel the eyes of nosy townspeople on his back, but didn't want to turn around and confirm his theory.

"That's not what I saw. Here's a little advice. I'd be careful with that girl."

Maggie plopped an egg-and-bacon platter with wheat toast in front of Harold and pointed a finger at the man's chest. "Doc Brennan told you to cut back on the fat. Maybe I should start serving you fruit instead of bacon."

His eyes opened wider. "A sixty-eight-year-old man's got to be able to enjoy some things in life. And don't be going and telling Claudia, either. She'll nag me until I have to turn my hearing aid off."

Chase chuckled until Maggie's steely eyes turned to him. "What are you smiling about, soldier? Couple of years, and you might look just like him."

"Maggie—"

"Yeah, you keep telling me you can still do a hundred push-ups with one hand behind your back, but I haven't seen it yet. And, you." Maggie pointed the coffee pot in Chase's direction. "Go careful. Ashley's been through a lot these past three years, being shut in with her sick mom. She's like a daughter to me. You hurt her and you'll get run out of town faster 'n you can spit."

What was this about her mom and three years? Both Harold and Maggie's expressions said now wasn't the time to ask. Both of them genuinely cared about Ashley, and the sentiment touched him, even made him a bit jealous.

"I was just fixing some stairs and asking her about a used snowmobile. That's all."

"Bull honkey," Harold coughed behind his hand, and grinned.

Maggie rolled her eyes and walked away.

Who was he kidding? Harold was right. He was interested. Too interested. At thirty-one, he knew the consequences of hitting on a woman. By Christmas, he'd be visiting

Bobby's parents and then getting back on a plane. He wouldn't see her again. But he'd sure remember her sweet face.

I need to fix that snowmobile. Least I can do, since she won't accept rent.

"Message received. Loud and clear."

"Good." Maggie dropped a plate stacked two inches high with dinner plate-sized pancakes in front of him. A dollop of creamy, rich butter seeped into the carb heaven. "Now, get some food in your belly so you can get to work."

Ashley needed to think about something, anything other than *that* Marine. She had too many things to get done, and for several days he'd created too much of a distraction.

On the way to the store, she considered stopping for a hot cinnamon roll with cream cheese frosting dripping down the edges and freshly brewed coffee. When she saw the gray Ford sitting in the café's parking lot, she decided a granola bar and instant coffee might be safer. That man was too tempting and dangerous. She didn't need any more bad luck, considering her morning had started off with the VW Bug refusing to start, which left her with her dad's extended cab truck, a giant, snorting monster of a machine that could tug half of Elkridge behind it and not slow down.

She opened the store door, removed her coat, and then studied the delicate Art Nouveau perfume bottle sitting on the counter. She wished she could keep that particular work of art. Then again, selling the beautiful items on eBay was her way of ensuring the treasures went to someone who'd appreciate them, rather than the bank or an estate liquidator...plus, having the cash to eat and pay bills was a nice benefit. Her mother had warned she hadn't prepared Ashley for adulthood. In her naiveté, Ashley hadn't comprehended how huge an understatement it had been.

After her mother became too ill to help, Harold and Claudia had helped Ashley figure out what she could do, given the fact she had no money, no place to live, not even reliable transportation. She and Claudia had worked through the calculations several times, but no matter how they approached it, the numbers made it clear that first, she had no choice but to let the bank foreclose, and second, she couldn't take any ol' job if she wanted to pay bills and student loans. Even if she split living expenses with a roommate, there might not be enough money to put food on the table. The big, bad adult world closed in fast.

The older couple sure had been a big help, but continuing to impose on people was the last thing she wanted. The endless quandary looped around and around.

Why did life have to be so damn complicated?

Her fingers trailed along the bottle's rounded ridges, a tactile reminder of Chase's sculpted abs. She stiffened and drew a deep breath, fighting for control. No matter how handsome the man, she hoped he'd leave soon, so she could concentrate on putting her life back together.

When the door opened, she held her breath, expecting Chase, and then released it when Jenna entered with a cheerful howdy and a bakery box in hand.

"Figured you might be hiding."

Jenna's hair, tied in a loose knot at the back of her head, made her look five years younger. Obviously, she'd just come from the café, but she didn't have a spot of flour on her turquoise turtleneck or tight-fitting jeans. Darn her for looking so ready-for-anything first thing in the morning. Ashley knew her faded jeans and worn university sweatshirt looked anything but flattering. She should do something about finding an outfit suitable for job interviews. And soon.

"I'm not hiding. Just need to package the stuff I sold on eBay and get the boxes to the post office."

"Wow. You sold all this?" Jenna pointed at the table filled with vases, bookends, and her mother's porcelain doll. "Your mom should have let you run this place a long time ago."

"In Mom's mind, no one could run this store but her. It was her baby. She loved this place. Every piece in this store was discovered and chosen by her and her alone."

"At least, she won't have to see the store close."

Keeping the store and house had been the goal, but as the bank account balances dwindled, the financial necessity to liquidate became obvious. Over the past months, the anger over having to sell the little shop had sagged into acceptance. She'd miss the place because it had played a significant role in her life.

Every day after school, she used to sit at one of the back tables and do her homework while waiting for her mom to close up shop. Ashley had daydreamed the afternoons away, selecting an antique object and making up stories about it. A hand-painted brooch might take her to France, a Black Forest hand-carved clock to Germany, or a linen napkin or tablecloth to Scotland. In grade school, she could spend hours sorting silver into piles, and get a thrill out of finding a matching piece. During the summers, she and her mom would go on road trips, never failing to stop for estate or garage sale signs. Back then, Ashley hadn't realized that her mom had created the adventures so they could spend time together. Sad, really.

"Mom was a trip. Never knew whether she was heading west or east."

Jenna dropped the bakery box on the counter and looked across the sea of antiques. "But preparing stuff to ship doesn't explain why you skipped dropping by this morning."

Ashley pretended to fuss with the coffee stain on her shirt rather than face her friend's scrutiny. "I wanted to avoid Chase. I've got enough to worry about without him sabotaging my brain and turning it into mush."

"Yeah, I get it. Just looking at him melts

my butter. He's in the café, melting a few more hearts right now."

Ashley swore Jenna licked her lips. Her eyes narrowed. "What do you mean?"

"Maggie's got him over there fixing the back door. There can't be anything sexier than a guy wearing a tool belt."

A little ping zapped her heart. Oh, God, was that jealousy?

"He can just stay over there. Fix the whole town if he likes. Just as long as he doesn't bother me."

"By bother, do you mean in the hot, sexy, kissy kind of way?"

Her head did a snap and lock on her friend. "I mean the go away kind of way."

"Really? You sure? Because rumor has it you were getting pretty cozy yesterday."

Heat singed her cheeks. "Does this town have nothing better to do than spy on each other?"

"Just thinking a guy like Chase might be good to blow out the pipes a bit. It could be enjoyable. When was the last time you could relax and have fun?"

Fun? "Not lately."

Jenna walked around the counter. "Okay. If you can't spare the time to hook up with that gorgeous man, can you find time to have a night filled with carbs? Let's do a girls' night. Nothing special, just you, me, and pizza."

"You sure that's a good idea? I wouldn't want to spike your sugar levels." The blush rolling up her friend's face made her feel a bit guilty for bringing up her diabetes. "Never mind."

"No. It's okay. You know how it is. I just don't like talking about it. I've been good lately. It helps having taste-testers."

"Pizza it is, then. How about later this week, and you bring some of those lemony whatsits so I can taste-test them again?"

"I think you mean Lemon Burst Tartlets? I was thinking about adding raspberry puree to the recipe, what do you think?"

"I think no matter what you do, it will be fabulous."

A rare sparkle lit Jenna's eyes. "Don't let a guy run you off. See you at the café tomorrow?"

"Tomorrow," Ashley agreed and watched the door close behind her friend.

The next few hours were filled with bubble wrap and packing tape and went by in a flash. She'd done a good job of getting Chase out of her head until she heard the sound of the snowmobile revving in the back alley.

That tingly sensation completely destroyed her concentration. Frustrated over her lack of mental control, and curious to see if the snowmobile actually was working, she picked up her coat and walked outside while shoving her arms in the sleeves.

Chase hovered over the sled the way she wanted him to hover over her. He was a handsome man, especially when he gave her a smile that said he'd just unwrapped the man toy he'd ordered for Christmas. He had on a gray T-shirt covered by a red-checked flannel shirt, tucked into a pair of jeans sitting just right. Every inch looked deliciously tempting. The excitement of getting the sled working might have caused his celebration, however, the joyous grin infected her, and she returned his glorious smile.

"You got it started." She wanted to give herself a swift kick for sounding so... so...blonde.

"Took some work. She just needed a new filter, some oil, and a lube job."

Lube job. Like blowing the pipes out. She groaned and felt a blush scroll across her face. The instinct to run like hell battled with the urge to kiss him silly. "I just came out to check on you. Looks like you're doing great. I'd better get back to work."

"Hey, wait." He launched ahead double time to catch up. "I thought you said if I got it working, you'd be my guide."

The guy had a memory like a stinking

computer. "You're right, I did. But maybe this girl has a right to change her mind."

"She does." The disappointment in his eyes made her pause. "Look, it's been a rough couple of months. Do you mind if I take the rig and do some exploring on my own? I promise not to break anything. It's a beautiful day. What do you say?"

She agreed. No place on earth could be more splendid than Colorado on a crisp December morning—fresh powder glistening in the sun, icicles dripping melting water, the air smelling of wood-burning fireplaces.

A hint of excitement surrounded a whole lot of sadness and made the excuses evaporate. She wouldn't be the one responsible for preventing his escape from whatever he'd seen on tour.

"Integrity is a window into a person's soul."

He cocked his head to the side. "Nice saying. It's almost poetry. I should write that down."

"The saying is my dad's. I made a promise. I need to keep it. I'll pack some food."

"I was hoping you'd agree, so I already ordered us lunch." He glanced back at the snowmobile. "We just need gas."

Ordered us lunch? Just thinking about where he might have purchased the food made a knot twist in her stomach. The obvious place would be the café, meaning the whole town knew about the outing. He didn't get small towns. The need for privacy. He should, since he must have lived in open barracks at some point. Maybe he just didn't care.

What would her mother think?

She paused, her chest tightening. Never again would she have to worry about her mom's opinion. The emptiness expanded, carving out another piece of her heart, before Chase's movements yanked her back to the present.

At least I'll be safe. The whole town knows where I'll be.

"I haven't allowed myself to have fun in a while. We both need a day off." She clutched the keys to her dad's truck. "We'd better get the sled loaded into the truck. You'll find a loading ramp and security straps in the shed." She tossed him the keys, and he snatched the ring mid-air. "I'll just get my boots and gloves. You need anything?"

"I saw a pair of heavier gloves and a face mask in the shed. Do you mind if I borrow them?"

"Take them. They'll just be tossed or given away soon anyway. And don't forget the helmets."

Questions filled his eyes.

Questions about her past and her present.

Questions she didn't want to answer, so she turned and walked back into the store.

CHAPTER SIX

*C*hase craned his neck to see past Ashley. He'd seen a lot of pretty places, but nothing this spectacular.

Fluffy white snow floated from the sky and whirled in eddies. The Rocky Mountains stretched out around them in an infinite display of unfolding peaks, deep gorges and stunning, ice-covered streams.

Ashley took the driver's position and zoomed up the old logging road, pointing out hazards while they travelled. His hands rested on her hips, and he worked hard to avoid scooching up and folding her against his body. He could feel himself reacting physically to her warm, soft curves.

Man, he needed to shove his ass in a snow bank. Permanently.

Concentrating, he studied the passing landscape rather than how her body felt. How her heat sent a tingle down his spine.

She pointed.

A group of deer standing at the tree line watched them whiz past. At another clearing, a female elk and her almost-grown offspring had gathered for lunch. Ashley gave the animals space.

The valley below reminded him of a snow globe he'd once seen at a foster home. He remembered letting his imagination take over, wishing he could live in the town where there was room to breathe, and people cared about one another. He didn't think life could get much better than Elkridge. People cared. As evidenced by the chest-pounding he'd gotten that morning.

He'd decided to back off, not pursue the attraction. But his head and body just couldn't quite put the decision into action.

Because here he was.

Enjoying her company.

Snuggling close.

After an hour, they decided to stop for lunch. He liked how she didn't need to ruin the sound of wind blowing through the branches or birds chirping with inconsequential conversations. For someone so tiny, she had an enduring strength. That spunky, almost defiant attitude was such a turn-on. And that scared him. Being scared pissed him off. Getting shot at or blown up was one thing, but being petrified of what Ashley could do to him scared him more.

Reaching another clearing, she dismounted and turned the machine over to him so he could have some fun, first pointing out off-limits areas. He took off, and twenty minutes later, he skidded to a stop a safe distance from where she stood, spraying her boots with snow.

"You have a grandpa license or something?" she laughed. "I've never seen anyone manage to putter along on a snowmobile like a creaky old grandma."

After always being the guy going mach five, he'd learned in Afghanistan never to go anywhere fast, always take it easy, and to never forget a bomb could detonate with the next step or roll of a wheel. The sights and smells of bloody bodies and the twisted wreckage surrounding Bobby's death haunted him. He closed his eyes and then dismounted to move next to her.

He pointed at the tracks in the snow. "What do you see?"

She squinted at the snow-covered field. A look of awe crossed her face. "You spelled my name."

Heat thrummed through his body and he shifted his gaze from her mouth to her eyes. Ashley's intense stare was similar to the one she gave him earlier in the day, but this time her gaze never wavered. The wind caught the ends of her hair, tossing strands in her face. She didn't notice. He wished he could read her mind. The need consumed his body. Her direct eye contact, the licking of her lips, the way she leaned in made him reciprocate. Suddenly, she moved away, taking off her helmet, and walking to the edge of the hill overlooking the ridge. He followed at a distance until reaching her side.

"Look over there. That's the café and the store. Just a bit closer is the grocery and hardware store. The big building to the left is the visitor center and courthouse."

"That looks like a sports field of some sort."

"It's the high school."

He pointed to a large estate just below the ridge. "Who lives there?"

"That house is for sale." Lifting her chin, she scanned the sky. Her emotions shuttered and dimmed her earlier joyous shine. "We'd better get back. The snow's picking up." Without another word, she followed the trail of footprints back toward the snowmobile.

The large house nestled against the ridge

attracted his attention again. Something about the house had made her shut down. He rubbed his hands over his face, uttering silent, frustrated curses, wracking his brain to figure out what the hell he'd said to send her into hiding this time.

He hadn't meant to turn her off.

He seriously considered throwing her over his shoulder and dumping her in a snow bank, and then tickling her just to see if he could get her smile to return. How insane was that? He leaned over and scooped a handful of snow, squeezing and pressing the frozen water together to ease his frustrations. Without thinking, he stretched his arm back and launched—bulls-eye.

His brain froze when she whipped around. The combustible playful passion in her features could only be described as spectacular. So magnificent, so distracting, he only had a second to respond to the threat of an inbound snowball. Dodging left, he tracked his prey with fixed determination. Ashley ran left, then right, launching snowballs as fast as she could make them. With every passing second, he slowly closed in on his target. She reached down for more snow, trying to hold him off, but when she reached her arm back, he rushed in and scooped her into his embrace, effectively disarming her.

She threw her head back and laughed. "Put me down."

He loved the sound of her laugh, an open and free expression of joy. Gone was the melancholy he'd seen moments earlier. She wiggled in his arms and brought his attention back to those luscious lips.

"No," he said.

"That's not fair," she complained.

He enjoyed watching her eyes fill with mischief. "What's not fair?"

"You're bigger than I am."

Considering he'd refused to respond to her relentless barrage of snow-bullets, he'd been more than equitable. Especially since a few of her balls had hit their mark. "Ashley, you're more than capable of defending yourself. I'm not falling for your weaker-sex excuse. Another woman tried that once. Let's just say I'm a quick learner."

She tilted her head back. "If I pout, will that work?"

"Nope."

"I'll promise not to throw any more snowballs, if you will." She laughed and pushed on his chest. "Let me down."

He reluctantly set her on her feet. She walked back to the sled and sat on the seat. "Where are you from, Chase? You haven't said much about your family."

And if he had his way, he didn't intend to. What could he say?

That his birth mother hated him for being too much like his father—the father he never knew? That his mom had finally lost custody after being arrested for the third time on meth charges, and the New Jersey court system had sent him to a foster home? That at six years old, he was no longer a cute baby someone might want to adopt?

His military brothers became his family.

Maybe they didn't have his blood running through their veins, but they'd shared more than enough blood in the field. He'd do anything for his buddies, including give his life—like Bobby had.

He took a deep breath, remembering and honoring his friend's sacrifice. He missed him, a lot.

He went over and sat on the snowmobile seat beside her, releasing the bungee cord holding a cooler, and handing her a bottle of water. "The military is my real family. I know you're not into the military, but the guys are like brothers, a bit wacked sometimes, but when the chips are down, they have my back. The Corps has provided me with stability."

"Stability. Really? You call moving every few years stability?" She gave him a direct stare, then something shifted. "Don't answer that. I'm being unfair, and biased."

"It's all right." Without thinking, he brushed snow from her jacket. "I see the look on some wives' and girlfriends' faces when we're about to deploy. I get it."

She swallowed a bite of her Reuben on marbled rye. "It must be hard fighting in a foreign country when people back home forget the events occurring on the other side of the globe. I'm sure when you are home, the dramas seem small compared to what you live with on a daily basis. It's no wonder your service mates become closer than family."

The understanding he saw in her expression amazed him. "Are your parents together?"

"Nope. Still married. From what my mom said, we moved five times in seven years, and were about to move again when my mom called a time-out and moved here instead. She wanted to build a place—a place for my dad to come home to—but with hindsight, I think she just wanted to plant some roots."

Chase took the last bite of his meal and stuffed the paper wrapping back in the bag. "I can understand wanting to stay put.

Soldiers relocate a lot. There's no reason their family has to."

"But then the kids grow up not knowing their parent."

The way her expression turned sad nearly gutted him. "Ashley?" he asked softly. He hated her sorrowful expression. He lifted a hand to her cheek and was surprised when she pushed his arm away.

"Please don't. Don't feel sorry for me. I don't want your pity."

Pity had to be the last thing he felt. Loneliness maybe, which made him ache for her. He understood just because a person surrounded themselves with people didn't mean they weren't lonely. Like him, she didn't have family support, yet she'd created one. She had a whole town watching out for her, caring for her. And she gave caring in return. Harold had filled his ears with stories about how she'd organized a local bake sale to support the race for multiple sclerosis, or donated books to the local library, and found homes for any stray animal that happened to get lost in Elkridge.

She had a lot to give. And he got that, too.

"There's no pity here."

"That's good." The smooth sensual response included a playful smile, before additional emotions flowed across her face and changed her mood. "Thank you for fixing the snowmobile. Today's been perfect."

But her perpetual, underlying sadness settled in again. Crap, her angelic eyes mesmerized him. Those beautiful and soulful eyes made him want things. Things he wasn't sure he could ever have. His eyes dropped to her mouth, and he leaned in before remembering the last time she'd run off when he tried to kiss her. He eased back.

"You're welcome. But like with the stairs, I must be honest. I didn't fix the snowmobile just for you."

"No?" There was that beautiful lift of the brow. She leaned in a bit more.

"No, I did it to stay busy. If I don't stay

busy, my mind tends to... Let's just say I need to keep busy."

She removed her glove and ran a hand down his face, her fingers stopping at the dimple in his chin. Her warm finger touched his lower lip.

God, he wanted to kiss her. Her gaze reminded him how he felt when he'd looked at his pancakes at breakfast. The thick buttermilk flapjacks with delicious, creamy butter and thick, sticky maple syrup running down the sides.

"Let's see if I can't keep your mind busy." Ashley moved closer.

CHASE GROANED, one of those hell-yeah sounds, and the next minute his hand moved to the back of her neck and guided her in.

His kiss tasted brown sugar sweet, and she searched with her tongue to taste. His tongue stroked and sampled greedily, while his lips and teeth nibbled.

She hadn't meant to lean in, but then she saw the same hurt in his expression she clearly felt.

His strong, protective arms surrounded her and held her close. His wet lips pressed in, a little bit hungry, a little bit determined. She let out a soft murmur. Strong arms crossed over her shoulders and then tightened, his hands caressing. Embers deep inside her ignited, and a whispered promise of something beautiful and magical fanned the flame. A hunger she hadn't known existed seized her. She wanted to stop the insanity, but his gentle yet urgent hands held tight.

She moaned and met his need. His arms created a strong, secure haven. She hadn't felt safe in way too long. He deepened their connection, and she groaned and concentrated on absorbing his warmth, experiencing the heat and hardness of every last inch of him.

She could feel the moment when his brain re-engaged because he started to tear away, but she wasn't ready to let go. "More," sighed from her lips, and it felt exactly right.

He let out a low growl and drove deeper. Her body hummed, and his arousal left no doubt he felt the same sizzle. The smell of cookie dough made her nuzzle closer to get a better sniff. She couldn't help herself. Stopping would have been like putting the lid back on the gallon of ice cream, and she couldn't do that. She trailed her kisses across his skin and found his ear to nibble on his lobe. He sighed her name.

His fingers wrapped gently around her neck and dragged her lips back to his. Just when she speculated he might come up for air, he dove back in for one last hurrah. Her mind exploded with excitement as he peppered her face with little kisses. She let her head fall back and allowed him to take his fill. The clouds drifting overhead made her feel like she was floating.

And suddenly she was slipping and

plummeting back to earth. Her mind screamed *no, no, no,* but it was too late. His taut muscles released her, his lips still reluctant to leave hers. Her muscles had turned to mush, and she had a hard time keeping her balance. Her eyes finally flickered open, and the raw desire she saw in his brown eyes warmed her all the way to her toes.

"Wow," he said, his voice a bit shaky.

Her forehead dropped against his chest. "That's all you can say? Wow?"

"Yeah." His hand had come to rest on top of her head. "I wasn't expecting that."

She had no idea what he was expecting. They had chemistry. Lots of it. She didn't need to take a college science course to know how explosive certain elements could be. Slipping from his arms, she stood and took a step to create distance.

She pressed fingertips to her lips to quell the sensations. "We weren't...I wasn't.... Well. Crap."

The need had been urgent. Like her life

depended on it. She'd clung to him as if he were her lifeline and she dangled off a hundred-foot cliff. She blamed it on his smell. Buttery rich and gooey.

He raised a hand, stopping her tumbling thoughts and stood, taking her hand. "This is my fault," he said, his voice thick with confusion and frustration.

"No, it's not. I'm the one who threw myself at you."

"But..." He didn't say anything else, just looked at her like he wanted nothing more than to kiss her again, which made her wonder why she hadn't wanted him to kiss her in the first place.

He's leaving. That was it. But did his leaving really matter?

Yes, she concluded.

She had no right to start on a journey she couldn't finish. Berating lectures from her mother filled her head. She turned and walked to the tree line to create some distance. For a moment, she stood watching the dry snow swirl on a wind current, trying to absorb the tranquility of the scene and ease the violent wave of emotions still crashing around inside her. The snow crunched behind her, and she felt the warmth of his breath on the back of her neck.

She was beginning to think maybe kissing and leaving shouldn't have anything to do with each other. Jenna had suggested she enjoy herself. Locking lips with this magnificent-looking, muscle-packed soldier blasted the top off the awesomeness scale.

Suddenly, he yanked her to the ground and covered her body before she even heard the sound of a rifle shot echoing through the hills.

"Stay down," he demanded.

She lifted her head, but he held it down. Another shot echoed off the valley walls.

"It's just someone target practicing," she assured him.

The intensity in his body eased. "And five, maybe six hundred yards away. Close enough for a friendly fire accident. That's too close for comfort. We should go." He inhaled a long, slow, scare-depleting breath. Then he hauled her up and brushed the snow off her jacket. "The sun'll be down soon anyway."

"You're right. I still have things to do back at the shop."

The tension in his body and the wild, intense look in his eyes should have frightened her, but it didn't. He walked back toward the sled. She followed him, securing her helmet. Seconds later, he joined her, letting the silence ease both of them back to reality.

Speeding down the logging trail, she couldn't help but feel she'd just missed winning the lottery by one number. The kiss had touched her more than she wanted to admit. The intense, sensual emotion—more than him leaving—had been the reason she called a halt.

Traveling in silence, racing toward the truck, she felt every inch of his arms and legs and chest nuzzling closer. She let the snow and wind pelt her face, hoping soon her body would go numb from the cold so she'd stop feeling the confusion and culpability seeping into her bones.

Lost in thought, she almost missed the movement in the trees, but then she eased back on the gas a little and scanned the tree line. There it was again. Movement—the first reason why things are seen. The list she'd memorized to get her dad's approval—shape, size, shine, texture, color, and shade—rolled on.

She slowed the snowmobile even more. Cougars and bears roamed the hills, and once in a while, the wild animals liked to chase and play with moving objects. She didn't want to get caught off guard, so she let the machine slide to a stop. Chase's arm came around her shoulder, his index finger pointing. She inched the machine closer to the edge of the tree line, spotting drops of blood. Ten feet away, she saw a pair of nervous eyes peering from behind the bramble bushes. When she whistled, the animal's ears perked her direction.

"I'll be back."

Chase's gloved hand tugged on her arm. "This isn't a good idea. That coyote or dog, whatever it is, could be rabid."

"If he snarls and I come running, it's your job to get us out of here. And I expect full throttle. None of that grandma driving." She forced her shoulders to relax and hoped the lack of outward tension would ease his concerns.

"I hope you know what you're doing." His warning made her pause and second guess. She held his gaze for a moment before facing the forest.

He didn't interfere, but his whole body went on alert, impressing her and boosting her confidence. Reaching into her pocket, she retrieved the plastic-wrapped strip of smoked buffalo jerky a hunter had given her in exchange for one of the knives in her mom's store. She'd intended the jerky to be her emergency provisions, just like her fire starter, but she supposed this situation constituted an emergency. Unwrapping the piece of dried meat, she tentatively approached the edge of the road, squatted, extended the food to the animal, and waited. Minutes passed before she heard a twig break, then more movement. Wind continued to ease through the evergreens. The temperature continued to drop as the sun sank lower in the sky. The fetid smells of blood and animal eventually wafted her way. She choked back the smell, breathed through her mouth.

"That's it. Come and get it."

A matted black dog hobbled forward, dragging a rear leg behind, blood smearing the snow. She waited.

"A few more steps. You can do it."

As the animal came closer, she could see the gaunt face and the protruding rib cage of what looked like a large shepherd. The more she saw, the more she was convinced this dog had almost been some predator's dinner. When she met the dog's gaze, something connected, and the dog walked past her arm extended with food and shoved its head into her chest before collapsing at her feet.

"That's a good boy." She stroked the fur, looking for broken skin and bones. A big chunk had been taken out of the dog's neck, and the back leg looked mangled. On closer inspection, though, nothing appeared broken, although several bite marks had penetrated the skin. She stroked the animal's coat with her gloved hand while she continued to whisper soft endearments. A few minutes passed before she felt a strong hand on her shoulder. She looked up at Chase. His hand held a large hunting knife.

Knife! Panic set in before rational thought defused the fear.

"What do you want to do?" He offered more than his simple words conveyed.

She looked at the dog, its eyes filled with pain, then at the seven-inch blade, which could quickly end the dog's suffering. She met Chase's eyes. "I can't. I just can't leave him."

The brutal-looking instrument disappeared immediately, and Chase returned to the snowmobile.

Relief, then fear shortened her breath. *How am I going to afford to do this?*

Medical supplies, shots, food—it all cost money. Money she didn't have.

I'll make it work. Somehow, I have to make it work.

She didn't think this situation was dire enough to contact her dad and ask for help. Mentally, she rummaged through the remaining store inventory, thinking what else she could put on eBay or sell to an antique dealer in Denver. Maybe she would make lots of money at the Christmas Bazaar. She certainly didn't like the alternatives.

Chase reappeared with the insulated safety blanket that had been stored under the snowmobile seat and spread it on the road. With his help, she carefully lifted and placed the dog on the tarp. Too weak to move, the dog remained silent except for one weak whine when they jostled him accidentally.

Chase's concerned eyes met hers. "You hold the dog. I'll drive. We'll keep him between us for warmth."

She nodded, straddled the sled, and waited for Chase to hand her the dog. Having Chase put the dog out of its misery might have been easier for the dog, and easier for her, but she couldn't do it. Day in and day out, she'd watched her mother suffer, feeling helpless to do anything except bathe her and give her more medication when she asked. She kept waiting for her mom to ask her to end her life, but thankfully her mother never did.

Caring was in Ashley's blood, her bones —a virus never to be eradicated.

When Chase approached the snowmobile, she held out her arms for the suffering animal. Chase said nothing, just looked at her with understanding. He settled in front, nestling the dog between, and began the slow descent down the trail. She hadn't cried when her mother died. She should have, but she'd been so relieved her mom was no longer in pain, she just couldn't. So why did the tears flow now? She let the tears come, doing nothing to stop them, and held on tight to the dog cradled in her lap.

The dog needed medical assistance and a safe place to recover. She would need Chase's help, which meant he would see her parents' house. It couldn't be helped.

He might judge her. Just like some of the other people in town. But the fact was, her mom had money. *Had* being the operative word. If Chase didn't understand, then let him be jealous or resentful.

But somehow she believed he would understand.

Since he'd fixed the stairs, Maggie's door, and the snowmobile, she trusted him. Besides, Harold had texted her about the heater not working in the studio apartment, and asked if she wanted to borrow his space heater. Chase hadn't said a word about the heat, and Harold wouldn't worry about someone he didn't like. Like Jenna had said, why not let him kick his boots under one of the beds? She did have several not being used.

The dog needed her. To help him, she needed Chase.

That was as simple as it got.

Right or wrong.

CHAPTER SEVEN

After loading the sled and dog in the truck, Chase drove them down the mountain road. Ashley sat in the back seat, left a message with the town's veterinarian, and did everything possible to comfort the dog while providing directions.

Pulling into the driveway of the palatial house—the large estate he spotted from the ridge—he studied Ashley in the rearview mirror. She met his gaze, then directed him to back the truck into a garage.

The four-car garage was immaculately designed, complete with a collection of wrenches and screwdrivers and power tools most men dreamed of owning, but could never afford, all covered in dust, unused. Overhead, two specially designed racks held snowmobiles and other ski equipment. The beat-up VW Bug sat in the far stall.

He turned off the ignition and walked around to the passenger side. Ashley gently relinquished the animal into his care, leading the way to the interior door while the garage door closed. She glanced back to make sure he followed and didn't require assistance with the dog, and then entered an oversized kitchen, which would have made a perfect spot for a platoon meeting, with plenty of extra room. She took a left into a living room filled with quality leather furniture and a river rock fireplace, and then another left into another, smaller room, just off the main hall.

Ashley pointed to a corner area piled with comforters and sheets. "We'll settle him there."

When the animal heard her voice, he

thrashed, and Chase tightened his grip, gently lowering the injured dog to the floor.

Ashley immediately reached for the dog's head, cooing comfort, and sat on the carpet next to a small stone fireplace.

She tried masking her concern, but there was soft sorrow lining her face. Like too many of the medics he'd worked with, she absorbed the patient's pain, creating a sphere of empathy.

"Can you start a fire?" she asked.

Logs and kindling were conveniently stacked in a metal grate, and a brass holder bolted to the wall held matches. If he couldn't strike a match, there was something seriously wrong with him.

The oversized family room didn't look like anyone had used it for a while. Mismatched pictures in various shapes and sizes and styles hung on the walls. A big area rug covered the center of the large room, with a small twin bed shoved to the side. A small oak desk and a wingback chair sat against the opposite wall. Something about the space felt odd, different.

The rest of the house appeared open, warm, and tastefully decorated, but this room, even though adequately heated, seemed morbidly chilly with a cold that crept into his bones. He leaned over to strike a long-stick match.

Once the dried pine caught hold, he stood back and watched Ashley stroke the dog's fur, talking to the animal in a quiet, gentle voice. He couldn't hear what she said, but it didn't matter. The dog only cared that he wasn't alone. Hearing a car arrive, Chase went in search of a door leading to the outside. When he found the right one, he opened the solid, thirteen-foot door.

A guy about the same age as Ashley, carrying a large leather case, slid his way to the front door and paused when he realized something was off. "I was expecting Ash."

"And you are?"

"Brad Clairemont. Ash texted something about a hurt dog and to bring supplies."

He expected as much, but the wool overcoat and tan loafers worn without socks raised his guard. Metrosexual didn't fit the small-town vibe, and the guy's return scrutiny didn't sit well, either. An ex-boyfriend, maybe? He didn't know, and cared more than he should. He would have liked to barricade the door, but he stood aside rather than let the guy stay on the front porch and freeze his delicate, undoubtedly polished toes off.

"This way," Chase said, closing the door before leading the way down the hall.

Ashley looked up when Chase entered the room. He pointed over his shoulder. "Vet's here."

"Hey, Brad. Thanks for coming."

The guy's eyes scanned Ashley the way a scanner rolls over a bar code, catching the intricacies of every line. Chase wasn't amused. In fact, he had the urge to toss the guy out the front door, headfirst into a pile of snow. But he managed to maintain an impressive degree of restraint. It was obvious the vet fancied himself a ladies' man, and he was glad to see Ashley didn't buy into the strutting peacock's act.

Ashley shifted the dog so Brad could take a closer look. After a few minutes of evaluating and assessing and leaning in a bit too close to Ashley, Brad gave the dog a couple of shots, stitched his neck and leg, and bandaged both. He took his time handing Ashley a pill bottle and bags of fluids and syringes, giving specific instructions. Too much time.

Finally, after an eternity of minutes, Brad closed his case. "That dog's lucky. He wouldn't have made it through the night. The next twenty-four hours will be critical, Ash. See if you can get him to eat. Right now, you need to keep him warm and calm."

Ashley's shoulders pushed back, silently communicating she had no intention of leaving the dog's side. Chase and Brad looked at each other, understanding passing between them before they stepped into the hall.

The vet handed him a piece of paper.

"Here's a list of supplies needed, but you might want to wait until morning. The dog's in pretty bad shape."

"The dog will make it." The adamant conviction in his tone left no room for argument.

"Just setting realistic expectations."

"Let's focus on the positive, shall we?" *Before I get arrested putting you out of your designer-jeans misery.*

Brad, however, wasn't totally stupid. He registered the not-so-subtle warning that said, *I'm a grenade, and in about ten seconds I'm going to go off, so move out of the way.* Without a word, Brad shot out of the house, slipping and sliding on the ice, which suited Chase just fine. Neither Ashley nor the dog would benefit from hearing doubt. Instinct told him if anyone could see the dog through the night, Ashley could. He shoved Brad's list in his pocket, closed the door, and made his way back to the nursing room.

A half-smile formed on Ashley's lips. "Thank you."

"For?"

"Believing."

He crouched in front of her and ran a gentle hand over the dog's fur. "You heard."

She rubbed the dog's stiff black ears between her fingers. "He'll make it. I know he will." Her voice quivered. "I'll give him a bath tomorrow. Tonight I think he needs to settle in. He's had enough trauma for one day."

A bag of fluids hung from a coat hanger on the wall and a tube extended to the dog's back. Combat training had exposed Chase to needles, syringes, and other sorts of emergency gear. He wondered how such a sweet-faced angel had come to know how to set up a triage kit.

Understanding dawned slowly, like the sunrise lifting into the sky. His gaze moved to the indentations in the carpet where another bed might have been. Her mother's. A twin bed in the corner. Hers. 24/7. Empathy for what this caring woman had gone through touched his heart, like seeing the hungry children in the streets of Kabul. Witnessing her with the dog, he realized she couldn't walk away from that dog any more easily than he could leave a wounded buddy.

He pointed at the open closet organized with towels, sheets, and other supplies. "Do you need another blanket or pillow? Can I get you anything to eat? Water?"

She turned her head toward the closet. "Another blanket might be good, and if you don't mind, a bowl of water for the dog wouldn't be a bad idea."

The offers meant for her were brushed aside. He was pretty sure she always put others before her needs, rarely ever considering her own needs or desires first.

He watched the slow rise and fall of the dog's ribcage, trying to decide if the mutt would hold on long enough for him to make it to the store and back. He didn't want Ashley to be alone if the dog died. He squatted and looked into golden-brown eyes. "She's counting on you to hang in there, okay, buddy? Don't disappoint the lady. You hear me?"

What he saw in the dog's eyes gave him hope and assurance. What he saw in her eyes made him want to tug her into his arms and make love to her until the worry went away. "I best get to the store before it closes." The appreciation in her gaze pleased him more than he wanted to admit. "I'll find something to put water in for the dog. You sure you don't need anything before I go?"

"No. I'll be okay. There's money in my wallet. Please, take it."

Not gonna happen. He'd rather be shot than take one cent from her. He tore off a piece of paper from the list Brad had given him and grabbed a pen off the oak desk in the corner. "Here's my cell number in case you think of something while I'm out." He placed the number on the desk, then turned to leave, a shudder passing through him as he walked out of the room.

He'd given her his number. Ashley might not have thought much of it, but he never, ever gave his cell number to a female. Even his mom didn't have it. Driving into town, he considered the handful of people he'd truly allowed in his life, none of them women. For the last two-plus years, he'd found even the simplest relationship with a female too complicated. So why now did he find it easy to get attached to this woman? Maybe because she seemed so sad and vulnerable, and his protective instincts kicked in. Or perhaps because he liked the intense emotions in her eyes—the willingness to help, care, and give of herself.

In the hell he'd lived in for the past several deployments, very little good existed. He wanted to feel all wasn't lost, that good still existed in the world, but he also didn't want to taint her with his pain and sorrow.

Right now, he wasn't whole. Bobby had left a big fucking gap in the middle of his chest, and he couldn't find a way to fill it. He needed to crawl back out of the trench and keep fighting. But right now he didn't know how. And he sure as hell didn't want the muck to stick to anyone else, especially her.

He stared at the Valu-Shop sign, surprised to find he was parked in front. If he'd gotten into a car and driven like that in Afghanistan, he might have not only killed himself, but taken others with him. He needed to strap down his emotions. He closed the truck door and moved to the store's entrance.

"There he is." Harold raised his hand in greeting when Chase took a step inside the door. "Heard you went snowmobiling today. Great day for it."

Wow, news travels. "Yep," Chase acknowledged, but couldn't get his happy on at the moment. "You got any dog or baby food?"

Harold gave him a wide-eyed, confused look, but he was kind enough not to ask. "Sure do. Back in the left corner."

Chase picked up a basket and began weaving his way to the back. Spotting the pet section, he entered the aisle, looked at the list, and then at the large bags of dog food, then the small bags, then the cans. He reached for the first bag, then paused, his hand suspended in the air, wondering whether he should get chicken and vegetables or liver and rice. So many choices. He rubbed his hand over the top of his head. Overseas, he got what was available. Once a month, if a soldier got lucky, the mobile PX truck would stop at their location, a friend might get mailed a package with stuff to share, or USO care packages might arrive. He dropped his hand in frustration.

"I think I know how you feel." He turned to see Harold standing at the end of the aisle. "I felt the same way when I came back from 'Nam. After eating the same crap month after month and coming home to a smorgasbord, I could never get just one thing. I ended up buying one of everything and letting my wife sort it out once I got home. She refused to send me to the store after a while."

"Is that why you own a store now? You needed to get rid of extra supplies?"

"That's a smartass remark for someone who's not too far off the mark."

Chase liked the understanding smile in the old man's eyes. He nodded toward the food. "Got any recommendations for an emaciated, injured dog that Ashley's decided to nurse?"

Harold shook his head. "That girl's got a heart as deep as the Grand Canyon."

The old man held out his hand for the list, and Chase happily passed it over.

"Here, take this." Harold dumped a few cans in the basket and walked to another aisle. "You might need these." The man began to fill the basket with bags and cans and jars.

"You trying to make Ashley think I've lost my mind?"

"If she's anything like my Claudia, she'll understand." The man's eyes softened at the mention of his wife. "Been married a long time. She's my miracle."

A miracle. Chase hadn't experienced one of those, and wondered if he might be due.

"I should mention, when we were out today, someone was firing off rounds. Seems a bit odd so close to town."

"Happens now and then. You should tell the sheriff. Joe would want to know."

"I don't want any trouble. Maybe when you see him you could mention it to him. Informal, like. We were on the ridge behind the Bryants' place. Sounded like a Remington 870, same one we use in the Corps. Two shots were fired, no more than five- maybe six-hundred yards out."

"The sheriff's brother was killed earlier this year. Authorities are still looking for the guy. I'll be sure to pass the information along."

Chase considered the worry in the old man's eyes, taking note, then slowly shifted his gaze to the cold cabinet filled with assorted packed deli meats and cheeses and other packaged items. "Any recommendations for dinner?"

Ten minutes later, he had a truck filled with groceries at the insistence of Harold, and leftover pot roast and peach cobbler courtesy of Claudia. He draped his wrists over the steering wheel, gazing through the windshield. The clouds had started to clear, and he located the North Star. A small piece of ice had broken off his frozen heart and begun to melt. In this little community, surrounded by people he didn't know, he felt humbled.

He'd driven into town a stranger and been instantly accepted by the townsfolk of Elkridge, no questions asked. He wasn't a drunkard or whore's son, or some stupid kid from New Jersey, or merely a Marine. It might have taken thirty-one years to get here, but he felt accepted—a person of worth.

It had been awhile since he cared about someone else's opinions.

In fact, he rarely cared what a woman thought, but he certainly cared about what Ashley thought of him.

He wanted Ashley to believe he was one of the good guys because he sure didn't like her view of him as a Marine, which translated into the equivalent of bad.

ASHLEY AWOKE to find Chase sitting in the chair across the darkened room, staring into the fire, lost in thought.

Firelight danced on his face and made him look exotic, and even more handsome, if that was possible. She hadn't made a sound, but he turned his head and stared into her eyes.

"You're back," she said.

"You looked so at ease when I got back from the store. I didn't want to wake you."

She touched the edges of the extra blanket covering both her and the dog, and then glanced at the closet, and then Chase.

"Thank you for the comforter." She tugged the blanket a bit higher. "Did you eat?"

"Claudia sent me home with pot roast. There's more if you want it."

She didn't know whose stomach growled, hers or the dog's, but she needed to get up or she wouldn't be able to walk in the morning. She'd let the shepherd sleep until the meds wore off, and then would try getting him outside to pee. She had absorbent pads somewhere, but finding additional supplies could wait until morning. She moved the dog's paw pinning her arm, and then piled extra fabric under the dog's head. His eyelids lifted.

"It's okay, Lucky. You're safe." The dog's lids blinked a few times before he relaxed back into slumber.

Chase's brow lifted. "You named him Lucky?"

"Actually, Brad named him by saying he was lucky to be alive. I figured it fitting." She studied the leather journal in his hands. "What are you writing?"

"It's nothing."

"Nothing. Right." She couldn't help the sarcasm dripping like sap, fertilized by her disappointment.

What was it about the Marines that made its members shut out the world around them? They honed their emotions to such a fine point that only small bits of feelings escaped from time to time. On the rare occasions when her dad did come home, he'd often stare into the distance. When asked what he was thinking, he'd give some generic answer, never a real, honest one. She pushed to her feet and headed toward the kitchen.

"Poems," he whispered as she walked past.

The desire to leave the room wavered, and she took a half-step back. "What did you say?"

"I like to write poems." Emotions and the firelight danced in his eyes.

"Do you have a favorite?"

"There's a poem by Rudyard Kipling I like. It's about what it takes to be a man."

A thimbleful of reminiscence got lodged

in her throat, making it hard to swallow. "My dad has a framed print of it hanging in the garage. It's his favorite. Have you ever read Maya Angelou's poem, *Alone?*"

Chase shook his head.

Nobody can make it out here alone. "Look it up on the internet sometime. You might like it."

Her body reacted to his openness, desire welled inside her. The heat and intensity of his gaze created a flow of sensation that seeped from her every pore. She stood mesmerized by his handsome face, remembering how his demanding, yet giving, lips felt against hers. She fought the impulse to walk over to him and curl up in his arms. Lucky shifted in his sleep, thankfully, and broke the connection.

Chase lifted from the chair. "I'd better go. It's late. Can I borrow your truck?"

"Stay." The single word came out so fast, she couldn't snatch it back, so she went with her gut. "There's plenty of room here, and I might need help with Lucky." She pointed at the dog, grasping for any excuse to avoid being alone in the giant house.

When attending her mother, she'd longed for the solitude, only to find once she got her wish, solitude wasn't really what she wanted. With her mother gone, the house felt like a crypt. She hadn't known how loud quiet could be until she even missed the sound of her mother's congested wheeze.

"You sure?" He took a step closer. "Earlier you didn't even want me to know this was your house."

"I can explain."

His warm fingers closed around her hand. "You don't have to. You like your privacy. I get that."

"It's not about privacy. It's about being judged. People see this house and they immediately decide my life's caviar. But it's not like that. My parents stretched to build this house. My mom wanted a perfect life, and decorated like she was aiming for a layout in a designer magazine. In the end, we couldn't even afford to heat the place, much less pay the mortgage. As a result, I learned that a house, a car, a nice wardrobe can be unnecessary accessories."

"I hear you. There are a lot of things in life people think they need, but they really don't. I get the part about being judged. People have put labels on me my whole life."

She crossed her arms to prevent her from fidgeting. "Try having an unconventional family."

"Try having a mother who's an addict. I don't tell many people because, like you've found, people make assumptions. My mother doesn't define me, either."

The cold tension she'd been holding turned warm. "So you do get it."

"I do. I take it your mom was sick."

She bit her lip contemplating what to share. How much to share. Or, whether she should share at all. She took a gutty breath. "Multiple sclerosis. But pneumonia took her life."

"Is that why you want me to stay? Because you don't want to be alone?"

She uncrossed her arms and took a step forward. "Are you asking because you don't want me to jump you again?" She tried pumping some humor into the serious conversation, but didn't quite reach her target.

"Seriously, I wouldn't mind, but I think you would. You don't seem the type to do casual."

"I'm glad you think so." She infused the statement with a bit of irony. "When I was in high school, I was willing to do anything to get under my dad's skin, and being sexually promiscuous worked best. Back then, I blamed him for being stuck here." *For not wanting me.* "Making friends was hard. Every kid wanted to one-up the next. Having lived other places, I had a broader view of the world and gave the impression I was different. Different wasn't good."

"I sorta like different."

The sweet honesty sent a sugarcoated thrill tingling up and down her arms. "I'm glad, but not every one does. To fit in, the dares got bigger and riskier. My dresses got shorter, the parties got wilder, and my grades hit bottom."

"Doesn't seem like you stayed there for long."

"Things changed in my sophomore year, when Harold dragged me out of a car filled with college boys who'd come to town for a good time. That night, Harold and Claudia sat my butt at their kitchen table and gave me a good talking-to."

"I've had a few of those in my life. Mostly from coaches and sergeants."

"It was a good wake-up call. I was in over my head and I knew it, but I couldn't get out of the self-abusing downward spiral. The thing is, Harold didn't lecture or make me feel small, like my mom used to do sometimes. Claudia only listened."

He nodded. "I've met Harold. He's good people."

Couldn't agree more. "Both he, and Claudia, helped me visualize where my life was going, which was nowhere. The next day, I dumped my boring boyfriend and discarded my red lipstick and four-inch heels for education, and indulged in my passion for art."

The weight of guilt holding her down lifted. Saying those things about her past was a reminder that history wasn't a predictor of the future. She wasn't that girl anymore. She was a woman who had a plan, even if fairly lame, which was now disrupted by a guy and a dog.

"Guess you didn't expect a confession." A self-conscious laugh accompanied the burn in her cheeks. *Fooled you, didn't I.*

"Like I said. No judgment here. Pastor Chris and Coach John would tell you a similar story about me. I was such an angry kid, always getting into fights, stealing things, pretty much flipping the middle finger to the world. You might live in a big house, but you and I aren't so different. We made something of ourselves."

His eyes turned dark and a soft smile curved his mouth. "And for the record, you didn't jump me. Plus, like I said, if you feel inclined, be my guest. There's no one here pressuring you to do, or be, something you're not. You have choices. And they're yours to make."

That's the problem. Mom always narrowed my choices to fit in with her wishes. Now how do I make good, healthy choices for myself?

"Has anyone ever told you you're addicting?" she asked.

He took a step toward her, but she stopped him with her palm out.

Keep those knees together, young lady. Her mother's soapbox diatribe blared.

"Marines can be lethal. My dad. He'd returned home—a week here or there, never on my birthday, maybe for Christmas if I got lucky. I miss him, and also despise him for not coming home to help." The emotions tangled together to the point she didn't know where one began and the other left off. It was negativity she didn't want in her life, and Chase was a reminder. She pointed at the ceiling. "At the top of the stairs, you'll find a guest room. I'll stay with Lucky and call if I need something. Good night, Chase." She hoped the forced fortitude would create the illusion that her life wasn't falling apart.

He hesitated and then took a step back. "Good night, then."

As soon as he disappeared, the vulnerabilities she'd been feeling most of the day doubled. She could have told him a lot more about her dysfunctional family, but how did you communicate such things without the other person wondering if maybe the dysfunction had rubbed off somehow?

Having him under the same roof could be easy. Or damn hard.

She'd learned long ago that living in a large house didn't necessarily mean having to cross paths. But Chase had a way of cutting a path directly in front of her. He'd be hard to ignore. He pushed her, making her think about things she hadn't thought of in a very long time. Like being with a man, and knitting pink or blue baby booties. And she didn't even know how to knit.

The floorboards creaked in the room above her head. "Good night, soldier man," she whispered.

CHAPTER EIGHT

*I*t was six in the morning when Ashley slowly awoke to find Lucky curled at her side, breathing easily. She delivered a silent prayer of thanks. After midnight, she'd helped the shepherd outside and managed to get him to swallow a pain pill, an antibiotic, and a couple of syringes of beef-flavored baby food.

Dragging her hand through his thick, matted fur, she'd discovered open sores that couldn't be comfortable. A warm bath today would do his muscles and her nose some good. After a couple more hours of restless sleep, she made her way to the basement storage closet.

Exhausted from a lack of sleep, she shivered, rubbing her arms and trying to generate some warmth. Sliding a box on the top shelf down so she could see the box hidden behind, she didn't see the lamp teetering on the edge of the shelf. When she grabbed to save the lamp, the ladder bumped into the shelf and created a domino effect of sliding boxes crashing to the floor.

Well, that's just typical, isn't it?

She let out a frustrated, teeth-clenching growl. It was meant to make her feel better, but it didn't. She climbed down the ladder and lifted the first box to look at the label, "metal working." And then the next, "jewelry making." Each additional label created a skip down memory lane. Grade school class pictures, progress reports, and adolescent drawings her mother kept. Too bad it was all destined for the landfill. She scaled the ladder to place the boxes back on the shelf.

"All right, Dad. Where did you put your electronics?"

"Need some help?" Chase asked.

She jerked and hit her head on an overhead beam. Grimacing, her eyes watering, she rubbed the tender spot while she turned around...to behold an unshaven and tousled Chase in the doorway, both hands on the doorframe holding him up.

"You scared me. Make some noise when you move around." She swatted a cobweb away from her face.

"I scared you? When I heard the ruckus down here, I figured I'd better get my ass downstairs in case the house was caving in. I could have used a blow horn to announce myself, but you wouldn't have heard me above all the racket you're making."

"I'm being quiet as a mouse."

"You mean a moose."

Damn that sexy brow. It raised ever so temptingly, challenging her, but he said not one more word. Evidently, she'd startled him awake because he'd arrived wearing nothing but his boxers, which sat low on his hips, every muscle on his chest thrown into relief from the indirect lighting. His arms and legs, too.

She also had a good idea about the rest since they'd spent hours on the sled together, and one couldn't quite avoid bumping into a few body parts now and then. When she'd felt the results, she considered popping in the boot camp workout video a bit more often, but decided that type of yumminess only came from physical labor and hours of hard work. Thinking about him wrapped around her and keeping her warm distracted her, and she shivered, not from the cold, but from the glorious, muscular splendor.

"Sorry I woke you." She forced herself to turn back toward the boxes. "Look at all this crap. You'd think an entire military division lived here."

The eight-foot shelves, four on each side and three in the back, looked overwhelming. No way would she be able to sort through the stuff in the next few weeks, so she planned to leave the chore for her dad's movers, whoever that might be. He couldn't expect her to take care of him like her mother had done most of their married life.

Her mother had pampered her father, doted on him when he came home. She'd loved him unconditionally until the day she died. An outsider might not see the love, but Ashley reluctantly had to admit her mother adored the man. The ache of wanting to see him and knowing she couldn't drove her mom into depression. On the few occasions her dad came home, her mother was bright as the sun. She'd fix fancy meals and open special bottles of wine, even throw intimate parties. Then when he left, because he always did, her mother would barely get out of bed, preferring to pull the covers up over her head and ignore anything and everything, including her daughter. Another reason not to get involved with a Marine.

"Can I help?" he asked.

She opened another box. "If you want.

I'm looking for a small hair trimmer to shave Lucky."

"Who used the shaver last?"

She discontinued searching to think of the last time she'd seen the razor. "Mom, I believe. When Dad came home, Mom liked to wash and cut his hair. Why?"

He pointed at the writing on the boxes. "You're looking through your dad's stuff. If your mom used the trimmer last, maybe it's with her things."

"Leave it to a Marine to use logic." She shoved the box back on top of the metal shelf. "Thanks."

"What's in this box?" He pointed to a plastic bin with her name on the side. His curious eyes held hers.

"It's nothing."

"Right." He turned to leave.

She hopped down from the ladder and hooked his arm, stopping him, remembering how annoyed she'd been when he refused to share his poems. His muscles contracted under her fingers and his body went still. He wasn't the only one shutting the door on inquisitive questions, but something inside her didn't want to hold back. She reached for the bin, set it on the floor, and unlocked the lid of her treasure box. She picked up the first box of china and opened it, revealing her first and favorite miniature tea set, complete with cups, saucers and teapot.

She picked up a cup and placed it into his outstretched hand.

"It's so small." He stared at the tiny object with wonder and nudged the porcelain with his finger. He looked into the box. "You have more."

"There are seven sets here. I've sold the others, but these are my favorites. I'll have to part with them eventually, but I wanted to hold on a little while longer. These miniature sets were the first things I looked for when we went to yard sales and auctions."

And now she'd have to let them go. Sell them and scatter them to the far corners of North America and beyond because she didn't have a place to keep them safe. She reached for the cup and swaddled the tiny porcelain object in tissue to put it back in the box.

He thumped the box with his knuckle. "I bet each one has a story to tell."

Her breath caught. *Oh. My. God.* He understood. He gripped the lid, locking it in place, and then gently put the bin back on the shelf like it contained the Holy Grail. Then he scanned the rows of bins.

"I got a little crazy."

"Crazy to collect something you love? No. That's not crazy. Letting a guy you just met kiss you? That's maybe a little out there."

He winked. He actually winked. Why did he have to be so adorable as well as hunky?

Spontaneity hadn't been part of her life for years, but it didn't matter because already her eyes were irresistibly drawn to his mouth. She wanted to collect some more of those luscious memories. The arousing heat overwhelmed the cold shivers from moments earlier. She wouldn't, couldn't go there.

Ashley never expected much from men. Her mom suggested their lack of brain matter was because the other sex made decisions with their stomachs and crotches, which also used up all their energy and brain power. But somehow Chase was different. He worked hard, didn't say much, but did say the things that mattered.

He finally gave her an electrifying smile. Besides the gold specks, his eyes ignited with a twinkle of humor as well.

Tipping a bit off-center, she decided to get back to the task at hand. Otherwise she would surely succumb to the way he was looking at her—like he wanted to crawl back in bed with her on top.

"When do you want to go into town to get your truck?" Ashley crossed her arms and looked past his shoulder.

"I was hoping to help with Lucky and then maybe go for a run, and then see where the day takes us."

"Us. Like you and me."

He picked up a strand of her hair and

tucked it behind her ear. "You have a lot of work to do, and I'm an extra set of free hands. All you need to do is point and provide instructions. Unless you have a problem with me helping."

Man, oh man, the guy could make a woman sizzle. If she touched him, she'd get baked. She wanted to feel his early morning stubble scrape across her skin. Feel his callused hands wrapped around her waist.

"Do you have a problem with me helping?"

"No."

His eyes made her grab onto the ladder to keep from falling over. The way he leaned in gave the impression he wanted some early morning fun.

"No? Then is there something you need?"

She tightened her grip because a whole lot of other things got weak, especially her willpower. But her brain engaged in the nick of time. She didn't need a man in her life who made her want to run her fingers over his glorious body while figuring out a way to wipe the smug smirk off his handsome face.

She appreciated his restraint. The white-knuckled grip on the doorframe was proof he was working overtime to keep from executing his desires.

"I need to shower," she said. "And before you ask, no, I don't need my back washed."

She swore his body pouted before he straightened and stepped aside.

As she passed, he asked, "Do you think your dad would mind if I used his tools?"

The image of him standing in her bedroom doorway wearing nothing but a tool belt slapped her in the face. The fantasy would have worked even with clothes on, but off...*oh, my!* She concentrated on closing the storage room door on the mess she'd made, but the image stuck. Her cheeks felt hot, like a lighter had been flicked into flame next to her ear.

"Need to keep your mind occupied?" she asked.

He narrowed the gap to within a slight

lean on her part. "Tell me you don't want to kiss me, Ashley."

She lifted her hand and placed her fingers on his lips. "No."

He took a sampling nip at her fingers. "Is 'no' the only word in your vocabulary?"

"No."

He laughed, a deep, melodic laugh full of tender promises. And she couldn't help going up on her tiptoes and pressing her mouth to his. He groaned and immediately reached for her, cupping her bottom and lifting her to deepen their connection.

Leaning slightly back, she wondered if he merely wanted to pass the time or turn off his mind. But the way he looked at her, his eyes full of desire...this wasn't about sex alone.

After she kissed him again, he took his time tracing the curve of her lips with his tongue. He maintained his restraint until she sighed and allowed him entry. Then he turned and braced her against the wall, freeing his hands to slide under her sweatshirt. Up and up they slid, until settling right below her breasts.

His eyes flared with the knowledge she hadn't taken the time to put on a bra.

When his hand cupped her breast, the need she was determined to avoid feeling came rushing back into her.

She didn't need just sex. She didn't want just a man. What she wanted was the man in front of her. "Chase," she whispered.

The plea didn't go unheeded. He lifted her higher and lowered his head enough to put his mouth on her nipple, playing, caressing, flicking his tongue and sending waves of sensations throughout her.

"Tell me you want this, Ashley."

She opened her mouth to holler, *hell, yeah*, but nothing came out. When he started to let her go, she dug her nails into his shoulders. His deep breath created a whole new sensation, and she loved it.

"Do that again," he demanded, his voice smoky with desire.

She crossed her arms along his back and

raked them across, pulling him closer, wanting him to feel the things she felt.

"Woman, you drive me to the edge of sanity."

He released her body and let it slide down his, then placed his forehead on hers and blew out a frustrated breath.

"Did I do something wrong?" She tucked her arms against her with self-doubt.

"No," he said simply. He gave her a peck on the tip of her nose and took a step back. "You need to go find that hair trimmer, and I think I need to take a shower. Now. An ice-cold shower."

Joining him in the shower crossed her mind. "I'll be upstairs."

He nodded and again said nothing when she passed. At the top of the basement stairs, she peeked over her shoulder. Sure enough, her eyes met a searing intensity that terrified and tempted her at the same time. She could feel the grip on her will unraveling. Every ounce of common sense told her not to get involved with the Marine, or make something out of nothing. But when she looked into his eyes, she saw a strong but wounded man. He tugged at her heart. She must find a way to stop this insanity before it truly drove her around the bend.

She turned and raced down the hall and up the back steps to put some distance between them. After a quick, fruitless search of the hall closet for the electric trimmer, she moved on to her mom's bedroom, which she'd managed to avoid since the funeral. Her mother's flowery perfume enveloped her like snow covering the ground. She made a fist, hiding the cut on her finger while placing her other hand on the walk-in closet door handle. Even after she'd taken four truckloads to the thrift or consignment stores, a precision row of blouses, slacks, and suits still lined the shelves.

She scanned the stacks of boxes on the upper rack and settled on a brown carton with potential. She set the dressing room chair in front of the built-in racks and climbed. Once she was eye level with the shelf, she spotted another container she'd never seen before. Curious, she reached for the box, which was wallpapered with forget-me-nots. Hopping down, she sat on the chair before removing the fabric lid. Inside were bundles upon bundles of letters and cards in date order, plus some ribbons, a few coins, and a pressed rose boutonniere. Letters and souvenirs from Dad.

A sealed letter partially addressed to her dad lay on top of the stack. The numbers on the back of the envelope made no sense, but the date underneath was the week prior to her mom's death. Setting the letters aside, she lifted each bundle, looking at dates. Then she put the box on the floor and climbed back onto the chair, pushing shoeboxes aside until she found what her instinct told her to look for—six more boxes stuffed full of letters. She climbed up and down until the boxes sat in a row on the tan wool carpet, and then she sank to the floor, dragging the nearest box closer. Selecting the ribbon-tied bundle with the oldest date, she opened the first letter to read.

My dearest Sally,

I should start off by saying you were right. Officer training is much harder than I thought. I get up at six and don't finish my day until sometime around midnight. You should be taking these courses. You're so much smarter than I am.

I understand why you wanted to move back to Elkridge. Yes, to be closer to the cemetery and our baby, who is safe in God's hands, but I feel you also moved back for me. You wanted to give me time to concentrate on my career. For that, I will always be thankful. I better go study. Know I'm doing this for us. You are always with me.

Your loving husband,
Dale.

ASHLEY READ ANOTHER LETTER, and another, frantically searching, hoping to find an answer. She didn't find another reference to a baby, with the exception of her, but she did discover her dad had a sense of humor.

Who knew?

She'd only known the serious, oppressive, quiet man. After a dozen or more letters, the perception of her father was transformed into something different. She couldn't find the previously-formed image of him on these pages. The young man who'd written these letters loved her mother—loved her more than anything else. He confided his dreams, fears, hopes. In the letters, he told his wife what Ashley had never heard him say in person.

She gently stroked the yellowing, tattered, tear-stained page. The passion had moved her mother as much as they touched her.

She opened another letter, which had been torn then taped back together.

SALLY,

I've tried calling for two weeks. Please pick up

the phone. We need to talk about this. I know you're scared. I've talked to the doctors here. They assure me you can live years with Multiple Sclerosis. Let me come home. Better yet, come back, bring Ashley, and live on the base. You'll have better access to medical providers. I want to take care of you and our daughter. We'll make it work. I don't care about my recent promotion to Major. You and Ash are the most important things in my life.

Call me. I love you.

Dale.

P.S. Thank my little Ash for the pottery ashtray she sent me for Father's Day. Tell her, I miss my little Ashtray's hugs and kisses and think of her every day.

HE MISSED HER? Hugs and Kisses? Ashley didn't know the man who'd written such touching and loving prose, but *that* man, she would have liked to meet. A father who managed to communicate. A man who wanted to be with the love of his life, but was required to attend to his higher calling. A strong yet tormented man. A man torn in half.

She removed her cell phone from the pocket of her jeans. And hesitated. What message should she leave? Hi, Mr. Bryant, this is your daughter. I'm calling to discover who you really are. Or, Hey, mister. I'm calling the FBI because you're an imposter. Or, Hey, Dad. Why didn't you ever come home? We needed you.

Do the right thing. Get your dad's address, and send your mom's letter. Don't think about it. Just do it.

She searched the contact list and dialed a number she'd tried to avoid calling for so many years. She held her breath and waited for the answering machine.

A sharp hello startled her.

"Dad?"

"Ashley, is that you? What's wrong?"

I was only wondering who you are, for real. I mean, I thought I knew, but now I'm not sure.

"Nothing's wrong."

Whenever calling, she got the inkling he

expected her to open with "I'm pregnant," or "I'm in jail," or "Please send money." Under any of those circumstances, she would have to be snacking on cookie crumbs to give him that kind of call, or any other kind of call, for that matter. He always seemed busy and in a hurry and surprised to hear her voice. She frowned at the phone. The temptation to hang up got stronger, but something stopped her.

She folded her legs underneath her and picked up the unopened letter. "I found your letters to Mom." She didn't know what she expected him to say, but listening to silence was a bit tough. "I also found a letter she never sent. It's dated only a few days before she passed."

She heard nothing. "Dad? Are you there?"

"I'm here."

"The bank collection agencies called again yesterday. Did they get in touch with you? They indicated they're starting foreclosure procedures." *Not that it will do them any good. There aren't any buyers for the house.*

"I spoke with the mortgage lender yesterday. Do you need anything?"

Nothing more than you, in my life, twenty-plus years ago. "Nope, I'm good."

She picked up the sealed letter, studying her mother's shaky handwriting on the outer envelope. The thick package created questions. The effort to write such a letter must have been exhausting. Whatever her mother had written must have been important.

"Dad, I need your address so I can send you Mom's letter."

She ran and grabbed a pen off her mom's nightstand when he began rattling off a memorized APO address. But then the silence on the other end of the line returned. She wished things could be different, but time continued to tick away, and after all this time, he wouldn't want to change. She'd accepted the facts long ago. No matter how much she wished for something different, longed to experience the Disney version of the father-daughter dance, it wasn't meant to be.

"I'd better go," she said.

"Ash?" Was that a plea in his voice?

"Yeah, Dad?"

There was a moment of silence, as if he was trying to gauge whether or not she was truly okay. "It's good to hear from you."

Her chest ached and she closed her eyes. She would trade her boxes of tea sets to hear him call her 'Ashtray' one more time. He probably assumed she'd outgrown the nickname, but she longed to hear the affectionate word, even once. She missed the early days, when he'd taken her fishing, or propped her on the toes of his boots, teaching her to dance. She wanted those special times back. She missed him, but didn't quite know how to tell him. The years of resentment and loneliness had burned the bridge that connected them once.

"I'll get this letter in the mail. Take care, Dad."

"Call anytime. I have to get back to my meeting."

Phone works both ways, Dad.

The line went silent, and she lowered the phone. All her life she'd been waiting to hear those three little words, but they never came. The word love wasn't in his vocabulary, not when associated with her, anyway. She didn't know why she waited, but she still did.

"Ashley?" Chase's voice echoed up through the stairwell.

She hurried to the landing and peered over the railing at the freshly showered man. "Is something wrong with Lucky?"

"Lucky's fine. I checked on him a minute or two ago. But there's some woman, a Rachelle, out front. Says she's a friend of yours."

Rachelle Clairemont. Must be a record. The temptation to check her watch was well-nigh irresistible.

Chasing men, especially ineligible men, had become a hobby for Rachelle. With a high-fashion-model body, she didn't have to try hard to turn a few heads. Rachelle's brother, Brad, must have tipped her off. Heaven forbid she set foot in the café. That would be slumming, and Rachelle would tarnish her high-nosed reputation. The diner was several pegs below Miss Fancy Pants's couture tastes.

"Would you please tell Rachelle I'll be out in a minute?"

Chase headed for the door, and she ducked into the bathroom to check the mirror. She brushed her hair, pinched her cheeks, applied lip-gloss, and snatched a shirt and pants from her mom's closet. Anything had to be more appropriate than shapeless sweats. She wasn't thrilled with the result, but given what she had to work with, they would do. She couldn't compete with the pageant queen, but she sure wasn't about to let the woman leave footprints on her back as she sauntered over her to get to Chase.

Skidding to a stop, Ashley adjusted her shirt before opening the front door, where she saw Rachelle, propped against the powder blue Mercedes, tilt her head back and laugh at something Chase said.

The way she twisted the blonde strands of hair around her index finger reminded Ashley of how she loved to twist men around her little finger. Ashley didn't understand why guys tripped over themselves to do her bidding. Rachelle was way too thin, way too perky, way too everything. The oversized augmentation her daddy had paid for with his real estate money didn't help. The women in the town referred to her as a stick with tits. Ashley agreed. The description was fitting.

She jumped down off the front porch and joined the laughing couple. "Rachelle, fancy seeing you here."

"Hey, Ash. I stopped by the shop, but you weren't there. I thought I'd deliver your Christmas Bazaar fliers here instead."

Since when have you ever stopped by the shop? Didn't know your car could find its way to that end of town.

"You didn't need to do that. You could have left them with Jenna since we're splitting the booth."

"Yes, but I wanted to personally make sure you got them."

Rachelle made one of those fake giggling sounds, a grating cascade which scraped the nerves. When Rachelle won the sixth-grade play lead Ashley coveted, that was bad enough, but stealing Ashley's boyfriend in high school had triggered an all-out war. She'd give anything to be a pebble in Rachelle's high-heeled shoe about now. Grasping for any excuse to send Rachelle packing, she remembered her irrational fear of dogs.

"I'd invite you in, but I have a sick dog inside."

"My brother did mention something about you finding a half-dead mutt. Brad was surprised you didn't put the poor thing out of its misery. Guess you don't mind seeing things suffer."

Ashley's jaws clamped because nothing

would be more satisfying than taking a bite out of Ms. Perfect, the woman who stole boyfriends, got her kicked off the cheerleading squad, and spread nasty rumors about her.

Then again, any attempt to damage Rachelle's perfectly styled hair or makeup might result in her calling the sheriff. Ashley didn't stand a chance against those flashy blue eyes, man-made hooters, and her dad's extra-large bank account. But then again, she had nothing to lose. She took a step forward.

Chase effectively cut her off. "We were about to head out."

Rachelle had clearly heard *we* because her eyes got a beady, squint-eyed look. "Then I won't keep you. Don't forget your promise, Chase."

The way she smiled at him made Ashley want to plant a boot against Rachelle's perfect chin.

She couldn't claim either Chase or the dog as her own. However, she certainly wasn't about to let Rachelle get her paws on either one. She needed to protect them. Rachelle had a way of destroying everything crossing her path, busting things into tiny pieces like her grandmother's china.

Chase stepped away from the car. "I won't."

Ashley snapped her head in his direction. "What promise?"

"To help unload boxes at the Bazaar."

Typical. Rachelle couldn't have designed a better man-trap. Ashley watched the car back out of the drive before scooping snow into her hand, balling it, and throwing it as far as she could.

She was standing, legs apart, hands on hips, glaring at the tire tracks, when she heard an unfamiliar sound. Chase was laughing. When she glared at him, he laughed harder. Not a simple tee-hee laugh, but a full-blown, shoulder-shaking, belly-wracking, eye-watering laugh. He bent over and put his hands on his knees.

"What's so darn funny?" she demanded.

He pointed. "You're jealous."

"Am not. I was doing you a favor. Rachelle's a first-class bitch."

"A favor? By putting me in the middle of two she-cats doing their best to claw each other's eyes out?"

She wanted to tell him different, but couldn't argue with the truth. "It's not nice to laugh at someone else's expense."

"Sorry. I really couldn't help it."

Whichever way she sliced it, jealousy had motivated her actions. Trying to find something witty or intelligent to say would only make her look defensive, or worse, catty. His laughter settled into a muted smirk. She'd stifled his joy and somehow felt bad for doing it.

Knowing where he had been, she wondered when or if he'd had an occasion to laugh with such unfettered freedom. She reveled in the pure joy beaming from his face and wished she could experience the same. She hadn't had cause to laugh, not in that deep, penetrating way, not in days, maybe weeks or months. Except with him.

The least she could do was give him a reason to laugh.

She nudged the gravel with the toe of her boot. "You should laugh more often. It looks good on you."

"Why's that?"

"Laughter makes you look less…"

He wiped the corner of his eye with the back of his hand. "Angry?"

She shook her head. "Haunted. For a moment, I saw the real you, not a ghost. You're a hard person to read sometimes." Embarrassment made her look away. "My dad always said I was too generous with my heart. Maybe if I could learn to be a little more protected, like you, I'd be better off."

"Don't say that." The anguish in his voice grabbed her attention. "He's right. You're the most giving and caring person I know. You shouldn't ever want to change."

A tingle of heat coiled through her, warming her extremities. She hadn't felt warm in ages, but only now realized how long she'd felt cold to her bones and uncomfortable in her skin. She couldn't name the jumble of feelings that filled her now, many of them awkward, yet satisfying at the same time.

She finally felt visible. He saw her.

"I'd better get moving. Lots to do." She turned toward the house, then paused. "If you want, you can stay here again tonight. I mean...Lucky is healing, but it'd be nice to have some help."

"I'll help." The earnestness assured her he'd help even if she didn't ask.

She nodded and walked into the house to put some distance between her and temptation. He was absolutely becoming more dangerous, in a warm, fuzzy way.

CHAPTER NINE

"What the hell are you doing?" Chase paced back and forth, talking to himself, puzzling over the woman in the house, and asking question after question of no one in particular. "Yeah, I'm an ass. I shouldn't have laughed."

He hadn't been laughing at Ashley, but somehow she didn't see it that way. He'd seen through Rachelle with the first flash of her pearly white teeth. He didn't need a warning. She had a sign hung around her neck saying 'boy-toys apply here.' Around the military base, he could find her type anytime, day or night. She fit the category of a woman looking for a little adventure, a buffed body, and a pressed uniform.

Some military marriages didn't last. He knew that. But it didn't stop him from hoping one day he might find the right woman, a reliable woman. A woman who could love him and give him a nice place to land while he traveled through hell and back. Finding such a woman seemed an impossible task, especially since he'd spent most of his time in training or overseas.

For the past twelve years, the military had provided him with a fairly constant adrenaline fix, and he thrived on being the best of the best. But jumping out of planes and playing sneak and peek didn't give him the rush it once had. The wear and tear on his body didn't help much, either. Every day, getting out of bed was a bit harder than the day before. And lately he'd been restless, and the nightmares and the triggered episodes were getting worse.

Kaboom. A loud crash reverberated from inside the house.

His heart about busted from his chest, but his body remained combat-ready calm. Entering the front door, he stopped to listen and heard Ashley's gentle voice. *God, woman, you're going to give me a coronary.*

Stubborn and independent. He could tell asking for help was like pulling a tooth without Novocaine for her. He was the same way. But the military had cured him of going it alone. Maybe he could teach her a bit about teamwork.

Entering the house, he moved toward the noise until he found her in an oversized bathroom off the main room.

She'd changed again. A gray bra strap peeked from under her navy blue tank top. White cotton underwear did the same from under her faded jeans. She looked flustered and adorable.

"Need another set of hands?" Chase asked over the hum of running bathwater. Ashley's head snapped around, her startled eyes engaging.

"Why do you insist on scaring me?"

"Sorry, forgot to stomp."

She scrunched her nose and turned back to her patient. In one hand, she held an electric razor. The other hand held Lucky's flank. The dog shifted back and forth, clearly uncomfortable.

After studying the dog for several seconds, she looked at him. "I'm trying to keep the weight off his hind legs. Can you keep him lifted so I can shave his thigh?"

"Would it be easier if he were lying down?"

She bit her lip, weighing his suggestion. "It might." She removed her arm from under the dog's belly, and Lucky collapsed to the floor. She gave Chase a surprised look. "You're such a problem-solver."

If only I could solve my own problems. If not the military...then what?

Her happy expression did odd things, like

making him think what he could do next to earn another smile.

When younger, he'd tried to make his mom happy by drawing pictures or bringing home a flower or leaf he'd discovered, but it never earned him the smile he wanted so desperately. The woman across from him appreciated the simple things he offered, but he suspected true happiness didn't exist for her. Not at the moment.

Details about her dying mom still hadn't been filled in enough to make a complete picture, but instinct told him her hurt went far deeper. The pool of sadness surrounding her made him want to work even harder to see if he could get it to evaporate. He sat on the floor at Lucky's head, working to keep the animal distracted. With each stroke of the razor, she gently removed a row of fur careful to avoid the tender patches of open sores. When the time came, Chase rolled Lucky to his other side so Ashley could continue.

While they worked in silence, he realized they were synchronizing their moves with complete confidence. They'd reached a level of trust he typically achieved after working with someone for weeks, sometimes months. Before deploying, his squad practiced together, exercised together, and often ate together. When a life depended upon a buddy being there, he didn't question whether the person beside him would watch his back. Building that type of confidence took time, practice, and patience. With Ashley, the assurance came naturally. She'd slipped right into the pattern of his life, like she understood, except when she decided to be stubborn and overdo it.

"Okay, Lucky. Ready for your bath?" The bright, upbeat encouragement in her tone did nothing to sway the dog, who looked at the tub of water like it was at the top of his absolutely-not list. She turned the taps off, checking the temperature. "Warm, but not too warm."

"How do you want to approach this?" Chase pointed at the shampoo and towels and water pitcher sitting on the toilet seat.

"How about you hold and I scrub."

Hold and scrub. Yeah, baby. There was a whole lot of Ashley he wouldn't mind holding and scrubbing. Inappropriate timing, yes, but his mind had to go there. When she leaned over to brush Lucky's fur into a pile, oh-la-la, the soft mounds of her breasts bulged from the top of her shirt and caused all kinds of commotion. That, coupled with her genuine, caring nature, meant he wouldn't mind at all being washed and scrubbed by this angel of mercy.

"Got it. Let me lift him into the tub so you can start."

She bent over to dunk the water pitcher and wet down the dog. Ten minutes later she was wet, Chase was wet, and the dog looked miserable.

The tiny, open sores looked raw and infected. Chase pointed at the largest lesion. "What do you think caused those?"

"Don't know. Mites or a fungal infection, maybe. The antibiotics and pain meds, plus the antiseptic and aloe vera balm, should help. I need to stop him from licking. Brad might have a collar I can borrow."

He studied the unadorned, functional room, and a niggling memory came back to him. He might not have recognized the modernized bathroom, with the low sinks and multiple-head shower with a roll-in basin, if it hadn't been for Sam. Two years ago, he went to see the young corporal. They were able to laugh together and spent a few hours remembering the good times.

Before Chase left, Sam had proudly shown his former sergeant the necessary addition to his parents' house after a training accident broke Sam's spine. A ramp now extended from the drive to the front door, the doorways were wider, the sinks lower, and ropes hung on doors so he could maneuver around the kitchen. Sam also showed off his newest toy, a racing chair he'd designed. Once the platoon's fastest runner, he wanted to beat some old records, feet or wheels didn't matter. Chase felt honored to call him friend, and to see how well he'd adjusted to life—better than Chase might have done, given the same circumstances.

The memory faded, and his thoughts returned to the woman lovingly attending her charge. He wondered if he was merely another of Ashley's strays.

"Harold told me your mom was sick for a while. It must have been hard losing her. I know how you feel."

Her lips puckered and her eyes squinted as if she'd bitten into a lemon, but then a deep sorrow scored the lines etched into her young face even deeper. "I don't mean to be rude, but how could you possibly know how I feel?"

"You're not the only one who's lost someone."

"See, that's the thing. People who've lost someone think they know, but they really don't know how the other person feels. They can't. They might know how *they* feel, but they don't know how I feel."

She brushed at clumps of fur on her

jeans, her frustration and annoyance crackling in the air around her, and then shoved to her feet. The dog, automatically trying to follow her lead, got up, shook, and sprayed the entire bathroom.

Two towels, one from Ashley, one from Chase, simultaneously went flying over the dog's back.

She held the three-foot cloth in place and then looked down at her drenched shirt, the wet floor and walls, and started to laugh. The contagious melody of her happiness made him laugh. Seconds passed before they both had dog-day-happy grins across their faces.

"Wow," she said.

"You can say that again."

"Wow." Mischievousness added another layer to her exuberant expression.

With a lot of effort and a bit of help, Chase managed to assist the exhausted dog out of the tub without a whole lot more shaking.

"Good boy, Lucky," she praised the dog while walking him back into the family room. The dog instantly collapsed on a bed of comforters and blankets.

"I bet you're wrong," Chase said, wanting to get her attention.

The tilt of her head suggested she'd forgotten what they were talking about. He could let the conversation about her mom drop. In fact, he should, but he didn't. "I bet I know a little of what you're feeling." He waited until her eyes settled on him. "My best friend was killed on our last deployment, and I buried him a few days ago."

Her head and shoulders fell forward, and she looked like she'd just dropped her birthday cake on the floor. "That sucks. It really does. There were times, I wished my mom would have died like that—quick, no pain, no lingering for three years, barely making it through each day."

"How can you say that? You got to be there. You got to say goodbye."

"There's a difference...never mind."

"No, not never mind." He understood

every person grieved differently. Almost always at the end of their rope emotionally, survivors could only hang on, clinging to life, until enough strength returned to climb back up. "Talk to me, because from over here, our wounds look the same."

"I really don't want to talk about this."

Would you talk to me, damn it? I need to talk about this.

Frustration prickled along his neck and shoulders and through his limbs. "You are so stubborn. I want to know what's so different, not to judge, but to understand."

She stood and started pacing, stopping at the window, which ran the length of the room and framed a spectacular view of the ridge. "No one understands."

Hauling bodies to safety after being shot, the smell of burned flesh, the weight of carrying an injured Marine to a medevac site came tumbling back. "Try me."

"What was your friend's name?"

His chest tightened. "Bobby," he whispered.

"From what you've said, Bobby was a good friend and an excellent Marine who died doing what he loved to do." She turned to look at him.

The emotion in her eyes ebbed and flowed so fast he couldn't get an accurate reading.

"For months, my mother rarely left her bed. When she did, it was for an hour or two to be bathed, or to work at the computer. In the final year, she couldn't even make it to the toilet. You don't know what it's like to watch a person's skin become paper-thin and their bones protrude from their body. She didn't have the desire to eat because she lost her senses of taste and smell, and it took badgering, threatening, even bartering to get her to eat Jell-O. I sat in a chair for hours, listening to mucus-filled, wheezing lungs, hoping the awful sound would end, but afraid to fall asleep because she might stop breathing. I also didn't sleep because I didn't want her to be alone when death came. I watched her die one heartbeat at a time. So don't tell me you know how I feel."

He opened his arms and stepped forward, but shrugged away. "This isn't me feeling pity, Ash."

"Yeah. Then what is it? Because I don't deserve sympathy or kindness. You see, I spent three years of my life, all day, every day, caring for a woman who constantly told me she hadn't raised me properly—that I needed to learn how to be an adult, make decisions, do something more with my life, take risks. Like I hadn't been trying." Ashley pushed her fingers through her hair, pulling the strands into a bundle to create a knot. "She basically told me all day, every day, that what I was doing wasn't good enough." Ashley took several pacing steps, her animated arms circling in the air. "Then there were times she'd cry all day, telling me she wasn't my responsibility and begging me to leave. I often seriously considered packing and going back to school, leaving her to suffer alone in some nursing home." Her hands fell silent to her sides. "Month after month I sat there and became increasingly angry and resentful. I couldn't go to the movies, or out to dinner, or see friends. I was a prisoner, and there were days I wanted her to die. I wanted her suffering to end. I wanted to be free. And eventually I got exactly what I wanted." Her chest expanded to take a needed gulp of air, before she let the breath exhale. "Now I'd give anything for even one more day, even if it meant listening to her complain and criticize and tell me what a pathetic person I am."

Her prison cell. The irony hit him. This was where she chose to bring Lucky.

She wasn't awful.

She considered herself pathetic.

Maybe the dog was her atonement for her mother. Whatever the reason, the dog seemed the right medicine to help her heal the caring part of her life.

"You came home to help. That's more than most people would do." And he respected her a great deal for that.

Her gaze lowered and the lines around her eyes softened with acceptance. "You're starting to sound like Jenna and Maggie. They said pretty much the same thing."

"Well, you know about the truth. If more than one person says it, it must be true."

"Is that so?"

Skepticism filled her eyes. Somehow, she'd created a truth, a truth that wasn't quite real. God, he wanted to demonstrate to her that she was special and desirable and needed. He wanted her to believe.

Believe in him.

"Yep. Marine's honor."

She rolled her eyes, which gave him a bold idea.

"When's the last time you had sex, the mind-numbing kind of sex?"

She choked. "Excuse me?"

That blew her mind.

"Stop worrying about the future and your plan. Think about this moment. Today. Now. Sex. You know...the wild kind, or the soft kind. Your choice. You have a lot of flat surfaces in this house needing to be initiated."

"Is sex all you military guys think about?"

When I'm around you. Yeah. "Being in the desert, knowing you've got a target on your chest and back, scaling buildings and sandy mounds to see what's on the other side does that to a guy. Your mounds are much prettier, and I'm damn sure they're much more fun to scale."

"Are you volunteering?"

"Hell, yeah."

Based on their kiss, he bet her body parts would be a thrill to explore, and he bet when Ashley let loose, she was going to make his temperature skyrocket above desert-hot.

"That wild sex, I've already tried it. It didn't turn out so well."

Curiosity made him daring. "Really? The guy couldn't be an expert, or was he a complete ass?"

Finally, he got her to laugh. "He definitely wasn't an expert. Guys can be assholes."

"True," he said honestly. "We can be

rather single-minded. Want to give it another try?"

She looked away, her cheeks turning the nicest shade of red. He liked red, especially red lingerie.

"I think I'll pass."

"Have you given up on men?" *Or is it me?*

"No. I haven't given up. It's me. I'm trying to get my head screwed on straight. Make some decisions. Work on figuring out who I am." Her eyes studied him. "I don't feel whole right now. And sex can be addicting. When I have sex, I want it to be for the right reasons."

He understood wanting time to figure out next steps. That's what had landed him in Colorado in the first place.

Chase lifted his arm, shrugged his shoulders. "Don't work too hard on improvements. You're pretty great the way you are."

Her eyes met his, and for half of a second he suspected she might jump on and scale up his body for a wild, hot moment, but then he could see an emotional disconnection take place.

He walked toward the door.

"Chase?"

He turned.

She rubbed her palms on her jeans and stared at his feet like his shoes needed tying. He might have followed her gaze if he didn't already know his boots didn't have laces.

"Your proposal. It's tempting. But I keep thinking you're going to go your way and I'm going to go mine, and I haven't worked out what to do about the spark yet."

"You feel it too, huh?"

Her guilt riddled gaze met his. "Since day one."

"Ashley, I have a lot of respect for you. I wouldn't intentionally hurt you. And that spark you talked about? I won't do anything about it until you decide to light the match. But I do think you should light it at some point, or else we'll both be left wondering for the rest of our lives."

She shoved her fingers in her back

pockets. He wished she hadn't made that last move because her round breasts pushed forward, her perky nipples front and center. He wanted to engage. He wanted to have those perfect mounds brush against his chest, feel her breath on his neck, her legs wrapped around his waist. If only she would allow him to hold her again, he would demonstrate how great sex could be. In her current state, she wouldn't let a fly close.

"How about I fix dinner tonight, and you can tell me more about your friend Bobby."

A woman offering to make him dinner. Now, there was a first. "Unfortunately, I already have plans. Maybe another time."

He could imagine her tumultuous bulldozer thoughts constructing a bridge to the wrong conclusion—Rachelle. He might look at Rachelle—because her plastic surgeon made sure she had something worth looking at—but he wouldn't waste his time on anything more.

He considered telling Ashley about helping Harold unload the store's delivery, but right now he wasn't feeling so generous. He didn't want to admit it, but her rejection had stung. Maybe he didn't understand exactly what she felt, but he recognized the emptiness, the longing for more time, the shock of having to live without that core person.

"Would you have time to give me a ride into town later?" he asked.

"Take the truck." Her tone had gone frosty. "I don't want to leave Lucky. Plus, I'm really behind. I've got stuff I need to put up on eBay and pack for shipping." Her arms crossed. Her eyes changed from turbulent to neutral.

Guess she doesn't like being turned down, either. "I don't want to leave you stranded."

"There's an ATV out back I can use if needed. If I run out of things to do, I can always work on my teapot wind chimes for the craft fair. Let's plan on swapping vehicles tomorrow. By then, I'll feel better leaving Lucky on his own."

There were reasons men stayed single.

One minute, she fit into his life like a warm pair of comfortable, dry socks, the next she chafed like a wet pair of boxers. "I'm going to change before I go. If you think of anything you need, you have my number."

"I'm fine."

Fine? Sounds like a 'fuck-you' fine to me.

CHAPTER TEN

I'm fine. Ashley scoffed at her own expense. *No, I'm not fine. Far from it.*

She contemplated calling Chase's cell to explain, but what would she say?

Forgive me, I'm still grieving and angry and not thinking straight? Sorry for being so bitchy? I apologize for not knowing exactly what I want to do with my life?

All excuses. She needed to stop with the excuses.

Time was running out. She needed to find her brave, and not be the person her mother expected—the directionless soul.

She had a plan. Money. Shelter. Food.

How did she get so distracted? She couldn't even manage to take care of herself, much less a dog or a boyfriend. But being distracted was no excuse for being rude.

She should have thanked him for helping with Lucky, for giving her a reason to smile the past few days. The idea had been buried by anger, and hadn't gotten her attention until too late.

Anger. So much anger.

Anger at her mom's friends who'd pushed her mom to the point of exhaustion. Anger at those who'd visit a time or two, then disappear. Anger at her dad for coming home to help, then letting her mother talk him into leaving several days early. She hated him for leaving. Not talking, only watching. Every morning he watched her go about bathing, clothing, feeding, and caring for her mother. After breakfast, he'd disappear, and she'd run into him fixing a sink or gutter or replacing tires. Once he fixed what needed fixing around the house, he'd left, abandoning her once again.

She didn't want to hate. Anything. Anymore.

Hate was exhausting.

And she didn't want to live angry.

She contemplated her hairy jeans and worn sneakers and wondered how her life had become blank. So easily erasable.

Her friends at school had talked about their dreams. Where were her dreams? Where was her black, bold Sharpie mark on the world? So far, she hadn't even made a pencil scratch.

She drew a deep breath, trying to feel a little ray of life. Of hope. For some reason, Rachelle popped into her mind.

Rachelle, a female who had it all—looks, money, and a no-give attitude that got her whatever she wanted. The minute the bimbo showed up, Chase was all happiness and laughter. Could it be he had a date with her tonight? It would explain why he wasn't available for dinner. Besides, why would he stick around for hamburger when he could have a sirloin?

Feeling sorry for yourself? You said no excuses.

A thump-thump-thump made her acknowledge the dog, whose tail was banging on the floor, his tired eyes gazing at her. Squatting, she brushed a hand over the dog's ear and down his neck. A surge of confidence hit her. "From now on, I'm going to do my best to stay positive and look toward the future, not back. I'm going to find my marker and make some plans. You in?"

Lucky lifted his head to nuzzle her hand and released a soft whine.

"That's my good boy. You keep me honest."

She moved to her desk and studied the plan she'd created.

Write thank-you notes.

Sell. Make stuff. Sell some more.

Look for affordable apartments.

Clarify what can be sold with Dad.

Fill out three job applications per week.

She'd at least gotten the first three accomplished, but she was running out of stuff to sell. Her dad probably had some things he wanted to toss, but that would mean calling him, and she'd rather stick a fork in her eyeball. The teapot chimes sold well, but she only had enough to make eight more. If only she could use the mismatched forks, knives and spoons.

Tapping the pen on the desk, she remembered a Pinterest image. She slid her computer toward the edge of the desk and typed 'things to make from silver flatware.'

A slow smile crossed her face. *Of course. Her high school metalworking classes were again going to pay off.*

Over the next few days she'd have to hustle. She could make stuff for the craft fair, and some special pieces she could hold back as gifts to show the members of Elkridge how much she appreciated them.

She picked up the phone and dialed the café, hoping to catch Jenna.

"River Creek Café," a familiar perky voice announced.

"Jenna, you up for beating the crap out of some metal?"

Jenna began laughing on the other end of the line. "What do you have in mind?"

She explained her idea of how she could make hooks, drawer pulls, key rings, and pendants. Her dad had the tools. All she needed to do was use them.

"That's brilliant. What if we decorate forks and spoons and bundle them with my pastries?"

Her friend's enthusiasm thrilled her. For the next ten minutes they hashed out the details, talking over each other and laughing in their excitement. Pretty soon the women had a plan, and Ashley had some research to do.

"Maybe you could get Chase to help," Jenna suggested. "He's mighty good with a hammer."

"No. He might have other things to do to occupy his time."

There was a pause on the other end of the line. "I doubt it. I bet he would rather help you than bust his butt helping Harold unload boxes and stack crates. He's over there now. And since when have you ever trusted anyone with your dad's truck?"

Relief broke through the annoyance with herself for having already decided he'd gone straight to Rachelle's. A slice of guilt slid onto her grandmother's chipped serving plates. Yep, her self-confidence was in desperate need of a Super Glue job.

"Hello? You still there?" Jenna's voice sounded in her ear.

"I think Chase needed a good ear to bend. I haven't been a very good friend. You should know that."

"When are you going to give yourself a break and stop berating yourself to death?"

She started to say something, but suddenly the negative, whiny words flew right out of her mind, and she couldn't remember what she wanted to say. Jenna had been there and heard her mom's reprimands.

She'd held her hand when she'd cried and told Ashley that, going forward, she'd bring only pureed Brussel sprouts, eggplant, and peas in retaliation. Her mom hated all three.

Ashley laughed at the memory. "How about I start today?"

"Really?" The shock in Jenna's voice was palpable.

"Really. Want to come over tonight? Have the pizza night you talked about? We can start hammering on things, or I might even let you win at Boggle."

"Listen, Queen of Webster, I can hold my own, thank you very much." Jenna's light, butterfly laughter assured her she was on the right path. "See you later?"

"Looking forward to it. Do you need me to pick up anything?"

"No. Most of the stuff I need is here. I've been boxing stuff to move into Harold's camper." Neatly stacked white boxes lined the edges of the living room. "I'm shipping my eBay stuff tomorrow."

"You've definitely got the hang of eBay.

Fred over at the post office is complaining about the extra work to anyone who will listen."

"You mean I'm actually keeping him busy enough to interrupt his afternoon nap?"

"Most likely." Jenna laughed. "See you tonight, then?"

"See you soon."

Ashley hung up the phone and counted her blessings for having met Jenna.

Jenna hadn't been in Elkridge long, but had quickly found her place in the small community, partly thanks to Maggie. She'd figured out how much Elkridge had to offer in less than a day. Before the end of the day, she decided to stay.

It had taken Ashley way too long to remove the blindfolds. Her only goal had been to get back to San Diego and what she thought was her life. But in reality, she'd been running to nowhere fast. Her mom's illness and death had tilted her world, and lately she'd been questioning a lot of things.

One thing she didn't question: Elkridge. The mountains had called her home.

She picked up the antique frame with her mother and father's wedding picture. Next month would have been their twenty-eighth anniversary, even though she seriously doubted they'd spent even half those years together. Still, they had stayed married.

The boxes of her father's letters yanked an emotional cord, but she needed to get started on making stuff to sell. The humorous, sometimes serious things he'd written to her mom made her more curious. In those boxes she might be able to find the answers she desperately needed. Maybe, in those boxes, she could find the strength to move on, the confidence to extend her hand and reach for Chase. But her dad would have to wait until later tonight.

She glanced over at Lucky. "Let's get you settled in the garage. It's not much colder than the house, and you can be with me while I work."

The dog's eyes tracked her and his tail thumped on the floor.

"Good. Then we have a plan."

She needed to make something happen.

Three more weeks might be all she had left before the bank came knocking. Then she'd have no choice but to leave. She needed to be ready.

CHAPTER ELEVEN

Jenna sat cross-legged on Ashley's kitchen island eating the last piece of homemade, supreme pizza. The island had a wash-your-hands sink at one end and a large, hand-thrown fruit bowl at the other.

Between bites, Jenna caught her up on town gossip.

Ashley filled Jenna in on Rachelle's visit and Rachelle's twirly-haired, pouty effort to get Chase to notice her. And the fact Ashley had gotten so frustrated she launched a snowball at Rachelle's car before she realized what she was doing.

"That's the way to do it. Good on ya." Jenna gave her a high-five and a smirk.

"What's that smirk about?" Ashley eyed Jenna with a thanks-a-lot glare.

"You're jealous."

"Am not." *But that's what Chase said, too.*

"You're green as they come, my friend." Jenna filled her wine glass. "Admit it. You thought he was on a date with her tonight."

She could imagine her head turning into a Granny Smith apple with a big brown stem, full of sour, juicy jealousy.

"I don't know why you'd be jealous of Rachelle. The guy only has eyes for you." Jenna winked at her over the slice of pizza. "Have you done it yet?"

"Done it?" Ashley choked. "What? Have we reverted to high school? Really?"

"I'm only asking. Geez, you don't have to get all huffy."

Ashley sighed. "I need ice cream."

"You need to get laid."

She paused midway to the refrigerator. "Don't start."

"Maybe that's it. You forgot how. Like how tab A fits into slot B."

Ignoring her friend, she retrieved a gallon of chocolate peanut butter ice cream. "Okay. I admit it. It's been awhile. And maybe, since my college boyfriend dumped me, I'm a little hesitant to get back in the saddle again."

"Men." Jenna lifted her glass of wine and took a long swig. "Every female has at least one asshole posting unwanted pictures on our Facebook timeline. We should make an asshole list. Those guys who broke our hearts, cheated on us, or downright crushed our souls. Mine would take a legal pad."

"Really, that bad?" Ashley asked. "How about having your picture posted in the boy's locker room labeled slut, just because you wouldn't put out."

"That would rank as pretty bad, if a line chef and I hadn't been caught having sex in the cruise ship's walk-in refrigerator by the head chef."

"You win." Ashley said, jumping off the counter to get another spoon.

Jenna scooped out a mound of ice cream the size of a baseball. "You want my opinion?"

"Would it matter if I said no?"

"Not really."

Ashley savored her ice cream, swirling the flavors and her frustration around in her mouth.

"There's something between the two of you. Both of you are trying really hard to deny it, and it's not working. Do yourself a favor and figure it out. Because opportunities like this, they don't come around often."

Confusion rushed in. "I've got to stick to my plan. Money. Shelter. Food. Nothing else."

"I get it. Keeping life simple. Blocking out everything but the essential. But sometimes it's not bad to let life get a little complicated."

A peanut butter chunk got stuck on her tongue, and she needed to wash it down. She leaned over and shoved her face under the island faucet. When her lungs cleared enough to choke down her astonishment, she said, "But he's leaving."

"You don't know that. He told Harold he was debating whether staying in the military was what he wanted. He might be a civilian by next year."

Ashley's emotions did a loop-de-loop. Now *there* was a game changer. "He actually said he was getting out?"

"No, but he's thinking about it."

Holy cow. What if he stayed? Her excitement stalled. "It doesn't matter. I'd still be his vacation fling."

Jenna laughed. "Okay. Try to say that again. This time like you really believe it."

"I'm telling you how it is."

"Well, then, your reality is slanted because when you two looked at each other, Hank's gas pumps could go up in flames and neither one of you would notice."

At that, Ashley shoved a hundred more calories of ice cream down her gob.

"I'm not saying you have to marry him tomorrow. I'm only saying you might give the poor guy a chance."

"I can't do long distance."

Jenna stared at her until an uncomfortable feeling set in. "He's not your dad, Ashley."

Well, crap. That transparent, huh?

Once again she wondered about the letters and the man she barely knew. "I forgot to tell you, I found several boxes of letters my dad wrote my mom." She let out a long, uneasy breath. "There's something there that doesn't fit with what I thought I knew. In the letters, my dad seems different. Kinder. More passionate. I don't get it."

Jenna looked away for a moment. "Nothing is what it seems. Trust me. You should keep searching for answers until you find the truth. Did you call and ask your dad if you could sell some of his stuff?"

"No. He knows the bank's about to foreclose on the house. If he intended to help, he would have reached out by now."

"I still think you should tell him how bad it is. At least you got the electricity turned back on."

Heat brushed up Ashley's cheek. "Mom kept telling me over and over again how sorry she was for not raising me better, for not giving me the tools I need to be an adult. I'm not a screw-up. It's just that I didn't think I'd be on my own so soon. I keep thinking all I have to do is sell one thing a day, and if I hang on long enough, I'll catch a break. For now, I have a roof over my head. And, thanks to a vintage perfume bottle and a silver coin collection, we can celebrate our friendship tonight."

Like a good friend, Jenna pushed both the tub of ice cream and the bottle of wine in her direction.

"Sounds like a good plan, but I still think you should talk to your dad. Knowing the truth is a whole lot easier to work with than making stuff up. The unknown eats at a person until nothing's left." Her normally easygoing friend spoke lightly, but with heavy conviction, hammering each verbal nail home.

"Chase is good at solving problems. Maybe I should have him help me solve this one."

Jenna only nodded because she'd shoved enough ice cream in her mouth to make her cheeks bulge.

The front door opened and then shut, signaling Chase's arrival.

Ashley hopped down from the counter and automatically began checking her outfit and pushing her hair behind her ear.

Jenna rolled her eyes, sighed, and eased off the kitchen island. "And you tell me there's no attraction. You got it bad, sister friend. I'm going home to let you two lovebirds talk about letters and the sex you're not going to have."

"Come on, stay."

"Nope. Got an early baking morning tomorrow." She snatched her multicolored hobo bag from the counter, dug out her lip balm for a quick once-over, and threw the tube back in the bag. "Hey, Chase."

"Hey, Jenna. Ashley."

Jenna put the lid on the gallon of ice cream and tucked it in her oversized bag. "You won't need this anymore tonight. And before you ask about my sugar levels, I'm good. Later."

Ashley walked Jenna to the front door, closed it, then slowly turned. "Hey."

His eyebrows lifted. "Hey, yourself. Did you have fun with your friend?"

"I did. She thinks you're hot." *Crap. How did that slip out? I'll blame it on the wine.*

"Really? And what do you think?"

Think fast. Think fast. Think fast. Ummm. "I think you need to take a shower." She eyed his surprisingly rumpled clothes. Thank goodness she had reconnaissance, so she already knew he hadn't been with Rachelle. The jealousy bug could really take a bite out of a person.

He took a step closer, placing his hands on either side of her head on the front door, effectively trapping her. "Interesting idea. You want to join me? You could light that match we've been discussing. Might be fun."

"Me? No." She ducked under his arm. "I've got stuff to do." *No matches. Lighting matches is dangerous.*

She swore she could hear a slight chuckle. She didn't dare turn around or look back. 'Cause if she did, she forecasted showers in the near future.

ASHLEY HAMMERED away her vexation on dozens of silver forks. Feeling good about making progress, she decided to spend the rest of the night looking at stars and making plans for the next day. While staring into the fireplace on the back deck, she went through her mental checklists made earlier in the day.

The sleeping dog beside her twitched,

and she inched the wool blanket over a few inches to cover Lucky's feet. Above the treetops, the stars covered the horizon. Soft winter air nipping at her skin prompted her to haul the goose down comforter out of the storage bin before settling again into the Adirondack chair.

Jenna's weird quips replayed in her mind. She'd laughed until she had tears streaming down her cheeks, and their bantering while playing Boggle reminded her of other good times. She recalled telling Chase he should laugh more. Maybe the same applied to her.

As if fate had summoned him, Chase opened the back door, flooding the deck with light from the kitchen. Even in the house's shadow, his masculine, sculpted form gave her heart a kick-start.

"Aren't you cold?" He closed the sliding glass door to keep the warmth inside.

"Not really. Not with the blanket. Why don't you join me?"

All afternoon, she'd wondered what to say when he returned, but nothing seemed adequate or fitting. She could only point at a chair and hope her brain would come up with something to say that might help him understand. But her mouth was too dry to speak. She reached for her wine glass to bolster her courage. She had to say something, but what? She took several big gulps and hoped for the best.

She tilted her chin up, looking behind her. "After you left, I did some thinking."

"The good type or the bad type? Because thinking isn't always healthy."

There was a tinge of sarcasm and humor, but what he said gave her the courage to continue.

"Ha. Funny guy." She rolled her eyes, and then waited for him to settle. "I came to the conclusion that I've been so fixated on making money and finding a place to stay, I haven't found time to enjoy what I have. I forgot how beautiful the night sky is here, the smell of the evergreens, the crickets chirping. Digging through the antiques, I remembered how much I loved old stuff, and finding a way to make it fit with the new. I've been so angry about the past, I've missed enjoying the simple things life offers. Also, I realized my anger hurts those around me. I'm sorry for that."

Chase moved his chair closer to hers. A giddy sense of relief made her toes tingle. She liked Chase. Liked him a lot, and didn't want to lose one of the few people with whom she'd ever found a comfortable rhythm. She pushed the edges of the comforter toward him to share the warmth. In the process, her hand brushed his thigh and sent a tingling sensation up her arm. The combined body heat and the intimacy of sharing a small space melted her apprehension about their earlier conversation.

He leaned closer, but she couldn't see his face or guess what he was thinking. After a moment, he pointed toward the sky. "When we patrolled at night, stars covered the sky. The lack of city lights made the sky intense. It was truly amazing."

"It's pretty here, too. Don't you think?"

In the pitch-black night, she couldn't see much, but she could see he wasn't looking at the sky when he said, "It's perfect."

The heat from his perceptions further melted the ice cream in her stomach. She tilted her head toward his. "What else is there to know about Chase Daniels?"

"There's not much to know."

"Sure there is. Like where you grew up, what's happened in your life, your dreams for the future?"

He sat back into the chair, clearly uncomfortable with having the flashlight directed at him.

"I grew up in New Jersey, joined the military out of high school, went through Marine boot camp, and that's pretty much it. Marines.com fills in the blanks. You should know the rest."

She did know. However, she'd read another bundle of her father's letters and realized she'd only seen the Marine, not the cherishing, providing husband, or the man.

"Chase, I'm working hard to separate the man and the Marine in my mind. Who is Chase Daniels? What does he want from life?"

The military had a way of tearing a person down to their fundamental strengths and weaknesses and building them back up from there. But in every soldier she'd met, a little part—the best part—remained.

"You sure you want to go there?"

"Yes, I really do."

He stretched his legs out in front of him like he wanted to stretch time. "I joined the Marines for a couple of reasons. I needed something to focus on. Plus, I wanted to get out of Jersey and find something to push my body and mind to the limits. I figured the Marines would do the job for me. After a few deserved ass-kicking sessions, I learned a Marine isn't about going the distance as much as it is about developing self-respect and confidence. Something I sorely lacked as a teen. The Marines made me a better person. I learned accountability, and how to be a leader and a good, solid team member. The Corps uncovered my best qualities and made me realize I had the potential to become the man I wanted to be."

"Have you found your calling?"

"Not sure. I've moved around a lot. I look around this place, and it's filled with a lifetime of memories. There are photographs on the walls and glass lamps on side tables. There's some great stuff here. The old leather chair in your living room is fantastic. It must be a hundred years old."

"It was my great-great-grandfather's, and you're right, it's a relic." *Too bad I haven't been able to sell it.*

"My point. The things I own fit into the bed of a pickup truck." He chuckled. "That's why I came in your store. I like looking at old stuff. Antiques have a history. My stuff is Ikea vintage, purchased current day."

"If you like antiques, I have a shop full of stuff you can buy at a real good price."

"And where would I put it? Naw. Sure, I'd like to own a French musket or a German beer stein, but to me, it's more about the history—who made it or who owned it, where it's been. History fascinates me. I like finding an object and learning its history." He nudged her with his elbow. "I thought you liked antiques."

"It's not that I can't appreciate a finely crafted silver set or hand-painted dish. You saw my tea set collection. But I think I lost interest once the excitement of the hunt ended with the Internet. My mom would get so excited when she found something rare, or a particular piece to complete a collection.

"The day I showed her three exactly like it on eBay, she got really mad and told me I didn't get it. And I didn't...get it, that is. In high school I begged my parents to let me go to art school, but they insisted on me going to business school. I think in their minds, a business degree provided a good foundation for any career path."

"Business? Not nursing or a medical degree?"

She shifted uneasily in the chair. "Health care? I don't think so."

"Why not? You're smart enough."

She'd considered the medical field, but she liked the caring side of nursing better than the technical side. Even thinking about chemistry and biology classes gave her hives. Plus, back then she'd considered creating masterpieces on canvas a perfect choice. Now she wasn't so sure. Eating tuna fish and rice crackers for the past four months kinda took the romance out of the starving artist gig.

She tilted her head toward the sky. "Something to think about. My immediate goal is to find a decent-paying job and a place to live."

"I get priorities, but it's never too late to work toward something you're passionate about. Caring for others is a gift, and you're good at it. If you want, I can put you in touch with a few of my buddies in the medical corps."

"Medical corps. Military. No thanks."

"Come on. The military isn't as bad as you make it seem."

He had a point, but she didn't want to go there.

Chase saw *her*, not the persona she'd created for her mom. His insights scared, yet thrilled her. In only a few days, he'd come to understand what her parents never had. He accepted her without questioning or trying to change her, only trying to help her see a better path.

She reached out to find his arm. "You're right. I'll think about it."

His warm fingers circled her neck and guided her toward the welcoming heat. The night's cool air brought a chill, but his breath warmed her cheeks. Fingers tightened on her arm, and he held her close. His lips touched hers, his tongue tickling until she opened to him. Hot embers ignited inside her. His tongue retreated and she chased the sensation, wanting more. He met her halfway and deepened the kiss, both fighting for a breath until the connection ended. He slid his hand from her neck, his thumb brushing her cheek, and said, "I've wanted to do that all day."

This kiss felt different, and took her places she wanted to explore. It had been too long since she'd seen intense desire on a man's face, and she wondered when she would again. She didn't want to what-if anymore.

Chase's kiss delivered an all-out warning. If they continued the foreplay, it would lead straight to the bedroom, and nothing or no one could stop the forward motion once they started. The wine consumed during the girls' night with Jenna encouraged her to lean closer, seeking a connection. She reached for his hand, lacing her fingers with his. "Does this mean you've forgiven me for my temper tantrum this morning?"

"I told you then, there was nothing to worry about." The huskiness in his voice spread across her skin like soft, silky lotion.

She leaned back, wishing she could see

into his heart. "I like you, Chase. I like you a lot, but I'm afraid."

"Tell me what you're afraid of."

"We get each other. I don't know about you, but I haven't felt free to speak the truth for a long time. I want to find the authentic me, and I'm not willing to give up whatever this is for one night of bliss."

"There's nothing more authentic than getting naked and exposing yourself to another person. Besides, bliss sounds like a lot of fun."

She laughed. "Tell me about it. Three years is a long time. Not that I'm counting or anything. And that's my other concern. Disappointing you."

He scratched his head and chuckled. "You can't disappoint me. Not possible."

"How do you know?" She shivered and goose bumps covered her arms, even though between the fire and the down blanket, she should be sweating. She gave him a tentative smile.

"Don't be afraid."

"Me? Afraid?" *You bet your sweet ass, I'm afraid.*

And her white cotton underwear, the type sold five pairs to the pack, reminded her why there should be no intimacy.

"Let me in, Ash." He stood and held out his hand.

He waited patiently, quietly. Unlike her mind, where a bomb had gone off, and fragments of thoughts were running around in a panic.

The way he looked at her was pure, tantalizing temptation, and made her mouth water. "I need to settle Lucky," she replied with a kick of pleasure for managing to say something at least half intelligent.

"That's the thing about dogs, they like to sleep." He stood and closed the grates on the fireplace, the embers outlining his body. He reached over his shoulders and in one motion pulled off his shirt.

Oh. God. "What are you doing?"

"Getting naked. Are you going to join me?"

"Um," she managed, while her mind still struggled to kick-start some brain matter.

She swallowed hard when his hands went to the top button of his jeans. *Lord help me.* As his zipper descended, her body pooled with the desire to connect to his skin.

"Chase?"

"Tell me you want this, Ash."

Please want me, she heard, although he didn't say it. In her mind, she responded, *Yes, and thank you.*

CHAPTER TWELVE

*A*shley made everything in his body go wild-ass crazy.

He'd been careful to not move too fast, forcing himself to slow down, but seeing her in the firelight, the stars above...he couldn't wait any longer.

She had a way of sneaking behind his defenses and surprising him, leaving him completely disarmed.

Until there he stood, vulnerable, scars and all.

Something in her eyes flared. "You're so..."

"You're so...what?"

"Perfect."

The breath he didn't know he'd been holding whooshed out like a dam breaking.

He'd worried about her reaction to the scars crisscrossing his body, but her lack of revulsion made him appreciate her more. An unexpected gift...which he should have expected because he'd seen her caring heart in action.

A couple of his scars came from his time in the military, but the rest were from when one of his foster mother's boyfriends held him down and stubbed cigarettes out on his chest. Some women got a deranged thrill when they saw his scars, fantasizing over how he'd gotten them and believing him to be a bull who'd give them the ride of a lifetime. Normally, he didn't disappoint. This time, however, the trip was going to be different. This time, he didn't feel like he had anything to prove.

He lifted Ashley from the Adirondack chair. "Let's go upstairs, Ash. I want to show you how perfect we can be," he murmured, kissing the soft skin below her ear.

"But—"

"*Shh*, no buts. Not tonight. I want to make love to you, Ashley. I want us to explore. I want you to feel everything I'm feeling."

Her body stiffened. He expected her to say no. He expected her to kick his sorry butt out of the house. But then her eyes shifted and softened. Her body relaxed. "What are we waiting for?"

He couldn't get upstairs fast enough. He kissed her and filled his senses with her citrus shampoo and luscious curves. He considered the comfortable-looking couch, but decided she deserved better. And maybe she deserved better than him, but he pushed the idea aside.

At the edge of the guest bed, he released her legs and gently lowered her to the floor. Her gaze lifted to his mouth and her tongue swiped over her lips.

Not wanting to disappoint, he slanted his head and captured her mouth, seeking, pressing deeper. "I want to see you," he said, his tone husky and a bit demanding.

When he gripped the hem of her sweater, she lifted her arms. Then her hands paused over the waistband of her jeans.

"Let me." He unbuttoned and unzipped and slid his hands inside to feel her velvety skin.

She released a soft groan, encouraging him and giving permission to slide her pants and cotton underwear down her smooth thighs. After she'd kicked out of her pants, taking her socks off at the same time, he cupped her face.

"You are so beautiful."

He deepened the kiss and got completely lost, nibbling, kissing, sucking. She snuggled closer, naked, only a bra covering those luscious breasts. Removing the barrier became a must, but she beat him to it, letting the nude nylon slide down her arms.

When she fully, freely connected to his body, she let out an erotic moan, and he went stiff.

"Ashley?"

"Uh-huh?"

He leaned back and looked deep into her eyes, searching for regret or indecision. "Make sure this is what you want because I want you more than I've wanted anything. I want to show you how special you are. If you give me the go-ahead, I may not be able to stop later."

In response, she wrapped her arms around his shoulders and climbed straight up his body. He leveraged her climb, but still wanted an answer.

"Ash?"

"For a guy, you sure talk a lot." Her trembling fingers settled on his lips for a brief second.

His mouth closed over hers, and he nibbled his way to her neck. "Tell me you want this."

"I want this."

He indulged in the roundness of her ass before letting his fingers skim her outer thighs. He wanted her to forget he was a

Marine, forget about making any decisions about her future, forget everything. Just be. He made his way from her collarbone to her ear. "Tell me again."

"I want this," she managed, even out of breath.

With her clinging to him like a formfitting glove, he leaned over to retrieve a condom from his wallet sitting on the dresser, and then moved toward the bed. He lowered her to the mattress before pinning her sexy softness beneath him, hovering his weight above her.

"I want you. I need this." His words were daring, exposing his real need. Her. He needed her. "Tell me how I can please you."

He leaned in. Let his tongue play with her nipple before indulging and sucking the turgid flesh into his mouth.

"Yes." The word floated out of her mouth on a sigh.

"Yes? You want more of this?" He switched breasts and provided the same tantalizing stimulation. He tugged and sucked hard on her flesh while he inched his fingers closer to her core. She wriggled beneath his hands, trying to get closer.

"Chase, stop talking," she pleaded against his skin, begging him with her body.

He laughed and slid his fingers higher, and then between her thighs, making her bring out the claws. She sank her fingernails into his back, dragging him closer while biting the exact right places. He moaned at the mind-blowing pleasure.

He applied pressure, experimenting, playing, and watching her reactions. Her kisses were doing wicked things to his concentration. He needed to hurry because his disciplined training was threatening to fail him.

She dropped her head back against the pillow. "Holy hell."

"You're not in hell, sweet Ash. I'm sending you to heaven."

She gripped his shoulders harder. Then her eyes rolled back in her head, her mouth seeking his. He let her feel like she was winning, but when she pulled back enough to take a breath, he lifted and nuzzled lower, kissing and caressing and nibbling until he found his salvation. He settled between her legs and let her knees drape across his shoulders.

"Oh. God."

"Nope. Only Chase," he sighed, before kissing each leg and caressing with his tongue. Her skin swelled and her breathing sputtered. He placed a hand across her stomach to hold her in place, to thrust deeper and deeper, until he felt her muscles tense and contract again and again and again. She wrapped her fingers under his arms and tugged. He kissed his way up her belly and then surrounded her with his arms. Her body had gone limp, but she pushed at his chest.

"I want…you…inside, now."

He didn't hesitate. After rolling on a condom, he lifted above her. "Lift your legs," he commanded. She readily complied. Unable to hold back even a second longer, he drove into her hard, and she met him stroke for stroke. *Amazing.*

Their combined groans were as stirring, as beautiful as the Hallelujah Chorus. The only thing he could see or hear or feel was her. Her body beneath his, fierce and brave and wild.

When she clenched around him, he erupted and emptied his need, holding nothing back. Giving her everything. Giving her what he'd always held back.

Giving her his heart.

He started to lift to relieve her of some of his weight, but she tightened her legs around his waist. "Don't leave. Not yet. You feel too good."

So he relaxed into her, letting the blood beating in his ears weave a complex rhythm with her heartbeat thudding against his chest.

No matter how many times he'd convinced himself he wasn't afraid while storming villages, looking for insurgents, and clearing rooms, he couldn't lie. Right now, with her in his arms, he felt afraid. Afraid of not being with her. Afraid he wasn't a good enough man. Afraid she might not want him in her life.

Never had he met a woman like her, and he didn't want to look any further. He rolled to his side, taking her with him. He'd had sex, but this wasn't sex.

After a while, her fingers began drawing little circles and curlicues on his chest around Bobby's tattoo and she released a little hum. "Did your tattoo hurt?"

"Not the tattoo, but the event which motivated it sure did." *Still did.*

She leaned in and kissed the tattoo, and then settled back by his side, letting the silence and her actions speak for themselves.

Eventually, she lifted her head and looked back at him. "I want to talk."

Shit. Here it comes. "Yeah."

"About my dad."

Wow. Didn't see that coming. Since the conversation wasn't about regrets, he wanted to pop a cork and throw a party. "What about him?"

"I...think I've been wrong about him."

He rolled her onto her back so he could see her better. She sat up and tugged the sheet up to her chest, hiding her body. Hiding from him.

Her slithering away wasn't cool. "You sure you want to talk about this now?"

"You're good at just about everything, including solving problems, and I thought... well, I thought maybe you could help."

Okay. That's better. He scooted up to the headboard and shifted the covers for warmth. She dropped her head to his shoulder.

She bunched the sheet in her hand, wadding and twisting the fabric. "For the longest time, I hated the Marines because they took my dad away. I assumed he loved the military more than he loved me, and that's why he stayed away. That he didn't want me."

"Ashley."

"No, let me finish." She folded her hands together. "I've been reading old letters my dad wrote to my mom. The more I read, the more my perceptions don't seem accurate. He loved me and my mom a lot. But my gut tells me something's missing. I have to find out what it is. I'm trying hard to keep an open mind, but a multitude of ifs keep tromping though. I want to concentrate on the future. But part of me almost feels like I have to discover my past, get some clear answers, before I can make solid future plans."

He gathered her small hand in his and wrapped his fingers securely around hers. "You shouldn't worry about what-ifs," he suggested, trying to hide the contradiction. He was a master of whirligigging, never letting his mind rest. Constantly running the possible outcomes in his head, anticipating the result. "I'm sure you've thought about asking your dad directly?"

"I could probably get more information out of Lucky. Marines don't like to talk much…unless they're having sex, as I've recently discovered."

"Funny."

"You think so, huh? You wait. Women know how to talk."

That paybacks-suck smile lit a fire in his groin. He'd made love to her the best way he knew how, and to prove they hadn't just had sex. At least it wasn't sex for him.

"Will you help me?" she asked.

Pastor Chris's advice came back to him. "I can certainly try."

ASHLEY LEANED her head back against the headboard. "My dad always said a Marine knows a Marine. Maybe you can help me understand him better."

"Describing events to someone who hasn't experienced combat can be challenging."

"Jenna said you're thinking of getting out."

"Thinking about it. My commanding officer's expecting my answer by the first of the year."

Thinking. But I doubt you will.

Ashley tried shutting the door on her heart, but the hinges were stuck. Chase might consider getting out, but she seriously doubted he'd make the big adjustment to civilian life. Most former military didn't adjust well. The government knew it. Thus the many services offered to transitioning veterans.

She refused to get her hopes up. Too many times she'd asked her dad to stay, only to be told he didn't have a choice. She remembered her eighth birthday. Running down the steps before dawn. Seeing her father loading the car with his kit box and duffel bag. She'd begged him to stay, promising to be a good girl and do whatever he asked. Her mother came, tugging her small arms from around her father's legs. It had been a long time since she thought about *that* day, but the memory still hurt.

The pain of the desertion and rejection.

After that, she refused to say good-bye to her dad. She wouldn't be put into the position to beg any man to stay again.

She tilted her head to see Chase's face. "But either way, you have to go back."

"I don't have a choice. Getting out requires paperwork and medical exams."

I don't have a choice. There were those words again.

He would leave. Then he might write or call for a while. She pondered the pile of letters in boxes. She refused to live her life like her mom, running to the mailbox, waiting for a letter to arrive.

"I'm sure it's a tough decision." She picked at the edges of the healing scab on her finger.

"Getting tougher every day."

The uncertainty in his voice she could empathize with, but she didn't want to get entangled in the troubled emotions. He'd recently lost his friend, he felt alone, separated from people who understood him, trusted him. When he got back to the base, he'd put these few weeks behind him, forgetting her, forgetting this place. Her heart couldn't take watching another person drive away in a cloud of dust.

If he couldn't keep the relationship casual, then she would need to find a way.

She pushed off the bed and swooped up her clothes. "I need to check on Lucky. Can I bring you something?"

"No." His body had gone stiff, his face closed like a storm door just before a tornado.

She picked up his jeans, pretending she hadn't just experienced the most mind-blowing sex ever.

"I'll get those," Chase said.

"I noticed you fixed the firewood rack and restacked logs today. You didn't need to do that."

That damn sexy grin spread across his

lips. "I like working with my hands…in case you haven't noticed."

Memories of his warm, creative fingers working their magic made her body flash red-hot and transported her back to a place she wanted to be, but couldn't go. She moved toward the door.

"I'll be up early to work on the stuff for the Bazaar. I'll try not to disturb you."

"Don't worry about me."

She wondered how long she'd be able to keep her emotions closed off. She didn't have the defenses Chase had. He'd learned to be an expert at keeping his emotions under control, and could weasel his way in and take her down effortlessly. She forced her foot to take a step back. She considered her odds against this easy-going, extraordinarily good-looking man, and figured she didn't stand a chance.

ONCE ASHLEY DISAPPEARED, he let out a long, steady breath. He let her go only because she wouldn't be able to go far.

She impacted him in ways he hadn't expected.

A fierce protectiveness made him want to build perimeter defenses around her to keep her safe, safe from him.

She had sound logic—he *was* leaving and had no choice—but that didn't mean the future didn't offer opportunities.

While he unloaded dry goods off Harold's delivery trucks, the storeowner had asked him the 'what-next' question. He didn't have a solid answer. Over the past year, he'd considered leaving the Corps now and again, until the idea began to poke at him, like a persistent knife point in his side. Usually he dismissed the idea, not knowing how to tell his gung-ho buddies about the visions taking over his mind and body. If they knew, he'd be out or told to suck it up—a war needed to be won.

The truth was, he didn't join the Marines

to kill bad guys. He joined to get away from his mom, to make a living, make some friends, possibly create a family. The Corps had given him much, much more and had far exceeded his expectations. Then there were the housing and medical benefits he'd be giving up. He didn't know if he could, or even wanted to, cut the strings, but then Ashley walked into his sights.

No matter where he pointed his riflescope, there she stood, directly in front of him. He'd never met anyone like her. He wanted to be with her. Every time he walked into the house, the first thing he wanted to do was find her, talk to her, make sure she was doing okay. He believed she was a good person even before she told him about her mom. After that, he knew she had to be the most generous person on earth.

She'd given him something to think about, too. He wouldn't have been able to put three years of his life on hold to care for someone. He could stick his finger into flesh to stop a bullet wound from bleeding out, he could carry a buddy three hundred yards with bullets whizzing past his head, but to sit in a room, day after day? He couldn't do it. She was right. That took guts. Courage. More than he had. Ashley had to be the strongest person he knew, and he wished she had a bit more confidence.

She'd make an excellent nurse or doctor. Maybe he could talk her into going back with him. They might be separated for a while, but they could work it out. Then again…

He squeezed his index finger and thumb against his temples. He'd always planned, prepared, and then proceeded down the road.

Since when did he go marching down the road without his gear? Since he'd met Ashley, that's when.

His life had fit in a nice, neat box. In a couple of days, she'd turned his kit upside down, and it lay in a jumbled mess at his feet. Funny thing was, he didn't mind. He'd watched other buddies make compromises for a girlfriend or a wife, but his life had no room for such foolishness—until now. Now he didn't think having Ashley in his life would be odd. In fact, he couldn't think how his life would work without her. With only a few days left till the new year and his deadline for making a decision, he needed to look at options, and fast.

CHAPTER THIRTEEN

"I'm here." Jenna struggled through Ashley's front door lugging two plastic bins. She shifted the burden in her arms, greeted Lucky, and closed the door. "Look at you, big boy! Your hair is growing out."

"Let me help." Ashley gently nudged Lucky aside and grasped the top bin by the finger holes. "Is it me, or is he looking better?"

"His back leg looks great, and he's put on weight. He does look a bit weird with those scabs and stubby hair, but pretty soon the fur will cover them and no one will notice."

Ashley patted the dog's head and got a tail beating for the pleasure. "You're a good dog. Yes, you are." She looked at Jenna. "I cleared the kitchen table and island so we could work."

Moving through the long, tiled entryway, Ashley peered back over her shoulder. "I forgot to tell you. I got a text from my dad."

"Oh, boy," Jenna responded with a tinge of weariness mixed with a heavy dose of protectiveness. "It's good news, I hope."

"I'm not sure if it's good news or not. The message was a bit cryptic, but I think he's going to send me Mom's letters. He said something about gaining an understanding."

Jenna paused her unloading of the labels, bags, and ribbons needed to prepare for Saturday's Bazaar bake sale. "What's up with your parents? They must be the worst communicators on the planet."

"I know, right?"

No regrets. That was her mom's

philosophy. Look forward. Only forward. Never back. But her mom often didn't follow the advice. She'd reflected on the past plenty, especially in the early morning hours when the house was quiet, and fever-fueled dreams made her have conversations with Ashley's dad or the grandmother Ashley remembered only from pictures. Her mom had regrets. Tons of them.

"I'm starting to wonder if I knew either of my parents," she whispered, but Jenna heard the sentiment.

"Better than me. I barely remember mine. I was seven when the car accident happened. I have an image of a man and a woman, but I don't know who they were."

The look on Jenna's face made her want to reach out and hug her friend, but Jenna wasn't the hugging type.

"Look at us. Today is supposed to be a fun day. I'll put on some tunes, pour us some coffee and we can get started. How's that sound?"

"Coffee? Did you say coffee?"

Ashley giggled at the lustful look crossing her friend's face. She wondered if the same expression crossed her own face when Chase walked in the room. *Probably.*

That morning, he'd looked darn handsome in his jeans and leather jacket. He was on his way out to do some touristy thing and visit a few ski towns farther west. The gossip mill also provided the intel that he'd be building a couple of shelves for Harold, and Maggie needed a tree stump pulled out of the ground behind the café. Keeping those amazing hands busy was a mighty good thing. He needed the distraction. And so did she.

Ashley poured a cup of fresh brew and added a touch of vanilla creamer. The bitter and sweet fragrance mixed in the air before she handed the cup to her friend. Jenna took a long draw from her favorite drink and Ashley turned on the radio. Zack Brown's voice resonated through the kitchen.

"Oh. Coffee." Jenna sighed in ecstasy. "If they could hook me up to a caffeine pump, I would be in heaven. Speaking of which, where is that heavenly man of yours?"

"I keep telling you he's not mine. And stop looking at me like that."

Jenna's lips quirked into a yeah-sure grin. "Keep telling yourself he's not yours. You better open your eyes before you run into a tree. You're blinded by the self-centered jerks you've dated in the past. Chase has feelings for you, and he's a nice guy who also happens to help people while looking sinfully delicious."

Ashley's skin tingled to the point she needed to bury her nose into the plastic bins to avoid Jenna's scrutiny. She wasn't blind. Her eyes were wide open. It was her heart having the misgivings.

Ashley groaned when Lady Antebellum's song 'Long Stretch of Love' drifted into the kitchen. *You make me feel alive* reverberated in her head. "Holy bejesus. I can't get him out of my brain. He's like an infection."

Jenna picked up her mug, probably to

hide her giggling grin, but her laughing eyes gave her away.

"Don't start." Ashley pointed her finger at Jenna.

"I didn't say anything."

"You don't have to." She placed a finger on the rim of Jenna's mug and pushed down. "Someday a guy's going to run into you, and I'm going to have my laugh, although it's not funny. I think I'm falling for this guy, and that's bad." *Really, really bad.* "He's taking up way too much brain matter when I've got to concentrate on my plan."

Jenna's mood sobered, and she grabbed a stack of bags and began attaching labels. "After this is all done, are you going to go back to college?"

"That's a whole 'nother pile of elk poop." Ashley lifted another stack of labels. "I was going to finish my degree online, but I got a letter back from the University of San Diego. The curriculum for my business degree has changed. Since I've been absent for three years, the administration's looking to determine if my credits are still valid. Plus, I've already got a pile of debt I want to pay off first."

"Are you even still interested in going back to school? Do you even want to start a business?"

"I have been thinking about it."

"About what?" Jenna nudged her arm, most likely with the intent to lighten her mood. It didn't work.

The house. The store. Moving. Paying bills. The pending house foreclosure made her feel like the brewing storm would only get worse. She forecasted an avalanche of hurt with a flood of tears coming soon.

"Everything. I keep getting this feeling something will happen that will change everything." She glanced at the boxes she'd worked so hard to pack and prepare to move. "I know I'm delusional, but I keep hoping there's some clerical error at the bank."

A warm hand wrapped around hers and

squeezed. "It will work out. You just have to hold on."

"I know. But I'm still going to miss this place. This is my home."

"But you're not leaving Elkridge. Right?"

"It depends. I haven't found a place I can afford that isn't a dump or doesn't require a hefty deposit for large dogs. And eventually the stuff I have to sell is going to run out. I'll need something more permanent. eBay and craft fairs are only temporary."

She looked out the back window toward the snow-covered ridge. She could almost feel the sun on her face, the cold wind nipping at her cheeks, and the chirping of birds asking her how her day was going. She loved living in Elkridge. She'd left for college because she hated her mother's suffocating control more.

"I've been thinking about what you said." Ashley nibbled at a dry piece of skin on her lip.

"I say a lot of things. What specifically are you talking about?"

"A couple of months ago you were bitching about us needing to get fresh blood in the city, and saying how so many townspeople are getting old."

"There's more polyester and Polident in this area than there are people under the age of thirty. Newer members are moving in because the schools are great, but this old mining town needs a serious facelift."

"My point. Folks have lived here forever. And most are stubborn as a beaver about wanting to stay in their homes, refusing to leave. The nearest elder or emergency care facility is way over in Minesville forty minutes away, and that's only if the roads are dry."

"Wait! Are you thinking about starting an elder care business?"

"Still working things out. I figure I should use the business classes I took for something. I did some checking, and there's this online homecare certificate program. I would have to go to Denver twice a month to complete some practical training, but it's cheaper than living in California, and I could help this community. Since I got all that experience helping Mom, the practical exam shouldn't be über hard to pass, and it's not as expensive as a degree."

A genuine, hundred-percent smile filled Jenna's face and, for once, ran all the way up and exploded out her eyes. "That would be *awesome.*"

"Don't go writing anything down in permanent ink yet. I still have to find a place to live and figure out how I can pay for the program at the same time."

"I'd say you could stay with me, but my place is so small, I even trip over myself."

"Can you imagine your cabin with me plus Lucky?"

"No," she sighed. "So your dad's not going to help?"

"I haven't asked. Mom was vehement about me learning to make it on my own." Ashley eyed the white box sitting in the second plastic bin. "I forgot. Here are the spoons and forks I decorated to go with your baked goods. I hope you like them because I couldn't sleep and got a little carried away." She handed Jenna modified utensils adorned with colorful glass beads and key rings attached to the end.

"I love them. And look at the little charms."

"I found boxes of craft stuff my mom kept. I figured no one else was going to use the junk."

Jenna continued to oooh and aaah over the pieces.

"Are those bakery samples?" Ashley pointed at a little brown box with a lime green polka dot bow.

"Oh, I forgot. My newest invention, cobbler cups. I brought strawberry-rhubarb, mixed berry, tart apple, and peach-apricot. I was trying to come up with a way to sell pie slices and discovered an easy way to make mini pie crusts."

When Ashley lifted one of the pastries out of the box, her saliva glands kicked into high gear. "I wonder if I can shove this whole thing in my mouth at once?"

"Worth a try." Jenna smirked. "I'm sure you've had bigger things in your mouth lately."

Thank goodness she hadn't put the pastry in her mouth yet, or pie might have come out her nose. "Jenna? Holy crap!" She put the berry treat back in the box and got up to fetch plates and silverware.

Her friend batted her eyelashes. "Just sayin'. I still think you should tackle that scrumptious man and have your way with him."

Crap. Ashley felt an urgent need to stick her head in the freezer. The heat burning her cheeks couldn't be a good thing.

"Wait a minute." Jenna squinted. "You've already done the wild thing and haven't shared. What's with that?"

The heat dipped to her toes and shot up again, and didn't stop until it hit her hairline. "I'm not discussing my activities with Chase."

"Wow. The sex must be exceptional.

You're blushing all the way to your blond roots."

"Stop. I'm not going there." She set the plates on the table.

"And here I thought we were friends. Nothing exciting happens in this town, and I don't have a TV. I'm going to have to stick with my romance novels and Bob."

She glanced up after dropping a pastry on a plate. "Who's Bob?"

"My battery-operated boyfriend. Comes in handy once in a while."

"We are *not* having this conversation."

Jenna gave her knee a light slap. "Did I mention I found a chocolate sauce that's meltable and stays liquid? Want to try some? It's scrumptiously delicious."

"It's not like that with Chase."

Jenna's jovial exuberance faded into the skeptical. "Hmm."

Ashley pulled the fork out of her mouth. "What's that supposed to mean?"

"You've got more than job and school problems. You've got man problems, too."

"Do not." Ashley responded a bit too quickly and a bit too defensively to cover her tracks. "Well, not really. He's leaving, so there's no problem. We're keeping things casual. No long-term attachments."

"Uh-huh." Jenna eyed her suspiciously. The tips of her fingers held a bakery label suspended in mid-air. "I still think you should be careful driving. Your *headlights* are definitely turned off."

Ashley's stomach did a flip-flop, and she pushed the pastry aside. Not because it didn't taste delicious or contained a thousand calories, but because Jenna had a point.

"Really, it's nothing."

"Guys like Chase don't show up too often in a town like this. He's alpha and hot and interested."

"He is nice to look at. And I'm so..." *Frumpy.*

Alpha and hot would turn a whole lot of heads. Heck, if Rachelle didn't stop pecking at and around him, Ashley might have to wring her neck. However, alpha and hot never were a good indicator of strong and stable.

Jenna gave her a nudge, and Ashley sighed. "...I'm so ordinary. Chase could do better."

Jenna slapped a hand on the table. "You, lady, are not ordinary. Not even close. And no, Chase can't do better. You have to get your mother's voice out of your head." The firm tone made Ashley take note. "Don't you dare let that woman destroy your chance at happiness! You deserve only the best."

"You're being kind, which is sweet, but you don't need to."

"No, I'm not. I'm not that nice."

"So you think hanging out with Chase is good?"

"If a guy as stellar as Chase came knocking at my door, I'd let my muffins burn in the oven. You only have one shot at life, Ash. Live it to the fullest."

Life was short.

Too short.

CHAPTER FOURTEEN

Chase looked at the list of unanswered calls and text messages from the past five days. He wasn't up to answering questions about Bobby, or when he'd be getting back to the base.

He'd driven around the ridge to think because the small blonde in his life kept planting landmines and blowing his mind. He scrolled through a list of numbers, pressed dial, and turned slightly to get the best reception he could.

Having driven pretty much every road leading to or from town, he was getting pretty familiar with the terrain. A river had carved out the narrow valley between two ranges. At the top, a panoramic view of the Continental Divide spread across earth and sky.

A gruff "hello" captured his attention.

"Coach. Hey, it's Chase."

"I was just thinking about you. How's life?"

I'm dangling off a cliff with no rope and no safety harness. "All right, I guess."

"Have it your way. We'll play at niceties for the next five minutes until you get bored and hang up. Spit it out. Something's on your mind. Otherwise you wouldn't have called."

Surrounding oneself with people who gave a damn kind of sucked because they wouldn't let the BS get in the way of having a solid conversation. Starting the conversation was the problem. He'd never been good at starting one, even though he'd finished plenty.

"You still there?" Coach's voice came from the phone.

"Still here. Just trying to figure out this thing about a girl."

"Girl, or woman?"

Ashley was six years younger, but like him, she'd survived. He had a whole lot of respect for her. "Woman."

"Ah." The heavy dose of humor in his mentor's voice made Chase wince. "You've come up against a good woman and your brain's gone all haywire. Now I understand."

"Great. Glad someone has a clue."

Irritation jangled his nerves and rattled through his bones. He didn't like being on edge. Every time he caught sight of Ashley, his body went on high alert. He swore his body parts were doing things they weren't supposed to be doing.

"So let me ask you a question." Coach hauled out his 'mentor voice.' The voice he used when teaching a lesson.

"I'm listening."

"What do you have in common?"

"Trucks. Adventure. Spontaneity." Just thinking about her folded in his arms made his body tingle with renewed warmth. "She fits. She's not too fussy, and I like the fact she doesn't wear a lot of stuff on her face. Although she's a bit stubborn."

"I see. Stubborn's not so bad, you know. Keeps a guy guessing and interested. Now, what irritates you when you're together?"

"She doesn't like the military. But I could fix that." *Shit.* Didn't mean for that to slip. Chase kicked a pile of snow and let the cold mountain air carry away his exhale. "But getting out of the Corps for her might not be the best option."

"I agree. You have to do what's right for you."

That niggling pain in his heart returned. A pain that wouldn't go away and had his mind asking repeatedly, *how will you get along without her?*

"Coach?"

"I'm here."

"Didn't you once tell me there were going to be times I'd have to compromise for the ones I loved?"

"I did. But when you make those compromises, make sure the person you're making the concession for would do the same for you. This woman takes exception to you being in the military. The military is what makes you tick, Chase."

Not true. "I joined the military because I assumed it was my only opportunity to be a part of something bigger. Over the years, I've discovered being a part of something doesn't necessarily make a person whole. I needed to be whole before I could contribute to something bigger than myself. And I don't feel whole. If that makes any sense." Chase gripped the phone a bit tighter. "Listen to me getting all philosophical."

"Yesss! I've been waiting for you to figure out that life doesn't give you only one option." The pride in Coach's voice was unmistakable.

"Why's that?"

"A boy can take many paths to finding his inner strength to become a man. I think you've finally discovered yours."

Great. He sighed. Finding his inner strength and knowing what to do with his newly discovered treasure were two different things.

"It may not matter. I'll be somewhere else in the world, and she'll be moving on with her life."

Excuses. Every one he'd recited again and again over the past several days seemed convenient and hollow. He'd spent his time working his body into exhaustion so he could shut his mind off, but no matter how hard he pushed himself, she continued to disrupt his thoughts.

"You have a decision to make. However, from this end of the line, it sounds like you love her. And if you do, you need to tell her."

Chase pounded his forehead with the heel of his hand. "Got any advice about how to do that?"

"Nope. Took me three months to get the nerve to tell Carol, and I still screwed it up. Here's the thing about love. Chances are, she already knows and is simply waiting for you to say it. So putting off saying how you feel out loud is a complete waste of time."

Chase had nothing to say. Absolutely nothing. Coach spoke the truth. She probably already knew he was hopelessly, head-over-heels committed. He turned to gaze out at the horizon while uneasiness jittered across his bones. The world could be a mighty big place without loved ones.

"Want one more word of advice?" Coach asked.

"What's that?"

"Not every woman you love will abandon you like your mother. I think it's important for you to remember that fact."

Well, shit. You had to go there.

Coach always had a way of getting to the meat of the matter. Slicing it down into tender pieces of sirloin and feeding it to the person raw.

"I know." Some of the irritation trickled away like magic. "I remember a 4th of July barbecue we had at your house. Carol cornered me in the kitchen. She said the same thing, in a different way."

"She was a mighty fine woman. And I think maybe you've found one for you."

"Maybe. Thanks for the advice, Coach."

"My pleasure."

He ended the call, put the phone in his pocket, and headed back toward the truck, but paused with his hand on the door handle.

What if he left the military and everything he knew, and it turned out he was wrong? She had been a bit distant the past few days. Then again, she'd been busy packing, getting ready for the Bazaar, preparing for estate liquidators.

He couldn't imagine the emotional toll of packing a childhood home and everything she'd known and loved for most of her life into boxes, and preparing to be ejected. He got tired doing nothing more than watch her struggle with the mountain of responsibilities and help out where he could.

But deep down, he had a hunch she was torn between his helping and his leaving.

The realization struck him like a sniper bullet to the chest. His skin vibrated with tension.

He had to pull out soon, but leaving didn't mean it had to be forever.

He needed a solution. A good solution. One designed to work for both of them.

He solved problems.

Why in the hell couldn't he solve his?

CHAPTER FIFTEEN

"Shit, I'mlateI'mlateI'mlate." Ashley came flying into the kitchen at mach four, in an oversized T-shirt, her feet bare. "Jenna's going to kill me."

Chase peered calmly over the edge of the coffee cup halfway to his lips. Ashley's bed head made him smile. Hair bunched to the left side of her head, with an amazing bed sheet imprint on her left cheek, combined to make her downright adorable. Both eyes remained half-closed, and her mouth was set in a pouty scowl. She reached for the coffee pot and a mug at the same time.

"Thank God. Coffee."

"Nope, thank me," he said softly under his breath, quite amused.

Her eyelids drifted shut while she indulged in the sensation of hot java now percolating through her system, but popped open seconds later. Her head swiveled left then right then left again. "Where's all the stuff I was making for the Bazaar?"

Chase put his cup on the table and pushed his breakfast plate back. "I've loaded everything into the truck. How about I fix you breakfast while you get ready?"

"But…"

"It's done. Everything is beaded and strung and labeled. All you need to do is shower…unless you don't want to." An I-could-kiss-you look drifted across her face. His body parts responded enthusiastically. "You keep looking at me like I'm a stack of chocolate chip pancakes, and I'll pour syrup on myself and let you lick it off."

Her soft pink tongue ran across her bottom lip while she contemplated his offer and made his body parts stand straight up and salute. "Tempting, but I'm already late. I lay down for ten minutes. Ten minutes. And here I am, four hours later. I can't tell you how much I appreciate what you did."

"After the antique selling, shipping, and making those silverware things, I'm not sure how you kept going as long as you did. It's the least I can do. You sure you don't want to take me up on my shower offer? It might be fun."

Her thoughtful eyes met his over the rim of her cup. "I can't. I promised to help set up for the Bazaar."

Disappointment filled his empty coffee cup, so he picked up his dishes and placed them in the sink.

He figured the craving to bury himself deep inside her would pass. Eventually. In the past, every time he got an itch scratched, the need went away. This time, the urgency grew into a full-on scratch attack until he could think of nothing else. He wanted her. He wanted to stay with her. Now if he could only make her want him and figure out logistics.

All week long, people stepped on or took advantage of her generous nature. She couldn't say no, not to anyone but him. And that just sucked.

"Where's Lucky?" There was a hint of curiosity in both her expression and tone.

"Asleep in the other room. I took him out for a walk before my run this morning." Her brows pressed together, deepening the lines on her face. Her facial expressions were becoming more and more familiar every day. He needed to find a way to help her relax to avoid damaging the perfection. "What's up?"

"You're working as hard as I am, yet you aren't fazed. You're up earlier. Go to bed later. There's something wrong with that."

"Habit. I get tired a lot, and I've learned to push through it. Besides, I've never been able to sleep more than a couple of hours at a time." *Habit and nightmares. Nightmares of bullets whizzing by my head, the panic of being pinned down by enemy fire, the spooked look on my buddy's face when I close my eyes.*

"Sleep is good for the body. Unlike carbs." She pointed at his empty plate. "Has anyone told you your blood sugar is high?"

"No. Why?"

"Because you smell sweet, and you look like you've been having headaches. You should have your blood checked."

"Now that you mention it, you might be onto something." He'd received a message to report into medical upon his return and wondered how the two pieces of information correlated. "And you don't think you should go into the medical field?"

"I've been thinking about our nursing conversation. Nursing doesn't feel right, but homecare is starting to become more appealing."

Bummer. A thread of disappointment stitched its way through his body. "It's good you're assessing your options." From the refrigerator, he pulled out a carton of eggs and an English muffin. "How about I fix you an egg sandwich to go?"

"First you put my stuff together, now you want to fix me breakfast? Are you real? Should I pinch myself to be sure?"

"It's not a big deal."

But it was a big deal. He'd never wanted to cook for anyone before, but he'd cook for her. He'd do a lot of things for her. For the first time in his life, he wanted to put another person first. He liked the satisfying feeling. He wanted to give her a lot of things, but giving still didn't mean she needed what he offered. What did he really have to offer?

"Stupid," he mumbled under his breath.

"Who's stupid?" Ashley asked.

I am, for thinking someone like you could need me. "No one," he said.

She walked to his side, lifted to her toes and kissed him on the cheek. "You're sweet. Breakfast sounds great."

When she took a step back, he intended to let her go, but his arms reached out and snagged her wrist. Her questioning eyes met his. Gently, she cupped his face in the palms of her hands and gave him a slow, I'm-in-no-hurry kiss.

He leaned back. "You sure we can't be a few minutes late?"

"You've got a point. Life is way too short." She leaned in.

When their lips connected, a fiery heat made his mouth tingle like barbecue hot sauce, all tangy and spicy. Her tongue caressed his lower lip, and then she sucked it into her mouth before she released him and drew back.

"Woman, you're going to kill me." She changed her mind as fast as she changed clothes, and he couldn't keep up.

"You talk too much." She tugged at the top button of his jeans.

Those beautiful, sexy eyes wiped out his self-control. He lifted the edge of her T-shirt and slid his hands higher to cup her breasts and brush his thumbs over the tips.

A soft, sexy moan drifted from those kissable lips. He lifted her to the kitchen island and then pulled the cotton shirt over her head. He went for her hardened cherry nipple.

"Chase? We don't have a lot of time."

Fully prepared in case of a yes, he fished a condom from his pocket, pushed his jeans down to his ankles, and rolled on the latex.

She reached down to tug his shirt up and off. "Don't think. Only action, Marine."

The statement made him pause because all he wanted was to think. Think about protecting her. Making sure she was safe—safe from him. When her words sank in, he started to lean back, but her fingers had a lock on his shoulders.

"Ash—"

"Don't you dare waste one more second with thinking or talking. Sex. Now."

He'd give her what she asked for, but it wouldn't be sex. Following her command, he stretched her underwear aside and sank in deep.

"Yes." She breathed a sigh and wrapped her legs around him to pull him closer.

How had she taken the tough career Marine and softened him, making him want simple little boy things again—like being held and cared for and loved?

This wasn't sex.

It wasn't even close.

He wanted to show her, demonstrate how making love wasn't sex. He wanted to knock her off her axis like she'd done to him. Show her a Marine could be more than a walk-away guy. He wanted to stick like he wanted her to stick.

The trust in her eyes made him want to give her everything. And he wanted her to feel his love—like a boy who draws a special picture for his mom. A gift. A special gift, meant for hanging on the refrigerator, not thrown in the trash.

He trusted her and wanted to give her anything she asked. Him. Deep.

Her eyes, full and excited and intense, reached in and squeezed his heart. She ran her teeth along his jaw, and he rocked his hips forward, again and again and again, until she arched back with a groan.

"Chase. Harder. Please."

Oh, baby. Harder he could do, and with a please and thank you. He cupped her bottom and tilted her to a better angle for full penetration. Her mouth moved to cover his nipple, and she sucked and nibbled harder.

"You are so beautiful." His voice held an urgent gruffness. "I want you. All of you."

"Chase, you so got me," she murmured against his skin.

His mind went completely silent. No shouting voices. No machine gun fire. No training steps rattling off in his head. She made the noise go silent. Only she existed. Her warm curves in his arms. Her hot breath on his skin. The soft whimpers in his ears. She made him forget, and made him feel like he was the king of the mountain, like nothing or no one could touch him but her.

"Hold on tighter." He braced her against the counter.

Her fingers pressed into his back. "Yes, that's it. More."

Her legs tightened and she breathed his name on her exhale. He watched her take his offered pleasure. He'd never seen anything more erotic or precious. She rocked back into him, her breasts touching his skin.

"Come with me," she demanded between short, sweet breaths.

No need to ask twice. He thrust deep and let go of everything he held back and captured his piece of heaven.

She slumped against his chest. "We're going to be late, but that was worth it." She turned her head and clumsily gathered her shirt. "I'd better go shower," she relayed on a short breath.

"Offer still stands."

"Oh, no. You're like my favorite cookie dough ice cream, only you're an endless supply of sweetness with no calories. Now I know how scrumptious you are, you'll be impossible to avoid."

His face stretched into a grin as big as a

dinner plate. "I think that's the nicest thing anyone's ever said to me."

"Seriously?" Her body language indicated she wasn't quite done with him yet, and he could hardly wait to find out what was next.

"How about I make you that breakfast now?"

"Sounds perfect. I need a cold shower. I'm a bit overheated."

"I forgot to tell you, I found a large package on the doorstep. It's over there. It looks like it's from your dad."

"He sent them," she uttered in disbelief. "He sent Mom's letters. Is there a card?"

"Not that I could find."

"There's always a card. Would you mind loading the box and Lucky in the truck? I can open the box on the way into town."

He hoped whatever the contents, the stuff wasn't set to detonate her emotions and send her into another tailspin. He wasn't sure she could handle much more.

ASHLEY COULD HAVE BEEN KNOCKED over by a puff of wind. First it was Chase's mind-blowing sex, and then her dad had sent her mom's letters.

In her dad's truck, waiting at the river bridge for a stoplight, she showed Chase the card.

These are yours to do with whatever you like. I've scanned copies. It's important for you to have the full story.

Ashley dropped the note back in the box. Frustration and confusion fisted her hands. "What does he mean by that?" A ball of uncertainty lodged in her throat. "Maybe I should call him."

Ideas danced in her thoughts, swaying, skipping, sashaying, as she tried to make sense of her father's message.

Only a few minutes late, Chase drove up next to the school's loading dock. Jenna was there, probably checking her cell phone for messages and dancing on her toes, waiting for their arrival.

"Our table's already set up." Her slight irritation and the lack of hello made Ashley cringe. Jenna plucked the first box from the truck bed.

Ashley grabbed the next box. "Sorry we're late. Chase had a hard time getting the dog to go potty."

"Nice cover. But your just-got-lucky glow doesn't help support your bullshit story."

Busted.

"She has a point." Chase shrugged.

Her eyes narrowed. "Whose side are you on?"

Chase didn't respond. His gaze was locked on the traffic jam of artists trying to get inside to set up. Lucky leapt from the truck bed, refusing to be anywhere Ashley wasn't. He wobbled momentarily to gain balance, but placed full weight on the injured hind leg.

"Did you see that?" Ashley remarked.

A thrill of seeing Lucky's progress buzzed

through her chest. She turned to share the excitement with Chase, but he was walking backward, his gaze locked on the parking lot.

Entering through the double doors, she followed Jenna. Chase lagged behind. Dozens of tables and chairs were butted up against the high school gym bleachers. Rachelle hadn't been joking about maximizing booth space and expecting record numbers. Reaching the designated table, Ashley set the stacks of items on the floor. Lucky leaned into her leg, not liking the noise of the crowd.

Chase set his boxes on the floor and, without a word, walked back toward the door.

Jenna leaned into Ashley. "Is Chase all right?"

"I think so, why?"

"I don't know. He seems a bit off."

"Lucky is agitated as well. I brought him today to start socializing him. There are more people here than I thought. I think I'll ask Chase to take him home." Ashley reached down and gave the dog a good scratch behind the ear. "You're a good boy. As soon as the truck's unloaded, I'll ask Chase to take you for a W-A-L-K." Lucky tilted his head off to the side in that normal shepherd way. "I'm getting the feeling you're so smart you'll be spelling soon."

"I love the way he looks at you." Jenna lifted the tablecloth and pointed at the space beneath. "He might feel safer under the table."

"Good idea." She squatted and guided Lucky under the seven-foot folding table.

"I'll be right back. I want to go get a stack of those brochures before they're gone."

Jenna walked away. Lucky circled under the table, then curled into a tight ball on the floor, his expectant gaze watching every movement.

"Have you seen Chase?" a feminine voice asked.

Ashley lifted her head and peeked over the table...and about choked.

She hadn't figured it possible for Rachelle

to lose track of any man, but obviously her boobs hadn't bounced off the chest of a guy like Chase.

"He should be back shortly," she offered, using the fewest possible words to complete the most amiable possible sentence.

"Good. I was going to ask for his help with moving some tables."

Rachelle scanned the jar- and bag-filled table. "I'm out of luck. No cherry jam this year."

Ashley couldn't guess how Rachelle might have come to that conclusion, since the woman's delicate nose was lifted so high into the air.

"There's cherry." Jenna's syrupy-sweet voice intercepted the conversation, as if she'd thrown a football right through the opposition's hands. "I haven't had a chance to set it out yet."

She placed a box on the floor and a stack of fliers on the table.

Suddenly, a loud crash made heads rotate towards the commotion. Two adolescents stood stunned, with guilt oozing off their bodies. Each boy looked at the other, hoping either could explain why the art display now lay scattered and broken, and the handcrafted items were spewed across the floor.

Lucky launched to his feet, the folding table lifting as a result. Both Jenna and Ashley reached for the table at the same time, intent on rescuing the shifting items.

"Whose dog is that?" Rachelle's manicured finger pointed. The sour grapes expression on her face meant any response wouldn't result in a pleasant outcome.

"Well, you see—"

"He's mine," Chase said in such a commanding tone, the three women stopped and turned.

Rachelle folded her arms under her breasts, making them swell. "Yours?"

"Mine." He stepped closer, so close Rachelle had to tilt her head back. "I just came to get him."

Rachelle's bullying brow raised. "You get

that dog out of here now before I call the sheriff and have him impounded."

Ashley gritted her teeth and squinted at her nemesis. "On what grounds?"

"Animals are not allowed in public buildings. That includes high school gyms. Besides, I'm sure that dog is the mutt you rescued. I can also have my brother check his records. If you haven't purchased a license, that will be an additional fine."

A low, rumbling growl began and grew louder when Lucky pushed from under the table and hovered a couple of inches from Rachelle's thigh.

Ashley froze at the shock of Lucky's menacing bared teeth. Rachelle slipped behind Chase for protection.

A look of amusement crinkled around Chase's eyes. "Looks like the dog took an exception to your threat, Rachelle."

"I'm going to have that dog put down."

Ashley pulled on Lucky's leather leash, and the dog automatically quieted and sat— his eyes intent, watching.

Chase turned and let his height do the intimidating. "No, you're not. And you want to know why?"

Rachelle's eyes turned black with rage. "Why?"

"Because you may like playing the town bitch, but under those layers of nasty thoughts and statements, you're a kind person. But you don't want anyone to know it." He leaned in, almost to the point of touching noses. "But I see it. So why don't you do us a favor and let me take Lucky home so you ladies can get on with selling your crafts?"

Ashley held her breath, wondering which way her nemesis would jump.

Rachelle took a step back. "You have five minutes to get that dog out of this gym."

Chase didn't move. He didn't say a word. He engaged the tenacious blonde until she turned and walked away. Victory. Ashley released a heavy sigh.

"That was exciting," Jenna said. "I'm going

to go get the rest of the stuff from my Jeep. Will you be okay for a minute?"

"More than fine." Ashley gave Lucky an ear massage to assure him he'd done the right thing. "Aren't I special? I had two guys coming to my rescue."

"You didn't need rescuing," Chase responded, "but I had a hunch I could ease the tension a bit."

"Do you believe what you said about Rachelle? That somewhere underneath all her bitchiness is an actual person, not a demon in disguise?"

"Yeah, I do. There's a girl like her in every town. She spends most of the day in front of the mirror, trying to convince herself she's special. She's no different from you or me, but she hasn't figured it out yet."

"Figured what out?"

"That when she gets out of this town, she's nothing more than another woman among three hundred million people." Chase's fingers brushed hers and took the leash from her hand. "I'd best get Lucky situated."

"Can you secure him in the truck and then come back? I'd like to show you something."

Chase nodded and stepped back with a tight, serious expression she couldn't quite read. He led Lucky to the bottom bleacher step, and waited patiently for the dog to maneuver the stairs before guiding him across the wooden slat toward the door. The kindness and patience he demonstrated brought a lump to her throat. She had honestly never met a more heroic man.

She closed her eyes and listened to the powerful beat of her heart. The pulse pounded in her ears, her chest, her hands, as a reminder that she lived. The sounds of the Christmas music coming through the loudspeakers matched the rhythm, becoming stronger, louder. Joy lifted her spirit. Her heart had begun to heal. Chase's presence had helped her find a way to put the little shards of her life back together again, so she could move on and begin to dream, and look toward the future.

"What are you smiling about?" Jenna shoved a small box of baked goods into her hands.

"I was dreading Christmas. Maybe it won't be so bad this year after all." Ashley loaded the table with more silverware crafts.

"It wouldn't have anything to do with a certain Marine, would it?"

"Maybe." A tingle floated across her skin. A sure sign she'd blushed Santa-red.

Jenna gave her a nudge. "You should see the smile on your face."

"Stop it. We're keeping it simple."

"Simple, huh? Well, that's a good thing because look at the people coming in the door. This place is going to be packed in a minute, and you won't have anything else you need to think about to distract you."

"Oh, my." Ashley began reorganizing the display table, adding the new items from the box and avoiding Jenna's scrutinizing eyes.

Jenna bumped her shoulder to get her

attention again. "Remember those red pumps? The ones you didn't buy when we went to Vegas for your twenty-third birthday?"

"The ones I went back to get and they were sold out of my size? I searched the internet for months trying to find the same pair."

"Yep, those are the ones." Jenna's brow lifted. "Chase is like those shoes. I'm thinking you might regret keeping it simple."

She really had wanted those shoes. But Chase?

To be part of a healthy relationship, she needed to be whole. And she wasn't. Not yet. The urge to get settled and understand her past pulled, and pulled hard. She wanted to unlock the answers to her parents' secrets. Find answers to the questions her mother had refused to discuss, and her dad had never been around long enough to ask.

Trying to stuff one more thing into an already overstuffed closet wasn't practical.

A mad rush of holiday shoppers yanked

Ashley from her thoughts. She pasted on her salesperson smile and helped Jenna bag, make change, and replace inventory.

Someone poked her shoulder. "You wanted to show me something?" Chase appeared behind her.

"Hi. Yes. It's over there. The next row over." Ashley captured his hand to start weaving through the throng of people, but he took one step, then yanked his arm back.

When she turned, the smile on her face did a one hundred eighty degree-rotation. Chase's face washed over with a grayish-green color. His eyes were quickly becoming wild and fixed. His fingers twitched. His hand reached across his body for things that weren't there.

"Chase?" She reached out.

He blocked her hand with his forearm. His eyes turned feral. Frightened. He took two steps and leapt onto the bleachers, running toward the exit.

"Jenna, will you be okay for a minute? I need to check on Chase."

"Go." Jenna's eyes were already wide with concern.

Ashley followed the route Chase had taken, searching the school's corridors, heading for the outer door. She hit the metal exit bar at a run and didn't stop until she was at the edge of the sidewalk. *Where are you?* Spotting her father's truck, she saw Lucky watching something in the distance. Instinct made her run, and then slow to a trot when she saw Chase pacing on the track next to the football field.

When she got close enough, he turned and held his hand out, forcing her to stop.

She let the concern drain from her body and compassion fill the gaps. Holding out her arm with the palm of her hand open to receive, she waited with hope.

Come to me, Chase. Let me in.

The crisp air sent a shiver through her, but she didn't flinch. She wouldn't. Those eyes, the anxiety, the terror...she'd seen the same thing too many times in the eyes of her father. This time, she wanted the man to allow her to be included—part of that inner circle of trust—like her mom had been for her dad. This time she wouldn't let the hurts of a child make her weak and indecisive. This time, she would stand strong as a mountain pine against the tide of an avalanche.

HIS STOMACH TWISTED, and he fought to keep from revisiting the pecan waffle he'd had for breakfast. His palms itched and the irritation started to spread. Sweat beaded his brow. He couldn't breathe. He blinked, trying to defeat the visions in his mind, to regain control and release the tension in his white-knuckled fists.

And then there she was, a flag waving in the storm, guiding him home.

He raked his fingers through the short stubble of his hair and down his neck, fighting, working to piece together every bit of patience he could find.

"I don't like crowds," he whispered, barely loud enough for her to hear. "I...it's just..."

"You don't have to explain."

He seized her hand and held on tight.

"Bombs go off in crowds. A soldier always has to watch his back."

"Chase—"

"No. I assumed in a town this size I would be okay. Back in Carolina, just going to the grocery store is hard."

Ashley's eyes glittered with tears. "I'm sorry. I'm so, so sorry. I put you in this situation. I didn't know."

He hoped she didn't start crying. She'd hate herself for it—hate him. He had to make this right. He needed to suck it up. She considered him a hero. He could see it in her eyes. He wanted to be, but deep down, he wasn't that person. He swallowed to moisten his dry tongue.

Put on a brave face.

He'd done it enough for his men, his buddies, and commanders.

Do it for her.

"I'm good."

Ashley lifted her eyes to his. "Are you sure?"

He pushed his determined shoulders back. "As long as bullets don't start flying, I think I can manage."

"Chase, we all carry around baggage. Maybe a different size, shape, or color, but at the end of the day, it's still full of crap that we can't get rid of. I have my fair share. You shouldn't feel like you have to face this alone."

"Like you said, we all carry around baggage."

"I like you, Chase. A lot. You're a good man."

He acknowledged her statement with a nod because the walnut-sized lump in his throat wouldn't go down. The cold air bit into his face. His breath swirled around his head.

She gave his hand a tug and began walking back toward the truck. "You should go. Run. Take Lucky for a walk. Enjoy the crisp mountain air. I'm thinking it will help clear your mind."

"Yeah. You need to get back inside, too. I'm sure Jenna's feeling abandoned." He stopped by the truck's tailgate.

The understanding in her eyes and the softness of her touch made him lean in, but his name being called rocked him out of his thoughts.

"Mr. Daniels?"

"Sheriff," Chase responded neutrally, wondering what the man could want.

"I wasn't sure you'd remember me. Do you mind if I ask you a few questions?"

Ashley stepped in front of Chase. "Did Rachelle call you?" she demanded, blocking Joe's way like a lioness protecting her cub. "Chase was on his way to run an errand, and he's taking Lucky with him."

The sheriff's semi-confused frown gave

Chase the impression the man had no idea what Ashley was talking about.

"Ash, it's okay." Chase settled his hand on her lower back. "Sheriff, what can I do for you?"

The man shifted and gave him an assessment similar to a drill sergeant's, slow and thorough, not missing a single detail. "Harold Talbott indicated you might have heard gunshots the other day on the ridge."

The sheriff seemed relaxed, but his eyes revealed the deception. Not the untrustworthy kind. The kind indicating he wanted more than just an answer.

Chase pointed. "We did. About five, maybe six hundred yards off, someone was firing a rifle and aiming in our direction."

The sheriff shifted and rested a forearm on his utility belt. "You sure about that?"

"Positive. Heard the crack and the bang. Both times. That would only happen if the shooter was pointing in our direction."

Joe's brow lifted into an arc. "Our direction?"

"I was with him," Ashley said. "We were up on Lonely Ridge, a bit west of the Hound's Tooth, at the back of my property."

"Did you see anyone?"

"Nope." Chase shook his head, and Ashley concurred.

"Thank you for your time. You've been a help." The sheriff turned to leave.

"Sheriff?" Ashley called softly. "Do you think the shots might be related to your brother's death?"

A flash of pain flickered through Joe's face before being blocked and wrestled back into a friendly state. "Murder investigations take time, and we're still processing leads. As my wife likes to say, if you can collect enough flowers, you'll have a nice arrangement. Once we have enough evidence, the killer will be brought to justice."

Chase assessed the man as he approached his patrol car. A heavy burden lay across his shoulders, but he bore it well, and Chase recognized him as a man he could respect.

Ashley's delicate fingers surrounded his callused palm. "Chase?"

He paused, but didn't want to meet her eyes. He didn't want her to ask questions. Questions he couldn't answer. An inhale of cold air soothed the anxious nerves enough for him to connect to her concerned gaze.

"Thank you for not pushing me away."

Her unexpected comment allowed the tension to ease, and his mind to de-clutter.

"One minute, I'm here. The next minute, I'm back over there. My mind takes over and I can't control it."

"That must be frustrating. Maybe a bit frightening. I'm here if or whenever you need to talk. No judgment. I'm a good listener."

In that one simple look, she tied a bow around his heart and made it hers. He couldn't fight the emotions he'd felt since he first set eyes on the beautiful woman and held her hand, blood running across her fingers. She could head west or east, he didn't care. Whichever way she went, he'd track her down. No matter how long it took, he wanted her in his life.

"You wanted to show me something?"

"Why don't I take a picture and send it to you? It's a coin with the Marine emblem carved into it. It's really cool-looking. If you like it, you can text me, and I can get it for you."

She understood, didn't push, adapted to fit his need.

A hero he wasn't, but if he could figure out how to be her hero, he would.

CHAPTER SIXTEEN

$\mathcal{A}$n hour ago, Ashley had arrived home to find the dinner table set, with two-inch thick steaks marinating on the counter and baked potatoes warming in the oven. The whole place looked and smelled heavenly, especially with Chase smack dab in the middle of the kitchen. Somehow, he'd even managed to select her favorite bottle of wine. However, he might have had some help from Jenna.

Now, she stretched her arms and yawned. "That was so good. I'm stuffed. Where did you learn to cook?"

"Here and there. Cooking mostly came from necessity. The first few years, I ate more burned meals than an average person eats in a lifetime. I like food, and my culinary skills sucked. Befriending the cooks in the mess hall helped."

"He cooks. He cleans. He fixes things. Is there anything you don't do?"

"I have a hard time letting people get close." He leaned closer and brushed his knuckles down her cheek before settling back. "I don't do that well."

"That makes two of us." *But somehow you niggled your way in.*

He stood and picked up her plate, then his, and placed the dishes near the sink. "Why don't you get a fire started on the deck while I clean up?"

"Sounds great." She might be completely full, but the way he looked in his stocking feet, jeans low on his waist, wearing a tight-fitting T-shirt beneath an untucked plaid flannel, made her hungry...well, at least for a few kisses and a snuggle. "I a...I intended to search for an apartment when I got home, but dinner made me sleepy. I'll have to review the new postings tomorrow. No excuses."

"Are you looking for something in Denver?"

"I'd like to stay here, but I can't afford to keep this place. Denver's not my first choice. It's too expensive. I need to find something I can easily afford."

"Would you consider coming back with me to North Carolina?"

Didn't expect that. Her heart pitter-pattered in her chest. "What would I do there? Wait for you to come home? I'm sure jobs on and around the base are scarce."

"I could support you." *That would be easy.*

"And that is the last thing I would want. I need to learn how to live on my own. Besides, I'm not a charity case, Chase."

"I know that."

"I've got to find my own way." She pushed back her chair. Lucky, sleeping by her side, sensed movement and stood. "Want to go outside?"

Chase turned to wipe his hands on a towel. "Ash. I didn't mean to upset you. I only want to help."

"I understand you want to help. And thank you for the kind offer." She didn't want to address the hurt in his eyes, so she contemplated Lucky instead.

Sliding the glass door open, she snagged her coat from the hook, and matches to light the fireplace from the shelf, then stepped out onto the shoveled deck, and felt optimism settle in her bones for the first time in years. She wasn't afraid.

She could do this.

Find a place to live.

Make a life for herself.

She so wished she could be the woman that Chase wanted her to be, but she couldn't. She understood military life, and knew she couldn't fit that lifestyle. Life had to kick her in the teeth before she realized trying to be someone you weren't didn't work.

Even though she'd received job rejections, she didn't feel like a failure. Unqualified, maybe, but not a failure.

Bottom line, her mom's voice wasn't as demanding anymore. Her own inner voice had started to take center stage and grew more confident with each passing day.

Lucky, when he finished his business, came to check on her. She pushed kindling and a new log into the brick pit and lit the nearest pinecone starter.

Possibilities had begun to form and evolve and feel good. Within the next few days, she should have her past boxed up, labeled, and put away so she could start discovering her future, a future that she needed to design. The goal setting book she purchased from the used bookstore in town might help. With the antique and Bazaar sales, she might have enough for the certificate program. Finding a job and roommates was the next thing on her list. Chase was a question mark.

She dropped her head back, listening to the soft, magical breath of the wind flowing through the trees, letting the stars mesmerize her, and the warmth of the down comforter ease into her weary bones. Lucky settled onto his wool pad while she sat in one of the Adirondack chairs and snuggled the down comforter to her chest. In the middle of processing things still to do, she heard the back door open.

"That's a serious look," Chase said, balancing plates and closing the sliding glass door.

"It's not serious at all. More determined. I was thinking that, going forward, the future is mine." *Not that I know how to plan that future, but it will be mine.* "My mom made plans for me, but none ever felt right. And I know going to North Carolina, as wonderful as it sounds, isn't right for me either."

"I wanted to give it a shot." He set a plate

of marshmallows, chocolate, and graham crackers on the table beside her. Lucky lifted his head to acknowledge him, then settled back into his normal position.

"So you're not disappointed?" Her head tilted to the side, her eyes narrowing, trying to read his body for clues.

"Of course I'm disappointed. It would be an easy solution, and I could help you. Life isn't that easy. At least it's never been easy for me."

Chase leaned in to stoke the fire and retrieve the hot dog sticks, great for roasting marshmallows. A bonus view of his backside ignited an inferno in her at the same time. The tinder popped, sending small flecks of embers into the air that quickly burned out.

"None for me. You really should be watching your carb intake." She laughed at the just-got-caught smile on his face.

The smell of pine, the wavering blue and orange flames dancing across the deck, multiplied the sensual kaleidoscope. The firelight flickered across his skin, contrasting with the night and casting his features in a mysterious aura. He sat beside her, and she picked up a whiff of a peppery barbecue tang that must have clung to his shirt from cooking dinner. The smell fit him to perfection. His muscular shoulder brushed hers as she slid the down comforter across his lap. The chilly night air sneaked in, but his body heat soon transferred, building heat in their down cocoon.

"Thanks again for dinner," she offered, after eliminating the other stupid conversation starters she'd managed to contrive.

"I figured you'd be tired after being on your feet all day."

"Last year, the Bazaar lasted two days and was right before Christmas. Between the Bazaar, the holidays, and my mom being critically ill, I don't think my feet ever got a rest. She had her first bout of pneumonia on Christmas Eve and didn't recover until the new year."

Chase leaned in. "My foot rubs are hard

to pass up."

So are the rest of your rubs. "Is that so?"

"Award-winning."

Visions of his touch elsewhere turned up the flame already heating her body. She slipped out of her slippers and stretched her wool-clad feet toward him without conscious thought, but then she scrunched her nose. "Wait. A massage isn't a good idea. My feet are smelly and disgusting." She started to pull back, but he caught her ankle and held on.

"You sure?" she asked.

"Absolutely sure."

Her body craved the feeling of his strong fingers. The exhilarating touch of his skin. Logic fought against the hormones besieging her mind. She conceded the battle. "If you don't mind, then..."

His eyes dilated. An overflowing need set her body aflame. His burning expression indicated he knew exactly how she felt.

Before she could say more, Chase adjusted his chair back until it was perpendicular and removed a lotion bottle from his pocket. "I came prepared."

She caught her breath when his hand wrapped around her calf, lifted her foot into his lap, and pulled off her sock. Her toes touched the cold metal button of his jeans and arched back before relaxing as he began the massage. "That feels so good."

The pressure bordered on the edge of pain, but it worked the muscles and tendons, releasing the knots, relieving her headache, her backache.

"Award-winning good?" His question and eyebrow both lifted on the last syllable beat.

"I don't want to know who the other judges were, but yeah, award-winning." A twinge of jealousy left a bitter taste in her mouth.

He shifted her foot closer. She soaked up the heat from his fingers and the fire. Closing her eyes, she listened to the horned owl hooting into the night, the inhale and exhale of her breath, her body adjusting to the tempo of Chase's movements.

Heaven. Pure heaven.

She tried to remember ever feeling such peace in another person's presence, and couldn't. Around others, she constantly felt the need to give, to make sure everyone else was happy. As a caregiver, she melded into the background, quietly helping. She never asked for anything, never felt worthy to ask for something. Chase's giving, without her having to ask, meant more to her than she could express. His attention made her feel wanted. And that was a big dang deal.

"Is the pressure good?"

"Past good and rounding the corner to stellar," she responded like a melody floating on an exhale. "If this is your version of foreplay, it's working."

The statement brought a smile to his face before it deflated and turned serious again. "You know I have to leave. I don't have a choice. But it doesn't have to be forever."

"I know you have to leave. I do. But waiting around? I watched my mom waiting for my dad to come home. The loneliness. The heartache. That's not how I want to live my life."

"Before I leave, I want to make sure you're okay."

She drew in a deep breath. Her happiness wasn't his responsibility. She wouldn't let him own it. Besides, she'd promised herself that no one would ever again be the master of her fate.

"It's in your Marine mantra to protect. But this time you're going to have to let go. I'll be fine."

He studied her for a long time, his emotions unreadable. How was it that she wanted to push him away, and at the same time, crawl into his lap and reassure him that both of them would be okay?

"Chase?"

"I'm good."

She arched her foot when his fingers found an extra-tender spot. "You are good."

She lifted her brows and winked. "I like when you touch me."

"Yeah, well, I like the feel of your skin. Maybe too much. Part of me is working hard not to touch the rest of you since I'm leaving. And the other part of me wants to burn your body into my memories. I feel like I'm being torn apart here."

Before Chase arrived, vivid memories of her past had spooled through her mind constantly, threatening to derail her plans. His presence had calmed the storm of images and allowed her to find stable ground.

"Sometimes I think the universe gives us gifts," she said. His fierce, laser-targeted expression focused on her, a question in his eyes. "Chase, you're my gift. You arrived just in time. You helped me understand that I'm not alone. I've learned that I can connect and be intimate without having to slice off a part of myself. I know you have to leave. I know."

"Then you're okay?"

No, she wasn't. Not even in the slightest.

"Let's simply enjoy what comes. I want to spend these last few days creating memories," *to last a good long while, and hope someday you'll come back to me.*

He eyed her skeptically, the protective Marine still wanting to make sure everything was locked down. Unfortunately, human emotions weren't that simple.

"Chase?" His gaze lifted to hers and his fingers tightened around her foot. "Do you ever talk about the war?"

"Not usually."

"The look in your eye today at the gym. Your reactions. You weren't here. You were back overseas. I'd think you'd want to talk to someone."

"Unless you were there, it's hard to explain. Bobby and I talked. We used to sit out on nights like this. Mind you, Bobby did most of the jaw-flapping while I listened."

Ashley honed in on his body language. "Do you ever dream about it...I mean the war?"

"Sometimes. It's weird, though. When I

dream, it's as if I'm watching through this haze. I can hear sounds, see shadows, but I'm only observing. But if I'm awake, I remember details. Crowds or lots of bodies in a packed space tend to set me off. I can feel the static of bullets whizzing overhead, the sound of a rocket, radio commands in my ear, and my heart pounds like it's going to jump out of my chest. That's when the adrenaline takes over, honing every sense and thought. Military pre-programming takes control and my body moves in predictable patterns. Clarity kicks in and I go to work. Then something will pull me out. A voice or sound."

"I wish I could understand."

"No, you don't. What went on over there needs to stay over there."

"That's where you're wrong. What happened over there is a part of you, same as watching my mom die is a part of me. What you experienced isn't something to hide or avoid talking about."

"Soldiering is not as glamorous as you

think. There's a lot of practicing, preparing to go and then waiting around. It's hours of interminable boredom punctuated by moments of sheer terror." He shifted uneasily like he was sitting on a rock.

"Chase, I'm not a reporter wanting you to give me some headline story." She untied the strings on the bagful of patience she'd come to rely on. "I'm a plain, simple woman who wants to know more about you. The good times. The difficult times."

His warm hands stilled on her foot while he gave her a considering gaze. "You're anything but plain, Ashley."

The playful look on his face made her want things, like his lips on her mouth. "Don't change subjects."

"What do you want to know?"

Something in the woods caught his attention, and she followed the direction of his look to the tree line. A large male elk, not yet settled for the night, lifted his head from the elder bush.

"There go Mom's shrubs." Sorrow sank

in. "I guess she won't care anymore. And I certainly don't give a crap what the bank thinks. Have a good meal, buddy," she called to the animal.

Chase tugged on her right big toe and pulled her sock back on. "I bet he appreciates you not chasing him off with pie tins like you did the other day." He tapped her left foot. "Next."

He made easy work of removing the other sock and preparing her foot for pampering. The pure bliss on his face made her wonder what the private man had going on in that thick head. Maybe if she shared, he'd eventually learn to do the same.

"My mom and dad's letters have this funny code on the back."

"So many letters get misdirected, damaged, or lost. The code might have been a combination of a date or a letter sequence. I'm amazed we get any mail at all."

The simplicity of the explanation fit. "My dad sent another coin with Mom's letters." Her fingers surrounded the warm object in her pocket and brought it out into the brisk night air. She held the weight in her palm, then extended her arm. A curious yet expanding excitement splashed across his face as he reverently lifted the coin from her hand. She watched, intrigued, while he tilted the metal into the firelight.

Chase tilted the metal into the firelight. "*HOLY. SHIT.*" His fingers skimmed across the numbers engraved on the back of the coin.

"What's wrong?"

"Do you know what this is?"

Ashley tugged the comforter higher. "I couldn't say for sure, but it looks like some presidential memento my dad picked up in a gift shop somewhere."

"Ash. You can't buy this coin. It's only presented to you. And it's rarely conferred on anyone."

"I'm sure you're mistaken. My dad always sends me these things. I have a whole box of them."

He passed the coin back. "Can I see?"

She could feel his excitement vibrating through her foot resting in his lap. The raw emotion startled her, and she didn't quite know how to handle the open eagerness, but she wanted to nurture his passion.

"Sure, if you want."

He jumped up like a cinder had lit his butt on fire. "I'll tend the fireplace and take Lucky for a whiz, then meet you inside." The words rolled out of his mouth with the excitement of a kid on Christmas Day. He canvassed the deck like he wasn't sure what to do first. She liked seeing him so excited that he didn't know what to do next. Strong emotions slipped past his guarded walls and helped her connect to him in a way she hadn't been able to before. Although she didn't dare hope it would last.

She pulled on her sock. "The coins are in my room somewhere. I'll look for them and meet you there in a few."

Halfway up the back stairs, she grabbed the stair railing and her feet leapt into overdrive, propelling her to the bedroom door. She unzipped and threw her coat on her desk chair, then lifted the bed dust ruffle, pushing and sliding packed storage bins, searching for the handmade cherrywood box. She rushed to her closet, which was filled with packed boxes, and scanned the upper racks. Nothing. With hands on hips, she moved to the room's center, perusing the empty dresser, bookcase, shelf, considering which box she might have packed the item in. After several minutes, her gaze landed on the edge of a thin box, hidden on her desk behind a pile of books, and her miniature silver picture frame collection waiting to be packed. Lifting the box, she turned. Chase studied the handmade treasure.

She sat on the bed, folding her legs in front of her. Thirteen coins rested in the glass display case. She lifted the inlaid lid and straightened a few before rotating the box for Chase to see.

His hand reached for the first treasured

piece her father had given her. He rolled the heavy bronze in his palm. She'd held it often enough to know the weight, shape, and curve of the coin.

"Ashley, where's your father now?" A touch of admiration softened his voice.

"I don't know. He moves around a lot. I think he's in Washington, D.C., but I can't tell by the APO he gave me. Why?"

Chase paced the room, agitated, glancing at her from time to time. When he paced close to the bed, she reached for him. His fingers were cold, and she tightened her hand around his to prevent him from pulling away.

"What are you thinking?"

"When you said your dad was a Marine, I assumed you meant a veteran, some guy who'd done his twenty and retired. Your dad's still in, isn't he?"

"Yeah. So?"

"So? If I'm guessing correctly, your dad's Brigadier General Bryant, one of the most decorated Marines still in the service."

"Sounds about right. My mom said something about a promotion. You have to remember, for the last five years, I can probably count on my fingers the number of times I've talked to my dad—don't even need to use my toes."

When he didn't laugh, she crossed her arms over her chest, feeling self-conscious. Her mother had mentioned something about her dad's big promotion, but her mom was in the middle of a really bad spell, and Ashley hadn't paid much attention at the time. Her days were filled with laundry, meal preparation, physical therapy sessions twice a day, and medications every four hours, and she didn't have time to think about the here-and-gone-again parent halfway across the country.

Chase stared at the box. He replaced the coin, lifted the box, and moved it to the nightstand. He knelt by the bed and took her hand into his. "I didn't mean to raise my voice, it's just...your dad's a hero. A lot of

Marines admire him. He's done a lot for the Corps."

He pointed at the box and proceeded to recite the history of a man she barely knew. She knew Marine movements, but she didn't recognize the hero Chase described. She'd only met the quiet, unassuming man. The man who, when home, went for long walks and spent hours shut away in his work area, fixing things, sometimes making a piece of furniture, or special display boxes. Chase's sincere awe raised the hair on her arms.

He poked at the newest edition. "This one is the president's coin. Only the president can present this medallion."

"Chase, my dad's a Marine. He doesn't talk much. And he never talks about work. Ever," she said, offering the twisted and pathetic excuse. "When he called home, all he wanted was to talk to Mom."

"He probably can't talk about his work, literally, with his level of security clearance."

She hated the sting in her eyes. Blinking, she fought the liquid hovering on the edge of her emotions, waiting to spill over and embarrass her. She pushed off the bed and moved to her desk, turning off her laptop and straightening the piles of letters, doing anything she could to distract her brain from engaging. Wanting to be anywhere else than in the presence of a guy who believed her dad was a hero, and an honorable man. A man she barely knew and had been angry at most of her life.

She didn't want to let a guy, thousands of miles away, who she barely knew, impact her anymore. "It's been a long day. Heck, it's been a long week."

"Ashley." He gently moved a strand of hair behind her ear and hesitated, as if choosing his words very carefully. "I didn't mean to make you sad. Just the opposite. I know now where you get your strength. You have it in your genes."

No, I'm not. I'm not strong. And, even if I were, I didn't get it from my dad.

He put pressure on her shoulders until she turned. A gentle finger lifted her chin until she had no choice but to meet his scrutiny. "You give so much of yourself."

She tried to push past him, but his strong arms held on, and she collapsed against his chest. Tears of anger, resentment, and fear welled up and crashed through the dam of anger and grief, forcing the emotions out, sweeping past and annihilating debris from her past, leaving little behind. She clung to him, a sword in the rock of her soul.

"Ash?"

"I'm not strong," she sobbed against his chest.

Her feet left the floor when he lifted her into his arms. She clung to him as if her life was about to shatter in a hundred million pieces.

His arms tightened around her. "Let it loose."

His soft lips pressed to her forehead and ripped a bigger hole in the dam wall. She couldn't stop the gush of tears, and didn't want to. And when the last drop of emotion floated out of sight, there came a sense of lightness, of freedom. Her past had been ripped from the deep ground and swept away in the storm of tears, leaving behind a vivid landscape of possibilities. She released her grip, trusting Chase could catch her.

She tilted her head back. "I haven't cried for months, then you come along, and I turn into a water faucet."

"Your tears fill my soul like a rejuvenating forest rain." The poem resonated from deep in his chest.

"That's beautiful. Is that from a poem you've read?"

"No. It's one of mine."

SHE'S NOT YOUR MOTHER. *Let her in.*

Chase could feel his heart resisting. His mother had blown apart his world until trust didn't come willingly. He'd built an intricate defense system to hide his love of poetry, guitar playing, woodworking, and anything else he cared about, making sure no one could call his pursuits pathetic like his mother had done.

He'd faced the enemy overseas. Maybe it was time to face the enemies at home.

"I love playing with words, arranging them, then rearranging then to find a different meaning. Would you like to write a poem with me?"

She lifted her head from his chest, her swimming eyes and red nose making him tighten his grip. "That would be..." She brushed the tears from her cheek. "I'd really like that."

The encouragement felt refreshing. "I like working with clay. There's something about working with materials from the earth, building and sculpting, creating something meaningful. I can tell your dad's the same. He's got an exceptionally nice collection of woodworking tools."

"Mom always bought him something new to add to his collection. He spent hours in the garage making things for her. A jewelry box. A lamp. A recipe box."

"I could only dream of having a setup like that. I can see why he spent so much time there."

"And just think. In a few weeks, all the tools will be boxed and put away, perhaps sold."

"Maybe someday he'll rebuild."

That's what I would do. Find my island of sanity.

Coming back to the States, Chase acknowledged it was time to make a tough decision. While fixing things, he put a list of pluses and minuses together in his head, trying to come to terms with what he wanted to do. He'd been thinking about it for the past year, not sure whether he could handle the mental strain of another tour. His aging body hurt more this tour than the last.

Ashley had been right when she said he'd seen and felt things a human shouldn't have to see or live with. The nightmares were getting worse. She'd not only been right, but she also made things more complicated.

She made him feel things. Welcoming things. Scary things. Things that made him want to go down to the local jewelry store and pick out a ring, plop it on her finger and drag her back to North Carolina with him.

But she'd said she wouldn't go. Did that mean ever? Or only for now?

Ashley poked his chest. "What are you thinking about?"

Her glistening eyelashes and stunning hazel eyes softened his heart. He smelled the sugary sweet scent on her clothes from working with baked goods all day, combined with dinner and the musk of the fire, completing a perfect combination of sweet and spicy. Her breath caressed his neck, and his arms instinctively pulled her tighter. With his finger, he brushed a stray strand of hair from her face. She waited for an answer, and he wanted to give her one, but he wanted honesty between them.

"What would you think if I got out of the military and moved to Colorado?"

Her body stiffened.

His silent alarm sounded, and his heart started racing.

He flicked the switch to drop into his marine-battle-ready-mode. He scanned every movement. He waited. The only problem? He couldn't anticipate.

She tucked her head to hide her face. "Gosh. That's a big move. What would you do for a job?"

That wasn't the response he expected, or wanted.

His fists tightened. "Good question. I don't know."

I'm good at solving problems. I would find something.

Her fingers, gliding down the side of his face, forced his gaze to return to her exquisite face. He'd fallen into her web. "That wasn't what you wanted to hear. Was it?"

Determination replaced his insecurities.

"I don't want you to shut me out of your life. Not yet."

"I won't. Not yet." Her lips curved into a smile, not a deceptive smile, but one he'd constructed a time or two when he wanted to ease a friend's mind but wasn't certain of how he truly felt.

He wanted to see that radiant glow again. He leaned in, and sure enough got his wish. He dropped altitude, took aim and found her mouth. Her mouth moved against his and scrambled all communication leading to his brain, causing his backup functions to kick in, and the backup brain kicked in with a jolt. Forgetting the reasons he'd laid out for not touching, he let his arms draw her closer and closer until he saw nothing but her.

His hand slowly crept up her back until his fingers could tangle into her hair, feeling the silk cascade through. His full-force arousal was uncomfortable, and he needed to shift positions to relieve the ache. He pushed her back and stretched out beside her, feeling her thigh against him. He moved closer.

She guided his hand from her waist to her full breast to greet her erect nipple. His inner voice told him to stop, but he wanted to feel her skin next to his, to close out the world around them and simply be in the moment with her. When a sweet moan escaped her, his hunger drove him deeper. He tantalized her mouth with his tongue and nibbled with his teeth. He explored her delicate curves while the kiss lingered on and on.

She tugged his shirt from his pants and ran her feather-light fingers up his spine.

"Talk to me." He ran a hand up her back. "Tell me what you like."

"Shhh."

He reached for her face and drew her lips to his once more. He groaned, responding to her thirst. He had a mind to pin her to the bed and make her beg for mercy, but instead rolled to his back, taking her with him. Since he was on the bottom, he could allow his fingers to caress the vast amount of sensitive skin he hadn't yet had the pleasure of exploring. He let his hands drift lower, and when his fingers found the edge of the cotton fabric, he pulled her shirt up and over her head in one swift motion.

His arms encircled her waist. "God, you're beautiful."

"So are you. Now stop talking."

Her tongue ever so slightly ran over her bottom lip while she riveted her attention on the top button of his shirt. Something about her fingers working each button, one at a time, gave him an immensely erotic rush. When she finished, she spread the shirt wide and proceeded to kiss his scars. Each one. One at a time.

What a woman. "Do you know how much I want you, Ashley?"

She groaned and sank her teeth into his chest, then used her tongue to find his nipple, wrapping her mouth around the sensitive skin. When she finished, she rubbed her chest against his and landed in the crook of his neck. His nervous fingers fumbled with her bra clasp. When the closure popped open, he traced the edges of the strap, pulling the elastic to him. His abdominal muscles contracted in anticipation. She pushed herself up off his chest so she could remove the impediment, and his breath caught. He let out a ragged breath and cupped her breasts in his palms. She fit him perfectly. Nothing more. Nothing less.

Her lips found his while his arms stretched around her, and he slipped his hands down inside the back of her tight-fitting jeans. His arms around her, he prepared to roll when 'The Halls of Montezuma' Marine Corps hymn rang out from her coat on the floor.

Using his chest as leverage, she broke free of his arms. She stared at her coat, a perplexed expression crossing her face.

"Don't answer that."

"But it's my dad. He never, ever calls. What if something's happened?" Indecision crossed her face for a tick of several seconds before she attacked her jacket, then pushed the phone to her ear. "Dad?"

Awareness came pummeling Chase all at once. Her dad. Essentially his boss's boss's boss.

The beautiful woman covering her chest the best she could, looking incredibly guilty, was talking to the general. Her father, who sat in meetings with the President of the United States.

What the hell was he doing?

He rotated and sat on the edge of the bed, his head in his hands. His body vibrated with frustration, and his erection pressed painfully against his zipper. He needed to get out of the room. He stood. The need to clear his head became primary.

When he'd nearly reached the bedroom door, she stepped in front of him.

"Dad, I have to call you back." She disconnected the call and glared at Chase. "Where are you going?"

"That was your dad. I wanted to give you some privacy and get my head around this."

"This? You mean you, me, sex? The fact that you think you know my dad doesn't change who I am." The anger in her expression sparked hot.

"Sex. Is that what you think this is? Merely sex? Is that all you want from me?"

Ashley shrugged. "Other than friendship, that's all there is."

"No, Ashley. That's not all there is. I'm seriously thinking about leaving the military."

"And if you do, it can't be for me."

"Why not?"

"Because I can't give you what you want. Right now, I need to work my plan. Find a place to live. Get a job. Make my life work. My mother always made choices for me. Now she's gone, and I have to figure out my life. I can't give you more, and you deserve more."

"You're right. I do want more. Namely

you, in my life. I don't want perfect, but I do want permanent."

"What are you going to do when you get out? What? What skills do you have that will translate into the civilian job? If you get out, you'll blame me, get angry, and eventually leave anyway. Same as everyone else in my life. You won't want permanent, because permanent is tough."

Gut punch.

She scrambled to pick up her shirt and thrust it over her head. "Just go. Go now."

The room contained only so many square feet, but she'd put a lot more distance between them. She stood with her back to him, looking out the large-paned window into the moonless night.

He took a step closer. "Ashley, I'm not leaving you. But I must return to North Carolina. I don't have a choice. I'm not leaving because I want to."

She glared at him, her face screaming, *no, but you will.* "We've already had this conversation. We don't need to keep having it."

The knuckles on her fisted hands had gone white with rage. He wanted to tell her she was wrong. He wanted to explain how deep his feelings were, but he seriously doubted she'd hear a word. She must have taken his silence as confirmation because she took a breath and continued.

"When you get back, the military will take over your life again. I will be pushed to the back of the line and become a distant memory. I don't want to be second anymore. I'm tired of people in my life demanding things from me without giving anything in return. Go ahead and go. It will be easier in the long run."

The raw honesty in her voice made him wince. "That's not how it is," he countered.

"Oh, really? You're going to promise letters, phone calls, tell me you won't die? Or will you lie and promise me you'll be by my side the rest of my life? That's not you, Chase. You don't lie. You tell the truth."

"You're not giving us a chance. And about dying—when my number's up, it's up. No one can play with fate or offer a bullet-proof guarantee."

She turned and looked out the window again, physically and mentally shutting him out of her life. He wrestled with the temptation to let her push him away, but in the end, he couldn't do it. He was a fighter. He took quick strides to reach her.

He saw her reflection in the window, but couldn't read her mirrored face. "You've lived a tough life, and your mom's death and the aftermath she saddled you with sucks. I understand. But it's not reasonable to always look for and expect the worst of people. Sometimes you've got to believe. Take a leap of faith."

He stood for a long time, watching her reflection, waiting for a signal.

When he'd about lost hope, she shifted slightly. "You think I'm strong. But I'm not. I can't do what my mom did. I can't wait around, hoping for the front door to open," she whispered.

He let his breath settle and his shoulders ease. "That's crap. You can do anything you set your mind to. I've seen you do it. I get you're hurt—pissed off at your mom for dying and denying you the life you deserved after all your years of care, and your dad for leaving. You deserve every kindness the world has to offer. And you are strong. But you haven't figured out how to tap into it yet. You're still young."

"You're bringing up our age differences now?"

"You're right. That wasn't fair. And I didn't mean the statement to come out the way it did. It's just that I'm pissed."

"Stand in line. I'm pissed. I'm mad at myself for getting sucked into this situation and distracted from my plan. I'm trying to get my life together. And meeting you now, when my life's all screwed up, sucks. I like you. I like you a lot. But I can't make plans based on promises you can't keep."

"What do you want from me?"

"I want you to face the facts. I have to put my life in order, and you have to go back to North Carolina. I get that. My life is a jumbled mess. I'm a mess. Maybe it's time for you to go. You're a distraction, Chase. A nice distraction, but a distraction."

"A distraction? You mean a nice sex toy to amuse yourself with." His jaw muscles bunched and released as he wrestled with her request.

"You're being unfair again. You know you're more than that. But no matter how strongly I feel about you, I can't see how it will work."

"I want to stay. Talk. I don't have to be at Bobby's parents' until after Christmas."

"What would change? Besides, staying would only prolong the good-bye." Her step back and away emphasized her decision.

"Don't do this, Ashley."

"Chase, you need to go."

He stood, waiting for her to change her mind, but fear and insecurities and survival told him she wouldn't. Finally, he saw no other option. "As you wish. I'll pack my things and clear out in the morning." *Give you more time to reconsider.*

His heart felt like it was being ripped from his chest. He couldn't breathe. He needed air.

He knew when to back off, save his ammo, and minimize the casualties.

With nothing left to say, he managed to walk away.

CHAPTER SEVENTEEN

Chase studied the bottle of tequila in his hand, wanting to break the seal to feel the burn and numbing sensation. Memories of Bobby's mangled body, dirt soaked blood, the sounds of the medics replayed in his mind.

He closed his eyes, clenched his jaw and willed the images to fade. He took a deep breath. His gaze spanned across the sea of white stone, unclenched his hand, and wiggled his fingers to bring back the circulation.

It should have been him in the ground. Not Bobby.

If he could slice away the guilt clamping around his heart like a steel animal trap, he would—no that wasn't true. He'd live with the pain. Honor the best man he'd ever known. Take the necessary steps toward being the person Bobby believed he was, not the angry and confused foster kid from the streets.

He considered opening the bottle again. Instead, he dug a hole in the snow where Bobby's grave marker would be in a few weeks and settled the bottle and two shot glasses on the ground.

Chase sculpted and compacted the snow with his bare hands. The cold landscape left him feeling empty.

"I miss you, buddy," he choked, blinking several times to keep his emotions in check. He gazed out over the fields of stones in even rows. "I'm going to visit your parents later today. I want to check in, see how they're doing." He stood and paced back and forth, back and forth, back and forth, his thoughts random, flicking between the past and present.

He glanced at the liquor bottle. "I met a girl. She's not like the others."

I told you, buddy, not to let women get behind the man curtain. Fucks you up.

"Yeah. I should have listened to you. She did a good job of messing with my head and took a big chunk out of my heart."

But you love her. Come on, admit it.

"Yeah, I love her. But she doesn't need me."

What? A stud like you? Where's that Marine attitude? Did you tell her you loved her?

"Hell, no."

Thought so.

The sun overhead created a field of sparkling diamonds on the undisturbed snow. He listened to the wind blow through the pines, and studied the oak tree skeletons standing sentinel over the graves, waiting for the spring to breathe life back into the place.

Go to her.

"Not going to happen. There are plenty of women back on base who'll be happy to see me."

I bet none are like her.

"No. She's different. Kind. Smart. Giving. Stubborn. Did I mention stubborn?"

So don't be a wimp.

"I can't." He lifted his hand to rub his aching chest. "I can't." He brushed the snow off Bobby's temporary name placard. "It's time to go, buddy. Say hi to the guys. Tell Brian he still owes me ten bucks, and that I'll collect someday." He managed a puff of laughter. "Hopefully not anytime soon."

Chase sniffed back his grief and heartbreak and trudged through the field of graves to the truck. The pressure on his chest made it hard to swallow. His hand tightened around the key ring while he turned to view Ft. Logan Cemetery one last time. In his gut he knew he wouldn't be back, but leaving Bobby would be okay because the man wasn't really there. He was in his memories and heart. Never to be forgotten.

He started the truck, put it in gear, and drove through the large metal gates toward the highway. He felt like he was being ripped apart, right down to his muscles and bones, by the pain of leaving Bobby and Ashley, and his commitment to visit the Hershams.

Ashley had pushed him away because she was scared. He got that. He felt the uneasiness deep in his gut. If she couldn't admit the doubt and fear, how could she heal and get past the pain?

She couldn't.

He understood loss. Bobby had left a great big fucking hole in his chest.

His friend had been right about not getting involved with a woman, but not totally. Ashley gave him a sense of home. A conviction that he didn't want to be anywhere else but with her.

Colorado called to him, but he had to move on. Only pain awaited him here.

He drove, turning and exiting where required, then turned right and left on residential streets, until he saw the majestic oak tree in front of a house with white shutters, light gray paneling, a dark gray door, and a two-car garage. The three recently shoveled steps led to the front porch. He shoved Bobby's truck into park and turned off the ignition.

Shit. I don't want to do this.

He'd been on funeral duty before, and witnessed the grief of mothers and fathers and siblings. When he visited a couple of weeks ago, the sorrowful faces had been more familiar, since he'd seen them in photographs and heard detailed accounts of their lives on long overnight watches.

Bobby had discovered at boot camp that Chase didn't have a family, and generously put his family on indefinite loan, telling him stories and making them real.

The front door opened, and the realness hit him in the gut. He took a calming breath and picked up one of Jenna's pies he'd purchased to ease the start of a conversation.

"How was the drive?" Wilma Hersham's

voice traveled over the snow-covered ground.

"A bit icy, but not too bad."

John Hersham and Lillia, Bobby's sister, appeared in the doorway. Chase snagged his duffel from the passenger seat and made his way up the slippery driveway.

"John, I told you we should have put ice melt down on the pavement."

"Stop your nagging, Wilma, you're embarrassing the boy."

Boy? He supposed children remained kids to their parents. Besides, embarrassment wasn't close to what he was feeling. He handed the pie off to Mrs. Hersham before beginning the three-step climb into the split-level house.

"Lillia, would you please put Chase's things in the spare room?"

Bobby's younger sister didn't appear withdrawn and small this time. At the cemetery, she'd been bundled in an oversized wool coat that hung off her shoulders. The grief in her expression had torn at his soul.

Today she wore jeans so tight he wondered if she could breathe, and a shirt that pushed everything up and almost out.

She was moving on, healing. Her hint of recovery gave him hope. She bent over to show off her full mounds and gave him an inquisitive, I'm-interested stare. *Not going there. Been there and got burned.* Thankfully, Mr. Hersham rescued him by shoving a beer in front of his face.

"Like football?" John Hersham sat in a leather chair that could have had his name engraved on the back. The overstuffed recliner said Man of the House like no other chair in the room. Bobby's dad was looking at the remote in his hand, obviously itching to turn on the sound.

"Depends who's playing. Would I get tossed out if I admitted to liking the Giants?"

"Only if they were playing the Broncos, which they aren't."

Mrs. Hersham appeared with bowls of peanuts, corn chips and salsa, the carbs he should start avoiding, according to Ashley.

The idea of her and the Hershams' attempts at normalcy made the sorrow inside him explode.

He turned to the woman who'd recently lost her only son. "How are you doing today?" he asked, wondering if she felt as lost and adrift as he did.

She rapidly blinked and took a deep breath, fighting for acceptance of something he could never understand fully, a mother's loss of a child. "I'm doing okay today." She pointed at the Christmas tree in the corner of the room. "Putting up the tree was hard. I found Bobby's first ornament, and the one he made in kindergarten. Ugly little thing, but very precious."

"This time last year, Bobby and I were eating dehydrated turkey in a blizzard. Bobby started complaining, which in turn started a snowball fight." Chase chuckled at the memory. "Bobby liked to stir things up a bit."

"That's my boy." Pride with a hint of

sorrow made John choke back anything else he wanted to say.

"Before I forget," Chase said to change the subject, "thank you for allowing me to use his truck. I enjoyed visiting the places Bobby talked about."

"What did you like best?" He met Lillia's curious gaze when she entered the room. Aiming for the couch, she missed sitting on him by a slim margin, squeezing in between him and her mother.

"I had a list of places to see, but I only got to Elkridge and a few towns close by."

"Elkridge?" John pointed a finger at his wife. "Isn't that the little town with that quilt shop you like so much?"

"There is a quilt shop there, but you're getting it mixed up with the one in Idaho Springs."

John gave him a pointed look. "So what did you find so interesting in Elkridge?"

Chase rubbed his palm with his thumb, wondering how much to say. Lillia reached directly in front of him for a chip and some salsa. The interest in her gaze was something he'd seen a thousand times in bars across the world. A kind of look that had piqued his interest only a few times in the past, and today wasn't one of those days.

"I met some nice people." *And a woman.*

"Oh?" Mrs. Hersham's eyes widened and her expression lit up like a Christmas tree bulb.

"That pie is from the café there. The baker makes awesome pastries and pies. I thought you might like one."

"Sounds lovely," Mrs. Hersham said.

"There goes my diet," Lillia groaned. "I have to get in better shape before I hit boot camp this summer."

"If you're not in shape beforehand, you will be when you're finished," he warned.

Bobby's sister gave him that look again. A look informing him he might need to lock the guest room door to foil an attempted overnight rendezvous. Some women seemed to get this odd image of a Marine that didn't always apply. Especially to him.

"Is boot camp as hard as people say it is?"

"I've heard regulations have changed from when I went through, but it's still pretty tough. You'll get to know your classmates pretty well. They'll become some of your best friends."

"Maybe my Lillia will find a nice military man and settle down." *And have grandbabies,* her mother, and wishful future grandmother, left unsaid. "Bobby was adamant about never getting married. He got his wish."

Yep, he got his wish. "Bobby was a good man, and he didn't want the distractions." Chase shrugged. "At least that's what he said." Because Chase had witnessed Bobby involved with plenty of distractions.

"Are you opposed to distractions?" Lillia asked, leaning in a bit too close.

I'm not. Ashley is.

"No. In fact, I met a woman in Elkridge." Chase looked at Bobby's little sister directly, hoping she got the not-interested hint.

"So it's serious with this woman," John concluded.

"You could say it's complicated." One hand gripped the other and he pushed his thumb into a meaty pressure point.

"Then why are you here?"

Chase looked at Mr. Hersham, and then Mrs., confused.

"I think what John meant is you are welcome here anytime. We invited you for Christmas to make sure you wouldn't be alone for the holidays. You don't owe us anything. If you prefer to be with your woman friend, we'd understand."

Gotcha. The way Lillia looked at him, any reason might be a good excuse for a quick escape, but going back wouldn't be one of them. Ashley needed time. He needed time.

"Like I said, it's complicated. Besides, I wanted to spend some time here, and whatever you have in the oven smells awesome."

The smell of roasted meat and spices and garlic had made his mouth water the minute he walked in the house. He'd been too distracted then, but now his entire body was onboard and wanting some food.

"I've made my special meatloaf recipe. It was Bobby's favorite. John's mother gave me the recipe, but I've spiced it up a bit."

"Wilma likes to cook," John remarked without taking his gaze off the muted football game, watching players run around on the field with no sound. "Storm's moving in. Expecting a foot of snow this afternoon."

The weather. Football. Food. Small talk. Chase knew about trying to bury pain with the mundane.

"So are we going to watch some football?" he asked.

The last syllable of the word 'football' hadn't gotten out of his mouth before the TV announcer gave the score. Chase chuckled at the delight on Bobby's dad's face. He needed the distraction. Just as Bobby's mom needed to cook. Chase suspected Lillia needed to get laid, but she was going to have to look somewhere else. He couldn't help her out there.

He grabbed a handful of nuts and settled back into the couch. The room was full of family, not just the people sitting on couches and chairs, but generations of family along the walls in eight by ten frames.

Bobby had been family. Chase had loved him like a brother. He missed his smartass remarks, his carefree smile, and his boundless loyalty. Nothing and no one would ever fill Bobby's boots. Bobby was certifiable, one of a kind, unique. He was his friend. And the loss would be felt as long as Chase lived. The sting behind his eyes made him clamp his eyelids shut. He'd spoken his piece at the cemetery. Alone. Privately.

Last night, he'd spoken to Ashley with animosity founded on his insecurities. This morning, he wanted to apologize, but Ashley had left the house early with Lucky without saying good-bye. He probably deserved it.

Things weren't finished between them. Not by a long shot. However, building a relationship took two, and she didn't want to go there.

Right now he had obligations to meet. Spending time with Bobby's mom and dad was something he needed to do, for Bobby, for himself. He'd picked out a few clean stories, ones he could share with family or a priest. He wanted to share the friend he knew, and get to know the son and brother his family had lost.

He wanted to see if he could stitch up the open gap in his chest a bit more, but more importantly, he wanted to help Bobby's family heal.

Chase popped a peanut into his mouth and draped his arm over the back of the couch to watch Lillia squirm. "So what's the score?"

"Who knows?" She rolled her eyes, more interested in him than the game.

"What are you doing to prepare for boot camp?"

"I've been running and lifting weights. One of my friends is entering the same class, and we've been working out together. Of course, now Mom's not too thrilled with me going."

"Working in the intelligence office, you most likely won't be on the front lines like your brother. You should be fine."

"That's what the recruiter said." She studied her father and said quietly, "He's having a really hard time. I don't think he's been out of his chair in weeks. He even sleeps there."

"Give him time. Everyone needs to heal in their own way."

"I guess."

Lillia talked about her hopes for her assignments, and Chase managed to keep the conversation away from other topics. He wasn't going to talk about the war, or killing people, or what it was like over there. She'd find out soon enough. After a while, she figured out he wasn't going to sensationalize his experiences or show off his battle scars, at which point she got bored and made an excuse to disappear downstairs.

Shortly before the second quarter finished, Mrs. Hersham disappeared into the kitchen. He'd spotted a sheen in her eyes he wished wasn't there, and felt the need to check on her.

"Mrs. Hersham?"

She stood at the kitchen sink, staring out into the backyard. He suspected she wasn't really seeing anything. He walked up beside her and let the silence settle around them.

"He was a good boy. I didn't know him as a man like you did," she offered in a voice so frail, he had to lean in to hear. "He didn't like coming home much. Said this town made him feel claustrophobic."

"He was a good friend. And well-liked. He was also a good Marine, but I think he was a better man."

Bony fingers reached for his hand. "I'd like to think he was happy."

Chase remembered the last few weeks of the deployment. Everyone was tired and miserable and waiting their turn to go home. Fights broke out easily. Some guys got drunk. Some gambled too much. Some hit the weights to relieve stress. Some disappeared into their inner worlds.

He and Bobby played cribbage to pass the time. Neither of them had been particularly thrilled about the conditions, and often voiced complaints about this injury or that ache or even a stupid toothache. Chase remembered bitching about his tooth and being questioned by one of the NCO's in the mess. If only. He couldn't allow the heavy burden of guilt to sidetrack him now. He had an obligation.

"Bobby was happy," he reassured Mrs. Hersham. "He was a good friend."

"Thank you for your kindness. But I worry about Lillia and John. Especially John."

"Lillia will have a good career in the intelligence office. The military needs smart people like her. And John? Right now he needs to escape, and football's a good choice, as opposed to the other options he could have chosen."

"You're smart. Now I know why my Bobby liked you." She patted his chest with a tired hand. "I better get the potatoes on. Can't have meatloaf without some good whipped potatoes."

Chase caught a glimpse of a list as the refrigerator opened. He moved to the take a closer look when Wilma had closed the door.

Change the furnace filter.

Caulk the back window.

Repair bathroom faucet.

John's to-do list.

The listless man in the living room continued to stare at the screen. Chase doubted he saw much, either.

Each family member had disappeared into their inner world to mourn and find peace. As he had, but his way to cope with grief was to keep busy. A slow warmth spread through his limbs. Fixing little things, those irritants in everyday life, might not be a lot, but he could ease a bit of John and Wilma's burden.

If only for a little while.

CHAPTER EIGHTEEN

Silence has a sound, an attitude. Ashley hadn't understood that before.

Before her mother had died, and Chase had left, she craved space. For two days, a dark and mindless depression raged. She'd breathed in the silence, lived inside it. She embraced the earth's pulse, the movement of wind and cloud and tree. She accepted the movement of her jaw muscles mashing food into swallow-size bits, but lost her sense of taste or smell. Experiencing anger and fear and loss, she curled up into a ball and slept, running from the nothingness, not wanting to worry about finding a job or a place to live.

When the morning sun rose, she opened her eyes to see a dog who needed her, eBay packages requiring sending, and a sink full of dirty dishes needing to be washed.

She couldn't escape.

If she couldn't escape, then she needed to do something about it.

She stretched her stiff body and willed her feet off the couch. Movement caught her attention. Out the front window, snowflakes floated, swirled, and fell to the ground.

She studied the concerned dog's face. "It's snowing. Tomorrow will be a white Christmas. You'll like the fresh, fluffy snow. Want to go out?"

Lucky's hind end jostled from side to side while she walked to the kitchen door to let him out. As she walked past the kitchen table, her footsteps faltered when her gaze landed on the box her father had sent. Moving to the living room, she lifted the plastic bins full of letters, and re-read her dad's brief, to-the-point note again. Tilting the first box, she noted the catalog card at the end—typical of her father. The same numbers and dashes appeared on her mom's envelopes.

She had an idea. The niggle of excitement started in her fingers then spread through the rest of her, body and mind.

Rushing up and down the stairs, she carried the rest of the letter boxes to the family room and then pushed the coffee table to the side of the room, built a fire, and invited Lucky to join her on the floor. If her family couldn't be with her on Christmas Eve, maybe she could be with them. Ordering the boxes by date, she pulled the first box in each pile toward her. Looking at the dates, she started with her mom's letter.

Her parents had met at a Fourth of July parade—her mom fifteen, and her dad eighteen and preparing to go to boot camp. Ashley got the notion her maternal grandparents weren't thrilled about the relationship because in the third letter, her mom hinted at missing correspondence. The next few were nothing more than *I miss you, why haven't you written*, and then in a letter her dad wrote, she found a treasure, the mysterious numbering scheme. The first few numbers indicated the letters being responded to, the second the sequence of the letter sent. She fanned the bundles from both stacks and found her mom's conclusions had been correct—six dated envelopes were missing.

Many of the letters were emotionally difficult to read. Passion fueled the words— the anger and frustration of being apart, of not being able to talk to or hold each other, yet their love and respect for each other underpinned everything. She saw her mother's absolute refusal to let go of the relationship. Her dad encouraging the love of his life to live, not wait.

Ashley held the crumpled stationery to her chest, feeling the anguish her parents had lived, when the doorbell rang.

Chase.

She rushed to the foyer, sliding on her stocking feet across the tile to rip the door open. "Maggie...a...hi." She plastered on a smile to defuse the disappointment seeping into her heart.

The woman brushed past her with arms full of packages and gifts to lay them on the kitchen counter. "When you didn't stop by the café for my special eggnog, which I know you love, I thought I'd better check on you." Maggie turned to say something else, but stopped when her gaze captured a living room filled with letters scattered across the floor. "What's all this?"

"Years of my parent's letters. I thought maybe...I could...um, understand what happened between them. You know... understand why my dad left. Why they didn't just divorce."

"Oh, hon." Maggie pulled her into her arms for one of her all-encompassing squeezes. "There's no sense in asking why. Even if you knew the answer, you'd only want to have more answers, and there isn't any satisfying explanation of why your dad didn't come home more."

Ashley sucked in a startled breath and the sting of tears made her blink several times, trying to clear the emotion.

"When we moved here, I thought it was because he didn't want us anymore. Then I discovered Mom wanted to be here. Weekly, she would disappear for several hours. One day, I followed her on my bike to the cemetery. There was a little headstone carved with the name Dillon Joseph Bryant. A brother I never knew. I knew better than to ask Mom about him. She wouldn't have told me about my sibling anyway. She didn't like discussing the past."

"No, she didn't. Tell me, are you just going to sit here all alone on Christmas Eve, reading your parents' letters?"

"What else am I supposed to do? Huh? It's the last Christmas I'll have in this house. For just one day, I want to be with my parents. Both of them. I want to get to know them, and the only way to do that is through their letters."

"Then what? Are you going to live in the past—get stuck—constantly questioning why?"

A searing fear settled in her gut. "I don't know." Her voice sounded so small and pathetic, she hated the sound.

"When Chase comes back from wherever he is, I suggest you turn on some music, dance, maybe make some popcorn, and watch a movie."

Longing gripped her at the romantic picture Maggie presented, but she quickly brushed the enchanting scene away. That fairy tale wasn't for her. "Chase isn't coming back. He left."

"What? Why? That boy's a rutting buck in love."

No he's not. He wouldn't have left if he loved me. "I needed to focus on getting on with my life, so I sent him away."

Maggie's fists pulled to waist level. "Now, why did you go and do a thing like that?"

"I'm not what he needs. I have to straighten my life out."

"And you think sitting in the dark, reading your parents' letters is the right way to do that?"

"What do you expect from me? My parents are gone. I don't have a job. I have no way of putting a roof over my head. My mother thought I was a loser because she didn't give me the skill sets to be an adult. And she's right. I am a loser. I don't know how to fix all this. I'm supposed to figure out what to do next, and I don't know how. I'm all alone, Maggie."

"What am I? Chopped liver?" Maggie's eyes sparked with annoyance, then softened. "I'm sorry your mom died, but you can't just sit here on the floor feeling sorry for yourself and reading your parents' letters the rest of your life. The only thing you are going to get is a numb butt, and a horrible, pathetic lonely life. You have a chance at something real and good. What are you going to do with your life?"

A flash of anger sizzled through her chest. "You're always giving people advice. You tell me what I need to do."

Maggie's brow arched up, just like her mother's had so many times. "Girl, you're the only one who knows what you want to do. You're not stupid. Figure it out. I've watched you these past three years do what ninety-nine percent of the people in this town couldn't. You kept a roof over your mother's head, kept her fed, relieved her pain. And I'm talking both her mental and physical pain. She needed you and you stayed. If I was honest, I couldn't have done it."

"That's not true. You take care of everyone in this town."

"Giving a person a meal now and then isn't the same as washing, clothing, and giving a person meds. Nor is it the same as taking the abuse she dealt. If someone talked to me like that, I'd kick their sorry butt out of my place."

Ashley shook her head in disagreement. "Anger. It was just her way of dealing with dying. I wish she were still here. She'd tell me what to do, like she always did."

"Would you just get your head out of your ass? You don't need someone else telling you how to live your life." Maggie's eyes narrowed with suspicion. "You want to wallow. Is that it? Have a one-woman pity party? Feel sorry for yourself?"

"You don't know what you're talking about."

"Oh, hon. I do know." A flash of pain crisscrossed her face. "I've been there. Tell you what. You get one day. One day to wallow. That's all you get. Then you start living your life. Promise me. No more of this sitting in the dark. You have to promise me."

"How about an 'I'll try'?"

"Good enough. Now come give me a hug."

Ashley readily stepped into the warmth. She missed that human connection. The feeling of another person accepting her, physically conveying she was worthy of love.

Maggie held on until Ashley stepped back

and pointed at the counter filled with stuff. "What did you bring me?"

"I brought a pint of my eggnog and a couple of my jams for you to try. There's wild blackberry and fig. Jenna sent your favorite cookies. Joe made some elk jerky. It's spicy, so watch out. Harold and Claudia said to remind you they're saving a place for you for Christmas dinner. And there's a little something extra for you. A couple of others chipped in as well. You open it when you're ready."

"Can I open it now?"

"If you want."

Ashley pulled the card from the envelope. On the front of the card was a glittered picture of a Santa on the back of a Harley motorcycle, holding a martini. The image somehow created a smile. When she opened the envelope and saw all the ten- and twenty-dollar bills, her heart paused.

"Oh. Oh." She fanned her face, feeling a rockslide of emotions tumbling down the hill, with no way to get out of the way. She shoved the card toward Maggie. "I can't take this."

"You can and you will, 'cause I'm not going to tell the people who wanted to give you a little something that they aren't appreciated."

Ashley's chin quivered as tears welled and flowed down her cheeks. Maggie kissed her on the forehead, and lifted her chin. "I meant what I said. You have one day, and only one day, to revisit the past, and then you have to move forward—become the woman you were always meant to be. No one can tell you who that person is, you have to discover her for yourself."

Maggie moved toward the front door before turning back. "And remember. You're only alone if you want to be. This town, even if unconventional, has a lot of love to give."

The door clicked closed before Ashley could say a word. Yearning, fear, and determination all competed for attention.

Lucky, sensing her mood, nuzzled her hand with his cold nose. She returned to the living room and the little space in front of the couch she'd carved out in the circle of letters. She lowered into a cross-legged position and the dog collapsed at her side, resting his head in her lap.

As the afternoon sun warmed the room, she read about her mom's multiple sclerosis diagnosis. Her mom buried the announcement in the middle of a paragraph, moving on to local news in the next sentence.

Her dad had wanted to be with her, but her mom believed he had a calling, and told him not to come home. He needed to train his soldiers well, to keep the world safe. She would travel to him only when in remission, and go into seclusion when flares occurred. He wanted to leave the military and take care of the woman he loved, but her mom flatly refused, always saying she was only one person, and he needed to save the many. The sheer stubbornness might have driven some men away, but not Ashley's faithful father. He'd loved his wife then as he loved her now.

For several more hours, Ashley read letter after letter of back and forth arguing.

Back and forth commitment.

Back and forth heartbreak.

Ashley lifted the next envelope and took a fortifying breath, but couldn't stand to read one more set. Each of them at the end of their rope, tugging and pulling, neither willing to let go, both holding on, fighting against a dying marriage. Holding onto a love that just wouldn't give up.

She rubbed her head as guilt squeezed and made her joints ache. The angry words and silent rejection she'd thrust at her dad for leaving her mom were unfounded, and he'd let her believe him the villain. Let her create a false belief that he didn't want her, when each letter proved over and over and over again, every day, that he carried both of them in his heart.

Anger and hatred filled Ashley to the point that she had refused to speak to him at the funeral. Her grieving father left the next day. The guilt over her actions chiseled to a fine, sharp point. She'd needed to feel his arms around her, feel his strength soak into her like it had when she skinned her knee.

How could she have been so wrong about her dad?

She lifted the note he'd sent. *These are yours to do with, whatever you like. I have scanned copies. It's important for you to have the whole story. Dad.*

The holes in Ashley's life filled at a rapid pace. With the knowledge came pain. With the pain came understanding, regret, and sorrow for the time lost. She pushed the boxes near her aside and reached for the last set. Living with her mother's stubbornness, Ashley regretfully understood both her parents suffered, neither winning, both losing.

She lifted the last note her mother ever wrote. The white typed page seemed cold and stark after reading years of handwritten prose on elegant stationery.

She skimmed the pages, remembering the documented events. Tired of delving into her parents' past, she started to fold the sheets of paper when her typed name drew her attention. Her gaze zoomed to the paragraph, reading, then re-reading for clarity.

...ASHLEY SITS ASLEEP in a chair across the room. I worry about her. She's so beautiful, it makes my heart ache. You need to help her venture out and spread her wings. I've made mistakes in raising our daughter. She is not prepared for a life on her own. In the months I have left, I'll try to give her the tools she will need to move on. I shouldn't have been so controlling, yet I only wanted the best for her. I wanted to protect her, allow only happiness into her life. I didn't have the strength to let her grow and reach for her dreams. As I lie here, I've come to realize I wanted Ashley to live my dreams.

YOU WILL HAVE to be strong for us, for your special Ashtray. Promise me you won't swoop in and save her like you always wanted to save me. Let her become an adult. Promise me.

I'M AFRAID FOR HER—TRULY scared. She pushes everyone away, closes her heart, afraid to open to possibilities. She doesn't know how beautiful and freeing love can be. I fear we haven't shown our daughter that a love like ours, even if unconventional, is the glue that binds the pieces of life together and makes a person whole. I've loved you all but the early fifteen years of my life, and I'll love you until the end. Love Ashley as you always have, and help her see what a truly beautiful daughter she is.

ASHLEY'S HANDS trembled and her mind stumbled over the events of the last three years, the heated fights, the accusations, the emotions that left both her and her mother drained, not speaking.

The crumpled piece of paper fell to the floor. The months of poking, pushing, prodding hadn't been due to a mother's disappointment or disgust, but done out of love and wanting the best for her. *She doesn't know how beautiful and freeing love can be.*

Lucky licked her face, soothing her, lapping up the tears as the drops plopped into her lap. She hugged her knees to her chest and lowered her head, thinking her parents were total idiots.

She'd been wrong about *everything*—her mom, her dad, their opinion of her. Her back and belly convulsed and shuddered while she recalled the frustration she'd spewed at her mother. She wished now she could take everything back—every harsh word, every act of rebellion—everything. But now, nothing, not one damn thing, could be done. Her bones melted and she puddled into a small, sobbing blob on the floor.

"Mom, why? Why didn't you just talk to me?"

Lucky pushed his way into her arms, his golden eyes worried.

"Oh, Lucky. What am I going to do now?

How am I going to figure out what I'm supposed to do?"

She wrapped her arms around the dog's chest, threading her fingers through his growing fur, letting the words she'd read soak into holes in her emotionally deformed heart. Deformed from the years of believing her parents didn't want her, like her, love her. The revelations didn't yet match their actions, but she wanted to believe, to fill her empty heart full of wishes and hopes for love.

Tears swelled in her eyes and dripped on the carpeted floor. She would have told her mother...told her...told her what? Defensive, curt words were so easy to come by, but when it came to fresh, honest communication, words abandoned her.

Her phone poked her in the side, and she removed it from her sweatshirt pocket. Entering the security code, she hovered her thumb over the phone list.

Chase came to mind, but stubbornness thwacked her on the ear and wouldn't allow her to reach out. Her thumb continued to scroll down the list until she pressed enter. The phone rang. And with each successive ring, the monster in the darkness loomed closer, gnawing and chewing at her insecurities.

She couldn't hold out any longer, and every muscle went numb. She couldn't listen to an empty ring, not anymore. The phone slid from her fingers to hit the carpet, and she curled inward.

"Oh, Daddy. What am I supposed to do now? I'm so lost."

In a few days, the bank would likely evict her from everything she'd ever known. She'd packed her clothes, bedding, a few knickknacks, and kitchen supplies. What choice did she have?

She would make something of her life. She would. But today she wanted to grieve for what she had lost. All those years of heartache.

Of miscommunication.

Of misunderstanding.

Of missed opportunities.

You have one more day to wallow. Promise me. Maggie's words returned. She picked up a box of letters. "Okay, Maggie. No more looking back. No more questioning why. No more searching for answers. I'm going to take Mom's advice and only focus on the future. No more regrets. No more anger. No more resentment." She opened the fireplace grate to place a box on top of the log and watch it catch fire. "I will not let the past dictate my future. I won't. Not anymore." Watching box, after box, after box catch and burn solidified her determination to release the haunting of the past. Her mother and father might have scanned copies of the letters, leaving her the originals, but she didn't want the past to chain her to what might have been.

Not anymore.

No more letting the past actions of her family pull her under.

Ever so slowly, while the letters burned,

the ache of the past dissipated, and the steps toward the future truly began.

Tomorrow. Tomorrow is a new start. My start. My new life. No more wallowing.

BOBBY'S TRUCK skidded sideways into the driveway and stopped a couple of feet short of the four-car garage. The windshield wipers swished back and forth, frantically trying to keep up with the falling snow. Chase finally let out a full breath.

He'd made it back.

The massive, dark and silent house loomed in front of him, and his battle-ready instincts were signaling caution. He clutched the duffel bag handles and waded through the knee-deep snow to the front door. Testing the handle, he found it unlocked, and went on full alert. With fingertips, he eased the door wide and scanned the hallway.

He should have called, but he'd been so hell-bent on getting back to Ashley, back to the one place he wanted to be, he didn't think. Pointing the truck in her direction, he'd driven non-stop, speeding to get back to the one person he wanted to see. Back to the place where he felt at home.

Regret lashed at him while he moved through the house, alert for movement or sound. The light from the embers in the fireplace drew him closer, and a soft whine stilled his breath as he studied the lump lodged against the couch next to Lucky. His pulse beat wildly in his chest as he pictured the worst possible outcome. He reached a tentative hand forward, aching for the visions in his mind to be wrong.

Heat. He felt her warmth and a shiver.

He smoothed the hair from her face. Her lashes fluttered in the amber light until her disoriented face turned to his.

"You came back," she croaked.

"I couldn't leave things the way they were."

She rubbed her eyelids with her fingertips. "I didn't want to push you way. I got scared."

"I realized after I left that you'd misinterpreted what I said." He circled his thumb on her cheek, working to erase the dark smudges under her eyes. "When I found out Bobby's parents had made me promise to visit for Christmas just so I wouldn't be alone, I explained I wouldn't be if I returned to Elkridge to a very special woman. I wanted to come back to you, Ashley. I want to be with you." *This is where my home is.*

"I'm glad you came back."

Woman, you don't know how much I've missed you. But he mustn't speak his heart aloud. For one, the intense feelings might scare her. And two, they would terrify him.

He placed the back of his hand on her forehead. No fever, but her nose could have doubled for an ice cube. "Let's get you off the floor, and the fire going again."

Her fingers clamped on his arm, and then let go while she pushed herself up. "I'm fine."

She wasn't fine. He could feel her shivering. Her eyes were red and swollen, and he noticed the family room was littered with empty bins. Something had blown up in her world, and he wanted to know what.

He tossed another couple of logs on the fire and returned to the couch, where she sat huddled in the corner. She reminded him of Lucky hiding in the brush, afraid to trust. While on patrol he'd watched people disarm plenty of IEDs, and he approached her with the same care.

"Ashley?" he said gently. He sat next to her, securing her cold hand, wrapping his fingers around hers to transfer warmth. "What's all this?"

She shriveled inward. *No, come on, talk to me,* he pleaded in silence.

Ashley studied their entwined hands, and he felt waves of something raw and daunting emanating from her. Something or someone had hurt her. He prayed it hadn't been him. The idea stung and sliced at him.

"Ash, I'm sorry I left. We don't have very

good timing."

"You shouldn't feel bad," she whispered, but her wounded expression said something entirely different. "I hate Christmas, but you didn't cause that."

He wanted to rip the hurt away and find the beautiful, caring woman hiding beneath the pain. He sighed, at a loss for what to do, and then let his body make the choice, reaching out for her delicate wrist, feeling her pulse, wanting to feel more. What was she thinking? Feeling? Would she push him away again?

Her beauty in the firelight made him breathless, even shy. Reverting to his schoolboy years, he, a grown man, had no idea what to do, say. He stroked her face with a finger, and a miracle happened. She leaned into his caress until her cheek pressed into his palm. He hesitated.

"If this is the time we have left, I don't want to waste it." Ashley stretched up to him. "Kiss me."

"I want you to know this isn't about sex."

He brushed a finger over her cheekbone.

"I know. Kiss me." She turned her head, her lips brushing the sensitive part of his wrist.

His whole body sighed, and he captured her trembling lips until her breath combined with his. He cradled her face, his tongue exploring. His world began spinning, while her breath became increasingly short and ragged. Adrenaline shot through his system. Jumping out of airplanes didn't compare, and he felt a sharp thrill of excitement race to his fingers and toes. She took him on an adventure like nothing he'd experienced before.

Her hand bunched his shirt and yanked him closer. Chase's lips trailed down her jaw while he stretched over her, pushing her deeper into the cushions. He pressed his nose to the soft skin beneath her jaw, smelling the sweetness of spun sugar, feeling the swell of her breast beneath him.

Ashley sighed.

He lifted his head, dragging himself away

from her warm skin. "Am I crushing you?"

"Yes. I mean, no." He started to lift away, but her arms clamped around his shoulders. "I want to go upstairs."

He didn't expect to hear those words, and for a moment he worked to understand the full meaning.

"I want to be with you, Chase. Do you have a condom?"

A white-hot blaze surged through him. He lifted onto his elbows. "Stay here."

He closed the glass fireplace doors, ripped his duffel apart to find the strip of condoms buried inside his mess kit, and made it back to her side in Superman time.

Lifting her in his arms, he sprinted up the stairs as if his life depended on it. He didn't want her to change her mind. If she did, it might just rip his guts out.

Ashley gave a shaky laugh as he bounced her down the hall. She bent her legs, but he had to back up when her foot got stuck on the door molding. He wanted to lay her gently on the bed, but in his excitement he tripped on the rug beside her bed, sending her flying, with him landing on top of her.

He lifted his head to apologize for his clumsiness, but her laughing lips were already on their way to meet his, her arms gathering him closer. He skimmed up her sides, flesh reveling in flesh. Arching back to explore the curves of her face, he pushed a strand of hair out of the way. Dazed with desire, he bent his head to her swollen lips and indulged, claiming all she shared.

"I've missed you," he admitted on a whispered breath. "You make me feel alive."

"Chase, you're going to be dead if you keep talking."

He laughed and slid his hands under her shirt, over her skin. She let out a half-sigh when he cupped her perfect breasts covered only by thin lace. He wanted this. He wanted her. Pulling the shirt higher, he pressed his mouth against the lace and blew warmth through the sheer fabric, then watched the result. Her back arched as she let out a choked cry.

With a flurry of arms and legs, they were both naked within moments, clinging to each other as if tomorrow was their last day on earth. While the blizzard raged outside, a storm erupted inside. His hands and mouth moved on instinct, keying into the subtle changes in her breath or skin, relishing the surge of pleasure pummeling his body. Ashley's fingernails raked his back while she strained for a closer connection, positioning him to satisfy a deep need.

He wanted her. Now. Lifting up, he secured the protection and dove back into action. He wanted to wait to extend her pleasure, but she didn't leave him the option when she thrust her hips closer.

Another piece of his stone heart chipped away as he slid into her, into the place he needed, wanted, to be. He hadn't fully realized she held his heart so tenderly until that moment. Being in her arms, surrendering entirely, without reserve, was the only place for him. She wielded the magic which had captured his soul. When she exploded in his arms, he couldn't hold on and dove off the end of the world to fly with her. Their bodies pumped, and then surged, before riding the stream of moonlight coming through the window back to earth.

He rolled to his side and pulled her with him, refusing to let her go. She looked lovely in her satiated state. He'd risked driving an unfamiliar truck through a blizzard to get to her, but even a whiteout wouldn't have prevented him returning. He'd set his heart's compass to home. To her.

She had the most serene look on her face when her eyelids drifted shut and she dropped into slumber. Her ability to fall asleep thrilled him. It meant she felt safe, protected. He settled a blanket over them and snuggled her closer, letting her caressing hair fall across his arm.

She still hadn't told him what had happened in the two days he'd been gone, but he could wait until tomorrow. He liked the sound of tomorrow—a promise of something more, something good...a future.

CHAPTER NINETEEN

Chase awoke to a cold bed. He'd never been a heavy sleeper, and his mind had difficulty wrapping around the time on the clock beside the bed. Perhaps it was the sunlight reflecting off the snow-blanketed ground and bouncing off the ceiling of the room. He slid on a pair of jeans and went in search of his woman.

His woman.

The concept popped into his mind so quickly, fully formed, it made his breath hitch. But it felt right, down to his bones.

Lucky and the smell of bacon greeted

him at the kitchen door before the sight of Ashley pummeled his senses. Rumpled from the night of lovemaking, she couldn't have looked more scrumptious. She turned with tongs in hand. Her eyes flared and the tip of her tongue touched her upper lip, clearly communicating she liked the shirtless view.

Eventually, her gaze met his. "What woke you? The smell of breakfast, or Lucky chasing a squirrel off the deck?"

"Neither, actually." He returned her undressing, intent stare.

Missing her body folding into his had woken him, but he didn't know how to tell her without scaring her off or causing her to push him away. But he couldn't help craving her touch, and moved close behind her. She must have seen the lustful look on his face because her white-knuckled hand, resting on the counter, gripped the pair of tongs so hard he wanted to take them from her.

Without touching her, he took in her musky smell and peered over her shoulder to watch the bacon splatter in the skillet. He wanted to turn off the burners, throw her over his shoulder, and race back up the stairs, but he needed to find out what was causing her tension. The bedroom would only put a Band-Aid on a wound which was obviously still festering.

The cup she'd assigned him still sat on the counter, so he went over to the coffee pot and poured. "What happened while I was gone?"

Her jaw muscle worked while she placed the bacon on a paper towel. She obviously wrestled with some inner demon, and he wasn't sure which side was winning when she set a plate of bacon and egg sandwiches down in the middle of the table and took a seat.

Her features were closed and confusing, and he didn't know how to get her to open up, so he walked over and set her cup of coffee in front of her. She examined the black liquid as if it would give her answers. He sat and waited for her to defeat the beast, or at least invite him in to do battle.

"I fixed my mother breakfast every morning," she said.

"I'm sure she appreciated it."

Ashley laughed. "Actually, no, she didn't. She hated breakfast. I forced food on her. I thought she needed to eat. I tried eggs, cereal, yogurt, even health drinks filled with vitamins, but she refused food. We didn't communicate well. Maybe that was my fault. Maybe that was her fault. But the fact remains...we talked, but never communicated. Ever."

Chase shifted, attempting to figure out the clues to the riddle Ashley gave him, but not understanding the rules. Emotions rolled across her face, changing faster than bullets firing from an AK-47. He wanted to jump in and fight for her, but didn't know the entry point.

He touched her forearm. "You did the best you could."

Ashley snapped her head to him. "No, I didn't. In my mind, my mother always made me feel like I wasn't doing enough. Cooking.

Cleaning. Finances. Wardrobe. Education. She was always pushing me to do more, and criticizing everything I tried. We fought all the time, and I couldn't help feeling resentful. Just to be cruel, I wouldn't respond when she called. Then I'd hate myself for days. There were times I just had to leave the house for a few hours. At one point, she told me to just leave. I stayed to spite her." Her fingers pulled on the loose strings of the frayed placemat. "I thought in time she'd come to appreciate what I was doing for her, but until yesterday, I never realized why she was bugging the crap out of me to do better. Not because nothing I did was good enough, but because she loved me and wanted me to be prepared for a life without her. I watched her die a little at a time. Every time she wouldn't eat, or take her meds, or let me bathe her, a little piece of me shriveled and died along with her. I could have done better. If I'd only known what she was trying to do. But I promised I wouldn't allow those regrets to take over my life."

His mind returned to the empty totes he'd seen when he walked through the door. "Is this about the letters?"

"The letters. Yes, the letters." She sighed and turned her hand over to hold his. "My mom said I was too much like her. She wanted me to take chances. Looking back, I see now that every time I stumbled, she was right there, helping me up, cheering me on. I finally figured out the fighting and bickering started when I stopped reaching for the future." The haunted shadows under her eyes deepened as she tumbled into a pool of guilt.

"If what you say is true—"

"It is true."

"Let me finish," he requested with a grin, tugging on her fingers, trying to lighten the mood. "If your mother wanted you to take risks and follow your dreams, she wouldn't have wanted you to be sitting at the kitchen table on Christmas morning, beating the crap out of yourself."

"Oh, my gosh, it's Christmas. I've never liked Christmas, for a lot a reasons. Maybe all those reasons don't matter anymore. I think I need to change. Today's a good day to start." Her wide-eyed astonishment took him by surprise. "We've got to get ready."

"For?"

"To celebrate."

Chase couldn't remember the last time he'd celebrated a holiday. Usually he volunteered to remain on duty, to occupy his time and let those with families celebrate the day, his gift to his unit. The obligatory call to his mom took five minutes, or less if the answering machine picked up, but he'd stopped making those calls years ago.

"Go." She gave him a slight nudge. "You need to get showered. We have things to do."

He pointed at the breakfast sandwiches. "Aren't you going to eat?"

"Later. You can take yours with you if you want."

Chase reached and wiped a smudge of butter from her cheek. The need to touch her grew too strong to resist. When he stood, he kissed her forehead.

"I should warn you, I don't like Christmas, either."

"Don't worry. That's why we're going out. Elkridge has a way of expelling the Grinch."

"That sounds like a tooth extraction."

She laughed. "When you live here, whether you like it or not, you get sucked into the family."

The family she referred to amazed him. Other than the military, he'd never had people he just met cover his backside. The town had knocked him upside the head with their generosity and kindness. He would miss them—miss her—when he left. In the meantime, he'd do what he could to protect the general's daughter.

"Sure you don't want to stay here? We could have our own celebration." The lift of the brow and the huskiness of his voice held so many promises.

"Go." Her stern voice in no way matched the goofy grin on her face. "We have places to be."

He was gunning for another kiss, but

decided her desires were a higher priority than his, and turned to do as she commanded.

ASHLEY GRABBED a set of freshly washed clothes from the laundry room and showered in the downstairs bathroom.

Visions of Chase never strayed far from her mind.

When he'd asked if she wanted to stay at the house, she about shouted, *yes, yes, yes, stay here forever,* but courage failed her.

Years of trying to please, to be the perfect daughter so her dad wouldn't leave, or the diligent student to enchant her mom, had become an unbreakable habit.

She braced her hands on the shower wall and let the hot water stream over every nook and cranny. She hoped Chase might stay till the new year, but he told her he needed to leave early to get ready for work. She looked at her five fingers. No more than a fistful of days, that's what they had left.

Pouring shampoo into her hand, she quickly washed her hair, rinsed, and grabbed a towel off the rack. A little bit of mascara and lip gloss and clothes finished the job.

Lucky waited by the door, and they walked together back to the kitchen.

Decisions. Decisions. Decisions.

It would take her a year or more to get situated. She could concentrate on her plan, but could she wait for Chase? She was not going to turn into her mother, a woman who spent three-quarters of her life waiting for the love of her life to return home for only a few hours, or days, or weeks.

She wouldn't do it. But could she wait at least a little while for Chase?

Yes, but not for long, breathed into her mind.

"That's a severe look. Anything I can help with?" Chase asked, walking into the room.

Freshly shaved, hair still damp from the

shower, he looked scrumptious. In fact, he looked downright edible. No man should look that handsome.

"Only thinking. No worries."

"You sure? 'Cause you looked like you were trying to solve world hunger over there."

His attempt to lighten her mood didn't go unappreciated. "You're right. Today's Christmas. It's a day to celebrate. We have five days together. You ready?"

His weary eyes met hers. "You never said where we were going."

"You'll see," she offered cryptically, on purpose, knowing he didn't like hanging out with a bunch of people. But Harold, Maggie, and Jenna were people he knew, she reassured herself. "I'll feed Lucky and then we can go."

After a quick dump of food and refresh of water, Ashley headed for the garage.

Chase followed closely behind. "Did you ever find a buyer for your dad's tools?"

The way he licked his lips when he

neared the equipment hung neatly on the walls was a reminder her dad still hadn't responded to her request. The tools were on the do-not-sell list, but she didn't know what he planned to do with the various sets. Another text message might get a response. Then again, maybe not. For all she knew, her dad might not be in the country.

"Not yet. I should know something soon."

He got into the passenger seat of the truck. "I bet it will be sad to see everything go."

"Yep. That's why Jenna offered to help me move. I'm having trouble deciding what to keep, trash, or leave behind."

"She's good people."

"Yes, she is."

She backed the truck out of the garage, closed the door, and backed down the snow-piled drive into a typical crisp Colorado morning. Blue sky. Barely above freezing. Over a foot of snow on the ground. When they drove around the bend, a group of female mule deer perked their ears in their direction.

"Speaking of people, how's Bobby's family holding up?"

He hesitated and stared out the window. For several seconds, she thought he might not have heard her, or didn't care to answer the question, but then his expression changed and his tension eased like a bathtub emptying of water.

"They're good. His younger sister's home from school. She'll be entering the military next summer. Her parents aren't happy about her joining, and asked if I'd watch out for her."

Her airways closed in and her heart beat a bit harder. The image of another woman in his life made her want to grow a set of talons. Three-inch claws, like the horned owl in her backyard.

"Huh. Bobby's sister's joining the Marines," she managed to say, without adding the *oh-how-convenient* jealousy.

"The Navy, actually. She wants to be an

intelligence officer, so she should pretty much stay stateside."

"And you're going back to see her before you leave."

"Ashley?" He tapped a finger on her thigh. "Pull over, please."

"Why?"

"You know why."

Crossing the bridge into town, she decided to postpone his request. "We're almost there."

She parked in front of the general store. A closed sign hung in the store window, but a half dozen cars butted up against the parking rails. Ashley parked her dad's truck in an empty spot near a pine tree and turned off the ignition.

With hands in her lap, she tried to calm her hyperactive thoughts. She didn't have a right to be possessive. Chase wasn't hers. But dang it. The idea of someone, anyone, in his life but her didn't seem right.

"Okay. I admit. I'm a tad bit jealous." She pushed out the brave admission.

"A bit?"

"Well, not a bit. A bit is a skinny slice of pie. I'm Jenna's entire pie rack."

The crack of laughter made her turn and give him a soft backhand. "That's not funny."

He sobered quickly. "No. No, it's not. Jealousy from a woman I've been trying to convince is special, and the only person I want to spend time with, is somewhat ironic, though. Don't you think?"

No. Maybe. Fine. "I suppose."

Chase unclicked his seatbelt, then hers, and pulled her over until her face was inches from his. "I mean it, Ash. There isn't anyone else. And I'm beginning to doubt there ever would be. You're kind, and giving, and like no one I've ever met before."

"Does this mean you're not interested?"

"Oh, I'm interested, all right. Interested in hauling you into my lap and kissing you until any jealous thought leaves your body. When I go back to Bobby's, I'll be returning his truck and then going straight to the airport. I'm not interested in anyone but you."

Her mouth formed into a small O. He put a finger beneath her chin until her gaze connected with his. "I wish you knew how much I do care about you."

Care, but not love.

"I care about you, too." She pushed away from his chest. "So much so, we'd better get in there before we fog the windows and Harold comes to drag us out of the truck."

Grabbing the door handle, she launched from the truck before she responded with something foolish, like the L-word.

That pivotal sentiment, even if it was Christmas, didn't belong in her vocabulary.

Not yet, anyway.

"READY TO GO?" Ashley peered in, then reached over the tailgate of the truck.

Chase snatched the oversized box of gifts before she lifted something she could barely wrap her arms around. He hip-checked the door and then stepped aside, waiting for her directions.

She pointed. "We need to go round the back."

Hearing Christmas music and laughter, he braced and focused on the back of Ashley's head while they climbed the outside steps. Ashley didn't wait to enter. She walked right in to be embraced in the cheers and greetings of a crowd.

"Here let me take your coats." Claudia held out her arms, and Harold removed the large box from Chase's arms and set it aside.

A mass of warm bodies crowded closer while Chase backed toward the door, scanning the room, targeting any movement. His palms itched and the muscles at the back of his neck tightened. His vision turned gray at the edges and began to close in.

Ashley whispered something to Harold, then stepped in front of Chase, sliding her hands into his while Harold gathered his wife to his side, creating a barrier.

His mind went postal and saw a press of Afghan people crowding in, and someone shouted, *he's got a bomb!* He looked, searching the crowd, reading faces, looking for movement. His training kicked in. He reached for his com to radio in his position and put his guys on alert. But the radio was missing.

He felt a tug on his arm, and he looked down.

Ashley squeezed his fingers. "I'm here. I've got you. You're safe."

He focused on her face. The wave of sensory overload receded. Blood returned to his extremities, and his breath evened as he looked into her reassuring eyes.

Harold's concerned and knowing expression connected to his. "How 'bout we take a walk?"

Chase shook his head. "No. I'm good. Give me a sec to get my bearings."

He squeezed the muscle in his shoulder

to get the tension to release and then swallowed, and swallowed again, to get the imagined desert dust from his mouth.

He blew out a long, tentative breath. "Let's get this over with."

The sadness tightening Ashley's beautiful lips tugged at him. "There's no reason we need to stay. I messed up again. I don't want you to feel forced to be here. We can go back to the house. We can celebrate Christmas together, the two of us."

She turned to Harold, but Chase held her back. He closed his eyes. "I want to stay, but I need your help. You somehow manage to keep me grounded."

Her hand flattened on his chest above his heart. "You sure?"

Nothing could get past the rock in his throat, so he nodded and hoped the gesture was convincing.

For the next several hours, he plastered on a smile, shook a dozen or more hands, and found trivial things to talk about while she moved him from person to person. Most of the people he'd already met or seen around town, yet he constantly sought to find her. Just seeing her was enough to ground him again.

Of course he recognized Jenna. Maggie and Claudia fussed over the overabundance of food while Harold and Bill Mason were off in a corner swapping stories. Ashley had introduced him to a couple of dozen more people before he figured out this was the gathering of the misfits—those who didn't have family nearby. In the city, a single individual might be forced to pass the day alone, but not here. He took a seat at a quiet corner table with his back against the wall so he could observe. Ashley brought him a plate of food, then another. For the next hour, he ate until his belly was full to near bursting.

Ashley leaned back in her seat, then turned and glared at the Christmas tree branch poking her in the head. He laughed and helped her untangle her hair from the prickly blue pine tree sporting an assortment of ornaments. He grinned when he noticed the tuna fish can wrapped in Christmas paper with a glittered cotton ball and a tree in the center. A couple of kids sat nearby, pointing at packages, speculating.

Ashley laid her head on his shoulder. "I wanted to make this a special Christmas for you."

"I'm not used to celebrating things."

"Living here, a person gets used to it. This town celebrates when a kid learns to tie their shoes."

A clandestine joy stole across her face, and he reveled in her teasing nature. When he left in five days, he'd be leaving a piece of himself behind. He wanted to find a mason jar and fill it with her caring spirit and laughter, like the rare bugs he used to capture and study as a boy. He gathered her close.

Jenna, in her usual direct manner, took a seat across the table. "So lovebirds, ready for some unwrapping?"

Chase was so ready for unwrapping, but he didn't think Jenna meant Ashley. Heat flooded his cheeks. He cleared his throat and sat up.

Jenna's face sparkled with delight, and she gave him a lopsided grin. "Better buck up because everyone's coming over."

Chase looked over her shoulder, and sure enough, everyone was headed toward the Christmas tree to take a seat. For the next several minutes, Harold moved from table to table, depositing gifts in front of the attendees. If Chase had been smart, he would have taken off when Jenna told him what was coming, but he hadn't been quick enough. When a wrapped gift landed in front of him, complete with a bright red bow and Christmas sparkles on top, a ribbon of tension encircled his neck and threatened to cut off his air supply. He surveyed the room.

Ashley nudged him. "Don't worry. Before we left, I labeled the tags from both of us."

Typical, generous Ashley. He knew people weren't stupid, but he wouldn't ruin the moment. He gave himself a stern reprimand and tried to relax back into the chair. He'd accept what the others offered, thank them, and figure out a way to make it up to them somehow.

Claudia approached carrying an antique crystal pitcher, the one he'd seen in Ashley's mother's crystal cabinet. The woman had a suspiciously damp shine in her eyes.

"I can't accept this."

Ashley returned the hug. "Yes, you can, and you will. The bankers will come to take the house in a little over a week, and I can't take much with me. I have no place to put it, and I want you to have it. Plus, you loaned me your camper."

"You are a dear." Claudia held the pitcher to her chest. Then the round, cheery woman pointed at the parcels in front of him. "Aren't you going to open your presents?"

"Yes, ma'am."

He ripped at the thin paper, then opened the plain white box. His breath hitched. He stared at Claudia and Harold. Astonished. A warm appreciation filled his soul. He picked up the heavy, round metal Vietnam coin and flipped it over. He'd been about to tell the man he'd come to respect that he couldn't possibly keep the precious gift, but he changed his mind. No Marine would give up his gear or the things he treasured unless absolutely sure.

He placed his other hand on the top of the coin. "Thank you. I'm truly humbled."

The older man nodded, and the couple walked away. When the right moment came, he'd find Harold to properly express his appreciation in private.

Ashley hadn't opened her gift, but she was looking at him the way Lucky did when waiting for a treat. Eager. Anticipating. She wanted him to open his gifts first. He held his breath while opening the next package, and laughed when the sardine label appeared. In a few minutes, a pack of gum, a chocolate bar, and a can of soup lay stacked in front of him. He chuckled imagining Harold gathering and enjoying selecting the grocery goods. He surveyed the spoils of the day then picked up the small rectangular box. For so long he'd believed no one wanted him but the military. In a few short weeks, he'd been proven wrong.

Ashley slid another box in front of him.

He eyed the package. "What's this?"

"Open it and see."

The red ribbon-wrapped package seemed too perfect to unwrap, but she waited, and he didn't want to disappoint her. He didn't rip the paper, instead taking his time to untie the bow and remove the tape. Pulling back the tissue paper, he found an antique hunting knife lying on a bed of cotton, a piece of paper nestled beneath.

Ashley's excited, impatient fingers took the document from the box. "I could only find a couple of pictures of my grandfather with the knife, but I know you like to know the history of where things come from. Plus, it's small enough for you to keep with you."

She handed him sheets of paper with old black and white photographs and words neatly typed at the edges. He unsnapped the sheath and removed the blade, noting the weight and balance. Ashley leaned in, pointing out specifics of the knife, but the smell of her hair and the press of her breast against his arm played havoc with his ability to hear her.

She turned her face to his. "I wanted you to have something of me, of my family, when you leave."

At that moment, the world slipped away, and he couldn't fathom even being a block away from this woman. Something about her made him forget the commitments and responsibilities he had.

For only a moment, life couldn't have been more perfect.

CHAPTER TWENTY

*A*shley struggled through the door of Gwen's shop, the stack of her mom's clothing reaching above her chin.

"Hey," Gwen said, coming from the back room.

"Howdy." Ashley lifted and plopped the mound on the counter. "I found the missing button to the short jacket." She placed the designer fastener on the edge of the cash register.

"Heard your man is leaving tomorrow."

Her man? Guess he is. "Yep, Chase leaves tomorrow. I can't believe the time flew by so fast. He needs to return a truck to a friend's parents and then catch a flight back to North Carolina." She glanced out the store front window. "There's a storm moving in. Hate to say it, but I'm wondering if he should leave tonight to avoid the weather."

"Make sure you tell him to stop by and see Jenna to pick up some pastries before he leaves. Might tempt him to come back someday."

Jealousy squeezed her heart. She hoped something besides Jenna's pastries would bring Chase back.

"Did I hear my name?" Jenna asked, entering the store. Gwen's face lit up when she paused beside her.

"Hey, Gwen." Jenna returned a genuine smile. "Made some chocolate drops this morning. I know you like them warm." She handed Gwen a pastry box and turned to Ashley. "Saw your VW out front. About time that man of yours let you loose. Did you come into town to try out my new ginger spice cookie recipe?" Her brows drew into a severe line. "Before you say no, I should warn you—I'll let the air out of your tires if you don't."

Ashley laughed. "Nice threat. Chase decided to go for his last snowmobile run of the season before leaving tomorrow. He's been working hard, helping me pack. He came here for some R&R, but all he's done is work, and he still seems a bit restless. I picked up the ingredients to make lasagna for dinner since he loves the stuff, and I can eat the leftovers if he leaves any." She again looked out at the clouds rolling in. "Weather forecast says there's a storm a-brewin'. I was just telling Gwen, I think Chase might be smart to leave tonight."

Jenna slipped her arm through Ashley's. "Is that your excuse for making him go so he doesn't break your heart?"

Jenna always had to get to the basic ingredients of life's challenges. "Whether he leaves today or tomorrow, I don't think it will make much difference. It will hurt either way."

Gwen's facial features softened in a puppy-cuddly kind of way. "Have a chocolate cookie. Chocolate helps everything."

Ashley reached up to hug her. "Thanks for being such a great friend."

Not comfortable with the attention, Gwen picked up the top piece of clothing. "I'll stop by later for a taste of those cookies. I want to get these clothes sorted and priced. On consignment, same as before?"

"Yes, if you don't mind."

"Gotcha. Let me get to work on this. See you two in a bit."

Taking the hint, Ashley moved toward the door.

Jenna gave her a scrutinizing glare when they stopped at the edge of the sidewalk. "You have that 'haven't slept in days sex goddess' thing going on, but that 'baby deer whose mom's gone missing' look has me concerned."

"Don't worry about me."

"That's my job, sister, and I'm glad I spotted your car. Maggie wants to offer you a job at the café. And one of her renters moved out. It's not much, needs some paint, but the cabin rent is cheap. You'll have somewhere to live until you decide what to do next. Maggie says she'll let Lucky stay with you. You can start moving in now if you want."

Laughter and tears threatened. "That's awesome. We'll be neighbors. But waitressing? Me?"

"If I learned to do it, so can you."

"I know Maggie's doing better at the café, but not well enough to hire someone until the summer, when tourism starts up again. Thanks, but I refuse to transfer my problems."

"The Bailiff sisters are looking for some home-care help. They were saying the other day they needed to find someone who can open medicine bottles and unpack groceries."

If she hadn't sold her car before she moved home from San Diego, she might have considered it. With the truck, any money made would be gobbled up in fuel. And her mom's VW Bug might not make it much longer. Plus, the spry Bailiff sisters might be more than she could handle.

"Jenna, I appreciate—"

"What about—"

"Stop."

Ashley couldn't take any more charity. So many people had offered help, help she couldn't ever repay.

With a place to live and store things, she could sell on eBay, and that gave her room to breathe. Enough room that she could afford to spend the next few hours with Chase until he left.

As much as it hurt, he was leaving, and she had to accept it. And she didn't need to be the forty-pound rucksack making his moving on harder. She should encourage him to go tonight before the snow hit. Encourage him to live the life he wanted, but let him know her decision to wait was part of her plan.

"Tell Maggie I'll take the cabin for thirty

days. I'm going to pay rent, and I'll paint the place if she wants. It's the least I can do." She opened the driver's side door.

"Then what?"

"I still have to find a job. Denver might still be my only choice. If I didn't have those student loans, I would be able to start a business here, but I don't think I can pay rent, the loans, eat, plus start a business."

Jenna pulled on her arm. "Ash, I know I'm selfish. But I want you to stay. Permanently."

"Sometimes life doesn't always work out the way we want. Tell you what. Why don't I come by tomorrow after Chase is gone, and you can ply me with your cookies? We can look at options and sift through the classifieds together. How's that?"

"Well, hell. How am I supposed to stay neutral? You know I'm only going to pick the ones that mean you have to stay in Elkridge." She let out a long sigh, like one of her precious soufflés had deflated in the oven.

"Yeah, I know." Ashley reached for her

friend's hand and felt the transfer of love and concern.

"See you tomorrow."

"Maybe. I want to see Chase off," she said, sliding behind the wheel.

On the drive home, Ashley spotted a couple of foxes frolicking in a snow-covered field. A hawk circled overhead in the fluffy-cloud Colorado sky, waiting for an unsuspecting rabbit or mole or mouse to venture out of hiding. Every curve of the snowplowed road she knew like the freckles on the back of her hand. The day couldn't be more perfect, but the black clouds over the Ridge reminded her things could change quickly.

Chase had packed up Bobby's truck in the morning, so it would only be a matter of convincing him to get going before the expected storm hit. He'd have a handful of good driving hours on clear, dry roads. Tomorrow, the asphalt would be snow-packed and icy. If she hustled him out the door, he could still get the Hershams to drop him off in Denver. Maybe do some sightseeing before boarding the plane back to reality.

She parked on the far right to make sure he had plenty of room to clear her truck when he left. Lucky's enthusiastic greeting helped keep her heart from shattering. Laying her keys on the counter, she called Chase's name, but got no response. While she scratched the dog's ears, she listened, but heard nothing. After opening the garage door, she searched for her father's snowmobile. The smaller, more manageable sled her mom used still sat on the storage ramp, but the other one was gone. The dog ran ahead, his nose tunneling through the snow, then leapt through the drifts to pee on his favorite tree. When she stopped at the shed, he raced back and nudged her leg for attention.

"No, Lucky. I can't play now."

The dog smelled the single set of tracks leading up the back trail to the ridge. He raced up the hill, nose to the ground. Ashley called him, and he reluctantly returned, but then immediately started wandering off again. Just over the ridge, the clouds looked dark and menacing.

Chase, where are you? You need to go, now.

Moving toward the house, she called the dog, but he stayed at the crest of the hill, insistently barking.

"No. I don't have time to play. Come on." She patted her leg and entered the house, knowing Lucky would follow.

Hitting autodial on her cell phone, she listened to the phone ring, an echo coming from inside the house. She followed the ringtone. Chase's cell sat on the counter, recharging. She considered the clouds, the black sheet of heavy rain and snow moving in, while frustration chipped away at her resolve. She retraced her steps to the back door. Lucky refused to come in, so she decided to leave him outside for a bit.

Unable to stand still, she retreated to her mother's room to pack a few more boxes and wait.

With each sweater, skirt, or pair of shoes she packed, she resolved to shed the past. Last night, she'd agreed to meet halfway, for now. She'd friend him on Facebook. Write him letters. Answer his calls. But instinct told her long distance had a way of destroying most relationships. She had witnessed the effects. She didn't want to be pessimistic, but in her gut, she felt it was only a matter of time before the intimate relationship unraveled, settling into a call here and there, maybe a Christmas card now and then.

Lucky's bark drew her attention outdoors. The first flakes of the expected snow were already drifting past the window. She sighed. She'd missed the time slot for sending Chase on his way. She might as well start preparing the lasagna.

When she opened the back door, the brisk wind chilled her core. "Come on, Lucky, it's cold. If you're going to stay out, I need to put your coat on."

The dog stood at the edge of the deck and

didn't move. When she patted her leg to get his attention, he refused to budge, then moved to the dual tracks in the snow and laid down in the ruts. His penetrating look put her on notice. He whined, his body wiggling with energy, wanting so badly to run. He looked at the ridge. In a moment of clarity, she understood what the dog had been trying to communicate.

Chase.

The sun moved lower in the sky with each passing minute. She rushed into the house, retrieved Lucky's coat and harness, and started out the back door, but then hesitated. Her dad had made her take a mountain rescue course before allowing her out on the snowmobile, and launching a rescue mission didn't mean taking off with a dog, on the sled, alone.

She deliberated. She needed to make a decision.

Ashley grabbed both phones and started dialing. Within forty minutes, trucks with snow equipment lined her drive. She'd already positioned her machine, run through a checklist, and worked out how to rig the dog to her sled. His nose might be needed, and she wouldn't leave him behind. Climbing on the rig, she started the machine.

"Whoa, where you going?" Harold asked.

She lifted her goggles. "The snow's already started covering the tracks. I can't wait."

"You're not going until we're ready."

Harold made a good rescue coordinator because he was a good people person, and he was respected enough so people usually listened, but his lip-flapping was wasting precious daylight. She wished Jack Burke would show up soon. As head of the volunteer rescue team, he would see reason. Standing around talking was a waste of time. Just when she was about to tell Harold to shove his head in a snow bank, Rivers Black, the local tracker, stepped in. The resident Native American, part-Cherokee, he could find nearly anything that moved on the ridge.

Rivers studied her with an intensity that made her skin twitch. "Do you have flares and the required emergency equipment?"

"Yep, packed and checked."

"Keep your cell on, and be careful with that dog," Rivers responded, and turned to Harold. "Let her go. She called us and waited until we got here. Plus, she knows this ridge as well as anyone."

Relief eased the knots between her shoulder blades. "Thanks for the help. I'll be careful."

Without waiting, she locked knees and arms around the dog. Guilt weighed her down. Why had she waited?

If Lucky hadn't been so persistent, she still might be waiting. Speeding over the terrain, she scanned the horizon. Rescue and survival techniques played like a YouTube video in her head. By the time she reached the top of the ridge, the wind had hidden the tracks, and she switched on the headlight.

With adrenaline flowing through her, keeping her tired body alert, she paused at the top of the ridge and looked back. The rest of the crew had begun their search. The minutes floated by like the snow in the wind.

Lucky tilted his head back and licked her jaw underneath her helmet.

She turned off her machine and lifted her visor. "Chase," she hollered, and then waited. She yelled again, and again. The dog's ears perked, then flattened. Neither she nor Lucky caught a sign or scent.

"Where could you be?" she whispered.

The memory of their first trip jogged her mind, and she started the sled and turned into the setting sun. Hoping and praying her instincts were right.

CHAPTER TWENTY-ONE

Chase's entire being fizzed at the power of the snow machine between his legs and the sting of the wind on his cheeks. Racing along the snow-covered trails expanded and freed his soul.

All afternoon, a ruthless restlessness had tracked and haunted him like a shadow. Now, he wadded the uneasiness into a tight ball and tossed the gnawing feeling over his shoulder, breathing in the richness of freedom.

He was packed, the trucked filled with gas, so there was nothing left to do but say goodbye to Ashley. And he'd do anything to delay that knife in the gut as long as possible. Ashley had asked if he wanted to run into town with her, but he couldn't find it in him to say goodbye to one more person. Saying the words landed like a fist to his jugular each time, and he couldn't bear one more emotional blow since he had yet to say good-bye to Ashley.

The last three-and-a-half weeks had created a fishbowl ambiance, the swimming around and around in circles, bouncing off the side of the glass bowl, questioning his judgment over and over again. Losing Bobby, returning to the States, the funeral, bumping into Ashley...his emotions reeled from taking one punch after another. His brain wrestled with his heart about what future he should choose.

Finally, the turmoil overwhelmed him.

He needed to experience the rush of speeding across the snow-covered landscape, if only for a little while. With a twist of the wrist, he propelled the snow sled faster.

Zipping across the open field, he headed through an Aspen grove toward the next ridge. Clearing the first hill, he climbed the next, feeling the euphoria. The snow deepened, the hill grew steeper, and the path between the trees narrowed. His thoughts returned to Ashley, and the way she'd looked that morning after he woke her to make love. She...

Dhuk-dhuk-dhuk-dhuck. *Machine gun. Fuck.* Dhuk-dhuk-dhuk-dhuck.

Tips of tree branches splintered to his right.

Dhuk-dhuk-dhuk-dhuck-dhuck-dhuck.

He steered left. Suddenly, the handlebars jerked, ripping his hands off the snowmobile controls.

Weightlessness, tumbling, confusion.

Pain.

Time stalled.

The pale blue sky and trees above whirled dizzyingly while his gloved hand wiped snow from his goggles. He blinked, trying to stop the rotating sensation while an elephant sat on his chest. He lifted his head. No, not an elephant, a five hundred-pound snowmobile. He worked hard to drag in a deep breath, but couldn't. He dropped his head and groaned. Dismay crowded his thoughts, but he fought back with ingrained training.

Think.

Stay Calm.

Plan.

Claustrophobia made his mind race. He couldn't move. Mentally, he retraced the ride. His mind registered the hidden mound under the snow. Ashley had warned him. He should have been paying attention. He should have stuck to the wider roads and trails. He should have stayed away from the same ridge where the last shots had been fired.

The wind picked up, and he hoped it wouldn't wipe his snowmobile tracks away. He shoved at the machine, frustrated. It didn't budge. A slow shadow of dread engulfed him.

He must survive long enough for someone to find him.

Someone, anyone, but who?

This was his own damn fault. In a hurry to get away, he hadn't left a note with a location or path, or any indication of when he'd be back. He knew better. There were a few other sets of tracks, but nothing fresh. He wanted to be alone, and he'd gotten his wish.

Totally alone.

Pain in his right leg sent tremors up his spine. At least he could still feel his legs. Or could he? He couldn't see below his chest, so he concentrated on wiggling his toes. The left foot responded, but not the right. *One foot. Good sign.* It was a comfort to know the snow-covered rock that had launched him backward off the snowmobile hadn't broken his back.

Was he bleeding?

A scared breath shuddered out. His lung capacity had been squeezed into a small space. He pushed angrily, and pushed again.

Drops of sweat beaded on his upper lip. Sweat, a deadly sign of hypothermia. His body temperature had dropped, and a cold chill triggered body tremors.

Shit. This can't be happening.

Putting pressure on his left arm, he leaned to the right and struggled to reach the nylon-padded shoulder strap of his backpack. The bone-crushing pain doubled, and black spots blocked his vision.

He lay back, his mind working to convince his body to ignore the searing ache and keep trying. He lifted again, pulling the strap. Several more tries, and the bag released from beneath his body. He removed his gloves and tugged on the zippers to open the sack. His large black helmet weighed heavy on his neck. He dropped his head to rest while he used his fingers to search the bag. Water. He lifted the plastic bottle to his goggled face. His eyelids closed and he sent a silent prayer to the heavens. Tipping back the container of precious water, he steadily drank until the bottle appeared half-empty.

Refilling the container with snow, he pushed the container toward the hot engine, hoping to melt the snow, knowing dehydration and hypothermia were his biggest concerns. Exhaustion blanketed him, but he needed to keep moving. Moving and thinking. He couldn't give up.

A Marine wouldn't give up.

He pulled the gloves over stiff fingers and spread the poncho liner over his upper half. His mind registered his worst fear, and he looked toward the sky. A snowflake landed on his goggles, setting off mind-melting hysteria. He'd already run the gamut of emotions—disgust for not being more alert, anger when he'd been unable to move the snowmobile trapping his body, then acceptance and the need to think and plan.

Despair circulated in his mind, trying to convince his body of defeat.

He'd had enough training to realize being trapped in more than a foot of snow under a gigantic piece of equipment, and with a storm moving in, couldn't be much worse.

Short bursts of breath partially filled his lungs. He fought for consciousness. With each passing minute, the battle to retain body heat intensified. He wiggled his fingers and the toes of his left foot, the snow eating away at what little heat he managed to generate. When he tried to yank his body free, the intense, burning pain nearly shoved him over the edge into unconsciousness.

The shadows from the trees lengthened, and the sun had about run out of steam for the day. The cold coaxed him toward slumber, but his training fought off sleep, since he knew only hypothermia and death waited at the end of the tunnel. He stretched the poncho, shielding as much of his body as he could from the surface wind, and worked to center his mind.

The earliest childhood memories clicked through his mind like a slideshow. Racing downhill on a cobbled-together bike, the hot summer sun pounding on his back. Falling in the lake, barely knowing how to swim. Camping with a foster care organization.

Boot camp. Staring at the television in horror the morning the Twin Towers fell. Each memory highlighting a cherished moment, a disappointment, or an image that never quite got erased.

The image of Ashley's face appeared with the memory of their first kiss. He'd been so shocked by the sizzling energy, he'd had to make sure it, and she, were real. His mind told him to walk away then, leave town, not look back, but somehow he couldn't quite move on. Right now, he wanted her soft lips on his.

Black dots filled his vision, and he tried focusing on dancing drops of snow. His delirious, agony-filled mind created a ballet of fairies fluttering in and out among the branches. Laughing, playing, swirling, dancing. Bobby's image appeared at the edge of the clearing. Chase blinked, his mind denying the illusion but craving the comfort of a friend.

Bobby crouched beside him. *Fight, Marine. You fight. Don't you give up.*

Chase laughed, a crazy, *this is bullshit* laugh. Here he was. A Marine. In Colorado. As a person who'd signed his life over to the military, he never considered he'd die on U.S. soil. He'd never contemplated dying alone in a heap of snow.

"Not sure I'm going to make it this time, my friend."

Suck it up, man. You still have things to do. It won't be long. Have some faith.

How long had it been? Fifteen minutes? Fifty?

Chase stretched his arm toward Bobby. He needed to connect to something, to hold on, but the shadowed image kneeling in the light faded.

More time passed. He tried holding onto consciousness, but wasn't quite sure he succeeded.

His thoughts drifted to Ashley and Harold and Jenna. His new friends. His new family. It really sucked that the minute he believed he'd found his paradise, he was going to die. At least he'd gotten to feel what it was like to be part of something bigger. Maybe this was Bobby's final gift.

Warm air blew in his face. He moved his head toward the sensation. A nudge of his head, accompanied by a soft whine, roused him. Another burst of warmth drifted across his face. Not an illusion. Chase fought for consciousness, but the effort was beyond his strength until an angel called his name.

"Chase?"

A yearning so strong and profound rolled throughout every limb. "Ashley?"

His lips cracked open to form her name, but no sound emerged. He'd give anything to see her one more time—to hold her hand. He'd tell her he loved her. He wouldn't hold back, or wait. He'd tell her with his entire being how much she meant to him.

"Chase? Wake up."

At the demand, he cracked his eyelids open.

A concerned, scared face appeared. "You're such an ass. Don't you know not to go in the mountains without your cell? What were you thinking?"

I was thinking about you.

Her voice drifted away. Another illusion. An aching loneliness filled his soul until warmth came to his fingers. He frantically held on, feeling a stinging and painful sensation return. After a tough negotiation with his mind, he willed his head to turn and got his reward.

"Ashley?"

"Chase. Help is coming. You better hold on. Hold on, please." Warm lips touched his. "Don't you dare leave me."

The distress in her voice moved him. He wanted to open his arms and pull her to him, but he couldn't quite figure out where his arms were. He could track her with his eyes, but that was all. A weight pressed onto his right shoulder. Heat. Glancing down, he recognized the hunter green wool coat and the black fur. Trusting golden eyes met his before he slipped back into the darkness.

His dream of seeing Ashley had come

true.

He needed to tell her something, but the words drifted away with the snowflakes.

His throat tightened to push out the word *love*, but he couldn't hold on.

Bone-chilling cold replaced the warmth and tore him away.

Far away.

"CHASE? CHASE, WAKE UP."

Ashley's heart pounded to a stop.

Removing her gloves, she reached, frantic to find a pulse. She forced herself to focus on anything other than the dried blood on his face. The swelling and bruising reminded her of the time the high school quarterback broke his nose playing football. Her heart kick-started again, pounding a frenzied cadence, pushing her to act.

She'd figured her life couldn't get worse.

She'd been wrong.

Apprehension restricted the flow of air reaching her lungs. Finding a weak beat of Chase's heart, she lifted her backpack from her shoulders. Using the emergency radio Rivers had given her, she relayed her GPS coordinates and asked Harold to call for a medevac helicopter. Lucky lifted his head and whined with urgency, but she couldn't take the time to calm him. Chase needed the dog's body heat. Her dad's voice filled her mind—*stabilization, warmth, hydration.* She opened her pack and broke four hot packs. Lifting the poncho liner, she unzipped Chase's snowsuit and shoved a packet under each arm and as far down his chest as she could reach. Gently lifting each arm, she checked for signs of damage, careful to not move his neck or spine, rubbing and warming as she went. Hearing the echo of engines off the hill, she considered the anxious dog.

"Lucky, get help." The dog's ears lifted, his head tilted to the side. Ashley threw her arm wide and pointed to the tree-covered ridge. "Go, fetch."

Fetch. Sit. Stay. She hadn't had time to teach the dog any commands. She hoped he understood because she couldn't leave Chase. With the wind now blowing snow into the air, there was literally no visibility, making the search and rescue job even more difficult. She couldn't save him on her own. She needed help.

"Lucky, fetch."

The dog launched to his feet and disappeared beyond the snowmobile, all her hopes going with him.

She removed the energy drink from her pack but hesitated to lift Chase's head, concerned his immobility might mean a spinal injury.

"Chase? Open your eyes, you jerk. You can't do this to me. Come on." She waited. "Come on, Chase."

A flutter of movement.

"That's it. You can do this."

Chase's arms lifted and sporadically

moved in the air. She grasped his gloved hand and rubbed it against hers. His pain-filled eyes opened, and he rolled his head.

Monitoring his movement, she made a decision. Unscrewing the bottle top, she slid her hand under his neck and held the bottle to his cracked lips. He choked on the first sip, but managed to swallow a little more before turning away. She released his head at Lucky's frantic bark and the buzz of machines cresting the hill, and then several snowmobiles appeared and glided to a stop next to them. Discussions took place all around her, but she never left Chase's side.

Within minutes, the snowmobile trapping Chase was lifted from his body, and Jack Burke took command, providing trained medical attention. He raced toward her, his booted feet crunching through the snow.

Bright red drops splattered across the snow like paint flung onto a canvas. Jack hovered over Chase's twisted leg, which was rotated at an odd angle. The bile in Ashley's stomach churned, making her look away. Jack relayed Chase's vital signs to the dispatcher, who transmitted the information to the helicopter crew. Jack continued to work on stabilizing Chase's lower half while she hovered over his swollen face.

Inspecting each inch of visible skin, she grew nauseous with worry. "Chase, look at me."

His eyes rolled uncontrollably, not able to connect to anything solid. He groaned. "Ashley?"

"I'm here."

"I'm sorry."

The surrender, the hopelessness in his voice produced a mind-numbing panic. Frantic, she tugged off her gloves and touched his face. He couldn't give up. By some miracle, she'd found him. He couldn't let go. Not now.

"Chase?" She pinched his chin to get him to focus. "Don't you dare give me that snivel, Marine. Your job is to stay conscious." She squeezed his jaw again. His lips contorted.

"You better do your part, or I'm going to take your balls and put them through a meat grinder. I'll do it, too."

Jack grunted, and Rivers coughed behind her, but she paid them no heed.

She leaned in, her lips touching cold, clammy skin. "You have a mission, Marine—stay awake. Do you hear me?"

His lips thinned in a straight line, almost like he knew the end of the line was coming. "Chase. Don't. Don't go there."

His glazed eyes finally managed to connect with hers. "You'd make a good drill sergeant."

She delighted in his response. "Is that so?" Her mind eased.

The constant metronome of time ticked by, like a steady drop of water in a steel sink, one second at a time, never rushing. Finally, the thumping, rumbling sounds of chopper blades filled the valley. She covered Chase's face with the poncho and her body to protect him from blowing snow and debris, but within minutes, she had to relinquish her position beside him to let the professionals do their job.

Lucky ran to her, wanting another command, but she didn't have any more instructions to give. She stood frozen in place. She could only hold the dog's collar and watch the emergency crew immobilize Chase's neck and body, prepare him for transport, and load him into the chopper.

An eternity passed before the helicopter rotated and tilted east. When the aircraft disappeared over the horizon, she prayed for another miracle.

Keep him alive.

The men moved off to confer in a small group. Her gaze swept over the mangled machine. She dropped to a squat and rubbed Lucky's chest.

"You're a good boy. You found him for me." Lucky licked her face and nudged her hair.

And it had been all Lucky's doing. Twenty minutes into the race to find Chase, the tracks had disappeared. She'd circled the area, drawing wider and wider circles in the snow, working to find a clue. Then the taut muscles holding Lucky had cramped, and she couldn't continue. Forced to stop, she'd stood, pounding her fist into the cramped thigh muscles, her mind begging the pain to stop.

She hadn't had time for cramps or weakness.

Suddenly Lucky leapt from the seat in front of her and disappeared into the trees. The fear of losing him as well had been what led her to Chase.

Now Chase had been found, she felt lost. A shadow fell across her path.

Harold held out his hand to help her up. "It will be dark soon, and a second storm front is moving in. We need to get off this hill. A few of us will come back for your dad's machine tomorrow."

She opened her arms and hugged the man. "Thank you for your help." She tilted her head back. "And for calling in a few big favors on my behalf."

She'd lived up on the ridge long enough to know how things worked. Chase hadn't been gone long enough for a search. The emergency volunteers were there because she'd asked. She'd helped and held enough hands through the night when called upon to know how much effort it took to be always on call.

Jack joined the group. "Chase's been taken to St. Anthony's Hospital."

Ashley searched the man's grave face. "Will he make it?"

Jack turned to look east. "I don't know what internal injuries he has."

Part of her wanted to strangle Jack. The only thing she wanted to hear was that Chase would be fine, that everything would right itself, but Jack never minced words. He saw the world in black and white—no color, no gray.

Chase's injuries, like her grandmother's china, could never be glued back together to make a perfect piece. Life had changed for him, and for her.

She nodded and tightened the straps on her gloves. "We'd better get going."

Harold squeezed her shoulders. "Life has a way of working itself out. Have a little faith."

"I hope you're right because from where I'm standing, it looks to me like life has just crapped on my front porch. Again."

Harold's bushy brows raised and he chuckled. "Stay strong."

She lifted up on her toes and kissed the old man's cheek, and then called for Lucky.

In those frantic moments searching for Chase, Ashley had realized she didn't want to be without him. He simply had to survive. He belonged to the Marines, but he'd captured her heart and held it hostage. She could do nothing but go to him. Care for him. Racing down the ridge to her home, she finally understood her parents' love.

Wherever Chase went in the world, he would have her love.

And she would support him, help him, love him.

CHAPTER TWENTY-TWO

*A*shley gripped the door handle of her dad's truck, concentrating on keeping the drive-thru meal in her stomach. Jenna drove in silence. The city's congested traffic pounded on her nerves.

Get out of the way, people. We have an emergency here.

Her left foot tapped nervously on the floorboard. Not knowing Chase's status was like a nurse aiming a needle at her arm. The anticipation shortened her breath.

When she finally spotted the hospital sign, some of the crushing anxiety dissipated. Jenna dropped her at the hospital entryway and left to park. The front doors swished open into an airy atrium. Any other time, the greenery might have been calming, but not today. She scanned the reception area. Spotting the information desk, she moved swiftly to the counter.

"May I help you?" The elderly woman peered over the purple-rimmed glasses balancing on the tip of her long, straight nose.

"I'm looking for Chase Daniels. He arrived by helicopter," she said, a bit out of breath.

Ashley bit her lip and tapped the counter in time with the receptionist's methodical keystrokes on the computer. Finally, the woman stopped typing and peered through the bottom of her bifocals at the screen. "And your name?"

"Ashley, Ashley Bryant."

"Are you related to the patient?"

Gentle eyes studied her while her mind whirled. *Oh, man, please tell me you'll release his status. I have to know he's all right.* She let out a gradual breath and pushed her shoulders back while her hands, out of sight below the counter, folded into fists.

"Yes, I'm his fiancée," she replied, forcing her mouth into a half-smile, hoping the bullshit sign didn't flash neon red. She'd been in and out of emergency rooms and hospitals enough to know if you weren't related, you didn't get patient information.

A little white lie wouldn't hurt, would it? She'd been fully prepared to barter away half her life to locate and rescue Chase, so she might as well keep trying to bargain with the powers of fate.

"He's not in emergency."

Panic sliced into her heart. Did he die on the way to the hospital? Why hadn't she stayed with him?

The receptionist continued to study her monitor. "Found him. He's in surgery."

A whoosh of air inflated her lungs.

"If you go to the elevators and head

toward the trauma area, the nurses should be able to direct you from there."

Ashley lifted the book she'd laid on the counter and headed for the elevators. She'd spent enough hours watching her mom sleep and knew enough to bring something to read, but she wouldn't be able to concentrate. At least the weight of something in her hand, an object to hold onto, helped.

Entering the elevator, she pushed the trauma floor button and then heard the patter of rapid steps approaching. She extended her arms to hold open the doors and Jenna slipped through.

"What'd they say?" Jenna's halting breath meant she'd run all the way from the parking structure.

"He's in trauma surgery." Heat burned her cheeks. "I told them I'm his fiancée."

Jenna must have noticed the grimace because she gave her a friendly nudge. "Don't worry about it. The shoe fits. It's only a matter of time, so you might as well use it to help now."

Ashley's chest tightened. "Here we go again."

"Yep. And I'll keep at it until you listen. I figure you're destined to be together eventually." Jenna wrapped an arm around her shoulder, a surprisingly intimate touch for her friend. "I think Cupid might have just bonked you on the head."

Ashley glared. "Never knew you for such a romantic. But you might be right."

The elevator doors opened, and Ashley approached the trauma nurse's station. "I'm here to check on a patient."

"Name?" the harried nurse asked politely, although Ashley suspected the woman wanted people to disappear so she could do her job.

"Chase Daniels. I'm his fiancée."

Beside her, Jenna picked up an insurance brochure and flipped through the pages.

"He's still in surgery. I don't have an update. If you'd like to go to the waiting room, I'll have the doctor visit with you as soon as he can."

"Thank you." With the lurch of apprehension limiting her breath, the appreciation wasn't delivered with as much sincerity as she would have liked.

Ashley pulled Chase's cell out of the pocket of her jeans. She'd brought the phone along, thinking she might need to call somebody...the base, a friend, but she realized she didn't really know Chase that well. She didn't know his friends' names. Their phone numbers. His commanding officer's name. Nothing. Nothing a fiancée should know. She didn't even know his password. But she loved him. That was all that mattered.

She and Jenna settled in the far corner of the waiting room, away from the blaring TV. Ashley curled into a chair, waiting and hoping. Feeling small and helpless, she began haggling again with fate for Chase to survive his surgery. And if he did survive, she'd barter again that he wouldn't be as broken as her grandmother's china.

Maggie appeared in the doorway of the waiting room, followed by Harold and Claudia. Claudia shoved an egg salad sandwich, an apple, and a bottle of water into Ashley's lap, and did the same for Jenna. Jack checked in next, and stood off to the side chatting with Maggie.

The last three years, she'd felt completely alone. No one in her life but her and her mom. Day in and day out. Looking around the waiting room, basking in supportive smiles from those she'd come to love and depend on, she realized again how far apart perceptions and reality could be. Whether or not she liked it, she would never be alone again.

When her tension ratcheted so tight she could barely breathe, she stood and paced back and forth while the clock arms swung in circles.

When the door opened, an anticipatory hush came over the room. Ashley immediately hurried toward the blue scrubs-clad doctor. She wiped sweaty palms across the pockets of her jeans before pulling her shirt down and taking a deep breath. Her body had gone numb anticipating the worst outcome.

"Are you Ashley Bryant?"

Even though she'd had a bottle of water shoved in her direction repeatedly over the past two hours, her mouth had gone dry. She couldn't even squeak out her name, so she just nodded.

"Chase's surgery went well. I inserted a titanium rod and a few pins in his right leg. He's in recovery now."

"What about internal bleeding?"

The forty-something doctor's eyes crinkled a bit at the corners. "Other than a broken nose, a cracked rib, and a shattered femur, he's a lucky guy. He might need some cosmetic surgery, but he's stable."

Behind her, a cascade of smiles and hugs began and ended with Jenna wrapping her arm around Ashley's waist, steadying her.

Ashley nodded. "Can I see him?"

"He's in recovery. I'll send a nurse for you when he's in his room."

"He's a Marine. Do you think the military will want to move him soon?"

"I highly doubt it. After he's released from here, he'll have to come back within forty-eight hours for a checkup before I'd be willing to release him for transport to Walter Reed, or some other facility."

"Right, so we need to prepare." Her mind started whirling with to-dos, then came to a screeching halt. "One other thing. Did you check his blood sugar levels? He might be diabetic."

"We did. It's part of our routine blood work panel. And you're right. He's borderline. Good call."

Right. Limited carbs from now on.

"Thank you, Doctor," she managed to say in spite of tears stinging and poking, clamoring for release. The empathetic surgeon laid a hand on her forearm and squeezed before he quietly left the room. Her cheeks warmed and she stared at the door unmoving, needing to be by Chase's side. Right now.

Her caregiver mind kicked into full gear. She had wasted so much time worrying.

"Jenna, I need your help." The word 'help' seemed so foreign, it skidded out of her mouth sideways. When her mom was sick she never asked for help, hated when people interfered. This was different. She drew a deep breath and set her pride aside. "Chase will need some clothes, something to go over his bandages—like track pants. He won't be able to handle stairs, can someone move the bed into the family room so Chase can have easy access, and…"

Jenna's hands warmed her cold, numb fingers. "He's going to be okay."

"I know." Ashley said with an uncertainty she wished would just go away and leave her alone.

"Now sit down and eat something. Here's your sandwich."

Ashley let the doctor's information roll

through her mind, while her jaw moved up and down, chewing on whatever had been shoved into her hand. She swallowed without tasting. Her toes wiggled in her shoes while her gaze lingered on the clock even more than on the doorway leading to Chase. Thirty-three minutes later, the door finally opened.

"Ashley Bryant?"

"Here, I'm here." She waved to the nurse before grabbing her purse and book. She jumped to her feet and then turned back to her friends. She should say something. Express her appreciation, but her mind went blank.

"What are you waiting for?" Jenna shoved her out of neutral and toward the nurse. "Go. Harold and Claudia have already agreed to work on your house. Maggie loaned me her phone to text Gwen. She responded immediately with a *no problem, got the perfect pants*. You ordered, and we delivered."

Jenna tipped her head toward Jack, who'd barely said a word, sitting quietly in the corner with his arms crossed, watching the sports channel. "Maggie already volunteered to bring back a change of clothing, since we know what a stubborn ass you can be, and Jack's going to bring his van when Chase is released. See? You're not the only one who can plan."

She couldn't breathe or hold back the tears any longer. Her shoulders started to shake, and the room folded in. Several sets of arms closed around her, but she couldn't stop the emotions from spilling out. She'd held on so tight for so long. Her heart opened and a tsunami of feelings released to wreak havoc. She leaned into the human embrace.

Jenna gave her shoulder a gentle squeeze. "You've got to stop or you're going to make Jack cry."

Ashley stared at Jack's hardened, resolved face and found the idea of him crying so silly, the rush of water receded. She laughed and brushed her fingers under her eyes. "Thank you," she responded quietly, letting her gratitude ride on the simple words.

She gathered herself, opened the door, and headed down the hall to the room with Chase's name quickly scribbled on the whiteboard by the door, wondering what revelation life would throw at her next.

Ashley stood in the doorway and watched two nurses buzz around Chase checking IVs and an oxygen tube, and placing heart and oxygen monitors on his arm and finger. An average person might cringe at seeing the tubing and machines and bandages. Odd. He looked better than expected, in spite of his pale skin and medical paraphernalia.

One of the nurses paused long enough to acknowledge her, but continued checking for a pulse and recording Chase's vital signs. Ashley moved to the far side of the bed to get out of the way.

White gauze strips padded his nose, separating the black and blue swollen eyes and lips. When the nurse lifted the edges of the sheet to check the bandages, red-black inflamed skin contrasted with the white wrapping and made her curious what lay beneath. After the nurses departed, the room was quiet except for the medical monitors.

Left alone with the machines, she felt the stirrings of a déjà vu nightmare of sitting day after day with her mom, trapped, waiting and wondering when the last breath might come. She could hear the constant, insistent beeping of her mother's heart monitor and the hum of the flow of oxygen.

Bile stung her throat, but she swallowed it back. *Chase's injuries are not the same as a terminal illness.* There'd be no lingering month after month. No withering away to nothing. His strong, virile body would heal.

She scooped her fingers under the palm of his hand, then closed them over the top. The touch of skin on skin, and the heat of their connection, brought her comfort.

An index finger moved first, then his eyelid muscles quivered. She leaned into the bed so he could see her and know he wasn't alone. He looked around the room, clearly confused. The instant he started remembering, his brow furrowed.

She quickly checked the monitors, studying the pulse rate and oxygen levels. She wondered if he needed medication, and squeezed his hand to get his attention. "What's your pain level?"

His lips parted. "Thirsty."

"I can help with that." She took some crushed ice from a cup and carefully slipped one little chip between his swollen lips. When she saw him swallow, she offered another one.

The big, stubborn, confident man she'd come to know appeared shriveled and helpless in the sterile bed. His bruised and battered body lay still, so silent she centered her focus on his chest. She held her breath, praying to see movement. In the past five hours, she'd prayed more than she had in the past three years. Although this time, the request was to save a life rather than to end suffering. When his chest moved, she released her breath on a silent prayer of thanks.

You can do this.

Jenna had been right. Cupid had most likely bonked her on the head. However, Chase's arrow must have missed him altogether. He'd never said he loved her, and if this hadn't happened, he'd be on his way back to North Carolina.

Was it fate?

She'd bear the hurt and pain when the time came. She'd done it before. She'd make it through again. Loving him, she decided, would be worth the risk of heartbreak.

His lips pushed and pulled in a tug of war with his facial muscles to respond to his mind's command. Gradually, his efforts raised his eyelids like a garage door slowly opening and revealing all the emotions trapped inside. "I'm glad you're here."

You scared the shit out of me, you jerk! "Where else would I be? You should try to sleep. Let your body heal."

"You saved me."

Yeah, I did. "Actually, it was Lucky who found you. Without him, we wouldn't have—"

He squeezed her fingers and cut off her nervous rambling. "You came. I'm not alone."

His swollen lips continued to move, but his words got lost when his medicated body was forced into slumber.

Through the night, nurses came and went. Shortly before dawn, Chase's shoulders and head began to move side to side, and his body twitched. She lifted from her chair and put her wrist to his forehead. The lack of heat underneath her skin was a relief.

No fever. Only dreams.

She rubbed the sleep from her worried face and leaned in, placing her lips next to his ear, and whispered. "I've got you. You're safe. Let go and sleep."

Chase's breath eventually eased, and he slid into a light slumber. She straightened his arm. Refusing to let go of his hand, she moved the chair closer to the bedside.

The quiet acceptance of each other's presence provided comfort. The burden of his survival lifted long enough for her mind to ease.

She drifted into sleep with renewed hope.

Humpty Dumpty was cracked and broken, but would mend.

CHAPTER TWENTY-THREE

hase fought off infection and learned to maneuver around on crutches so he could be freed from the uncomfortable bed, white walls, and constant noise.

He awaited further military orders. The doctor expected at least six weeks of physical therapy and another eleven weeks of healing, but warned him each person healed at different rates. Plus, he had a diet change coming. Borderline diabetes meant he wouldn't be eating any of Jenna's famous cinnamon rolls anytime soon.

During the past twenty-four hours, he'd

grown unbearably restless. Ashley told him he reminded her of a Bullmastiff because his face had become permanently wrinkled and grumpy, and he'd begun to growl at people.

Everything in the civilian world had to be a production, made way too complicated by too many opinions. On tour, his life had been simple. Walk, fight, eat, and when necessary, sleep. He craved the simplicity of those days, even if he didn't like the constant moving, dust, and bloodshed.

Being back in Elkridge released the strangling tension that had almost suffocated him the past three days.

Harold shoved his head inside Jack's van to assess Chase in the far back seat, legs stretched forward where the middle seat would have been. "You okay there, buddy?"

"Yes, sir."

"That's my man."

Claudia moved in. "Move back, old man. Let Rivers and Jack help him out."

Jack poked his head in next. "Need help lifting that leg?"

Chase shoved his crutches toward the van's sliding door and reversed the process of getting into the vehicle, which seemed twice as hard when applied to getting out. A little nudge here and a shove there shot pain up his spine. How he managed it without passing out, he didn't know. He should have taken the offered pain meds, but too many of his friends had gotten hooked and were now going through withdrawal.

Good thing Ashley and Jack took Bobby's truck back to the Hershams' for him, 'cause he wasn't likely to be driving anytime soon. Ashley still hadn't mentioned Lillia, Bobby's sister, and he wasn't about to bring up the sore subject.

He made his way up the cobblestone path and through the door, where he found Ashley holding a wiggling, delighted dog and pointing at a bed. She'd given him her mom's old room, and the haunted look in her expression gave him pause. He understood how old memories could still cause pain, and he gestured toward the family room.

"I can sleep on the couch."

"Harold and Claudia worked hard staging this room for you," she said, with a direct and revealing expression.

After being in the town for several weeks, he understood her message clearly. *Don't offend the natives.* He hopped over to the bed and sat on the edge, lifting his leg to the mattress. He stared at what appeared like half the population of Elkridge and worked to find something to say. When he finally opened his mouth, a commotion at the door caused everyone to turn.

"Sorry I'm late." Jenna came through the door. "Maggie says hello. She made everyone sandwiches. They're in the kitchen."

"Any roast beef?" Jack asked.

Jenna reached up and patted the scruffy man's cheek. "Made 'specially for you, Mad Jack."

The announcement of food emptied the room with the exception of Jenna and Ashley. The two women stood guard, one on either side of the bed. When he lay back, both women reached for the pillow. All three laughed, and Jenna relinquished her hold.

"I'm going to make sure everyone's fed and leave you in peace. Want something to eat?"

"Naw, we're fine." Ashley laid her hand on Chase's shoulder.

When the door clicked closed behind Jenna, Ashley slowly sank onto the mattress. He was troubled by the black circles under her eyes and the pale version of her normally vibrant skin.

He reached out and covered her fingers. "You should eat something."

"I already did. Do you want something? Water? A pain pill?"

He patted the edge of the bed. "Having you here is all I need."

Ashley stretched out beside him, careful to avoid his ribs. Her head heavy on his shoulder, she let out a long, deep sigh.

He kissed the top of her head. "I can't believe half the town is here."

A short burst of air from her nose landed

on his neck. "They like you and care about you. You couldn't keep them away if you wanted to."

"They care about you, too."

"I've come to realize that. I'm thankful Maggie's letting me pay her for living in one of her rental cabins. At least now I have a place to stay for the short term."

He drew a circle on her shoulder. "Sounds like you've been thinking again."

"Guess I have. Elkridge is my home, and where I belong. I didn't understand the essence of home before. I may have to leave for a little while to find a job, but I'll always come back here."

A twist of regret formed in his chest. "So coming with me is off the table?"

"Yeah. Sorry. I want to help people, but being a nurse isn't for me. I'll leave the life and death bit to others—if that makes any sense."

"Yeah, I get it. I like working with my hands, but for something other than digging trenches."

Ashley released a sigh. "My entire days were filled with washing and cleaning and cooking and medicating until I could barely move. Since I don't have those things filling up my day, I feel anxious. Like I need to be doing something. But after I've finished packing and moving, I'm not sure what it will be."

"That perfectly describes how I feel about the military. If I get out, what would I do? My whole adult life I've been trained to do one thing, defend this country with my mind and body. I don't know anything else. And I didn't like school the first time around, so the idea of going back for more makes me cringe."

Ashley pushed to her elbow, scanning his face. "You don't have to go back to school, and deep down, I think you know what you want to do. You fixed the shop's staircase and repaired Maggie's benches outside the café. Harold's been mighty glad to have the help at the store."

"You found out about me helping Harold, huh?"

"When that out-of-town drunk smashed Jack's barstools, he was very glad you could glue them back together."

Jack had gained Chase's respect that day. The guy took down a drunk the size of a tank, but not before the oversized idiot had decided to smash a few things and taken a couple of swings at locals.

"All that's little stuff."

"All that little stuff adds up and creates a big pile of work. Work that people need help with and are willing to pay for."

"Then we'd both be in the same place. No place to live. Starting a business. Trying to heal a broken leg. With this leg, I won't be fixing things for quite a while. Besides, the government dictates the next several months."

Disappointment over not being able to convince her to come with him sank in. He didn't need her help with rehabilitation—the military would help—but he'd come to rely on Ashley, her unending devotion, her giving nature, and her hundred-degree temper.

"I might take you up on the offer of food and a pain pill."

"You got it." Ashley rolled from the bed. "The doctor said you could take up to two."

"One will be fine."

A knock at the door drew their attention. Sheriff Joe's head appeared through the crack in the door. "I was hoping to get a quick word with Chase."

"Great timing. Another fifteen minutes, and one of those pain pills would have knocked me loopy." Chase tried to shift higher in the bed, but ceased all movement when excruciating pain called a halt to his efforts.

Joe walked closer to the end of the bed while Ashley left the room. Chase loved the sexy swing of her hips, and he got a full view while she disappeared through the doorway. "What can I do for you, Sheriff?"

"I came to check on you and to confirm some information. Rivers said you were mumbling about hearing automatic fire up on the ridge."

Uneasiness made his chest tighten. "The thing is, Sheriff, I've been in a combat zone for a while. I've seen some horrific things, if you know what I mean. And lately I've been having flashbacks. They seem so real. Post-trauma type stuff." Chase clutched the sheets, bunching them in his hand. "At the time, I could have sworn I heard machine gun fire, but the truth is, I can't be sure."

Admitting his failing out loud triggered both shame and guilt, along with a taste of relief and freedom. He took a long, deep, unrestrained breath.

Sheriff Joe took a step closer to the head of the bed and reached inside his coat to an inner pocket. He extended his arm, holding an evidence bag containing a dozen or so metal shell casings along with yellow disposable ear plugs. "Found these up on the ridge about three hundred yards from your snowmobile tracks. Rivers also found a couple of bullets lodged in some pine trees.

Based on the evidence, I'm thinking you hitting that rock might have saved your life."

Chase locked onto the bag in the sheriff's hand. "You got a problem on your hands."

"S'pose so." The sheriff gave him a direct and pointed stare. "I'd appreciate if you'd keep this conversation between us. I don't want to scare the townsfolk or get them all riled up."

Chase extended a hand to the man. "You have my word."

The sheriff gripped and then released his hand, then shoved the bag back inside his jacket. "Take care of yourself, Gunny." He gave Chase a nod and left.

Ashley passed the sheriff on his way out of the room. "What did he want?"

"It was a friendly visit to check on me," he said, not wanting to stir her fears.

He'd protect her. Any way he could.

His body reacted. He couldn't help needing her.

Every time he woke up in the hospital, she'd been there, watching his back, silently supporting him. She didn't fuss or add a burden. The constant longing to touch her filled his lungs and pushed the air aside. His hands clenched, wanting to feel the strands of her hair falling through his fingers, or the soft curves of her body brush against his.

He had to go back, but how could he leave her behind?

He reached out, and her fingers so perfectly folded into his that he pulled her hand to his lips. And just like that, his body eased. Bobby's voice echoed in the far back reaches of his mind. *But you love her. Come on, admit it.*

Chase's response reverberated. *Yeah, I love her. But she doesn't need me—I need her.*

CHAPTER TWENTY-FOUR

The Colorado night had a nip in the air. She craved a moonlight walk, but with the fresh snow, Chase couldn't have made it to the end of the driveway even if he'd tried. New Year's Eve was supposed to be romantic, filled with parties, and drinks, and kisses at midnight. But somehow she didn't feel like celebrating.

He was leaving tomorrow.

Chase had received word from his administration office. He'd been ordered to Buckley Air Force Base, where he'd take a medevac repositioning flight to Walter Reed for his continued therapy.

The last two days had been magical. The love fairy must have been dropping extra dust because Ashley had fallen completely in love, hard and fast, faster than her more conservative values had time to translate into modern-day terms. She'd gotten the feeling Chase understood time was short because he didn't want to sleep.

Adjusting her position, she cringed when her elbow landed wrong on his ribs, but he held tight, refusing to let go. She wished the night would last forever so she wouldn't have to say good-bye in the morning.

Chase reclined on the overstuffed leather couch. The twinkle of the white Christmas lights she'd hung on the mantel, the music playing in the background, and the soft glow of the fire gave the room a cozy feel. In his arms, she tried forcing impending reality to fade away.

"What are you thinking?" His breath

caressed the skin below her ear, sending tingles to her toes.

"Do you think anyone's ever figured out how to make time stop?"

He chuckled. "Don't know, but stopping time would be pretty cool."

She liked the playful tone of his voice, and lifted her head from his shoulder to be sure of his mood. Her brow lifted in question. "What would you do with that time?"

His hand lowered, cupping her bottom, and pulled, rubbing her against his growing need. His need matched hers, and she wished he wasn't enveloped in head-to-toe bandages. She'd been about to make the suggestion they turn in early when an agitated voice stalled her thoughts.

"Is there a reason you have your hand on my daughter's ass?"

Ashley rolled so fast she landed on the floor. Chase grabbed his leg, gasping.

"Dad?"

Chase's head snapped toward her Dad

who stood, hands on hips, on the living room landing. The light from the kitchen framed his body, sharpening his outline.

Her dad's disposition hadn't changed. "I asked you a question, Marine."

Marine? Her dad knew Chase was military? Odd. Then again, military could always spot military in a weird, spy-sense kind of way.

"Yes, sir," Chase responded.

"And that would be?"

"I love your daughter, sir."

Ashley's jaw dropped and her head snapped back. "That's just great. My dad shows up, and in less than three seconds you tell him what you've never told me? Marines. Can't communicate worth a damn, but you end up loving them anyway. I'm so screwed."

"Ashley." Her dad's menacing tone meant her word choice was inappropriate.

"Here we go." She rolled her eyes. "No double standards. You haven't been here. You don't get to judge me anymore. That privilege was forfeited a long time ago."

"Ashley, I'd like to have a discussion with you in the kitchen. Please."

If her dad hadn't stumbled over the word *please*, she might have refused. She hadn't known that particular phonic existed in his vocabulary, and could easily imagine how difficult it had been to get it past his lips.

She tilted her head back and studied his steel-rod posture. He looked stunning in his pressed uniform. His medals and ribbons were precisely positioned and displayed in a rainbow of colors. But his face was so sad.

She wanted to turn back the clock to a time she once stood on her tippy-toes in patent leather shoes, cupped his face, and told him she would get him well and make the boogeyman go away. But those times were in the past. Anger and resentment had worn away her store of compassion.

"Fine." She pushed from the floor. "Will you be all right?" she asked Chase.

"Not going anywhere."

A nauseous tension filled her as she walked to the kitchen. Why was her dad here? What did he want? Either way, he wouldn't stay. The earlier she found out what he expected from her, the sooner he'd leave.

She ambled to the kitchen island, biding her time, then turned and crossed her arms. "Why are you here?"

His shoulders lifted in a simple yet defeated shrug. "This is my home. Or at least it was."

The last sentence created an understatement. "Funny you say that because you haven't lived in it much, and the bank's about to repo it."

"I didn't come here to fight with you, Ashley."

"No? Then why?"

"I wanted to see you." The sharp edge of his tone had softened. "To make sure you're okay. To ask your forgiveness."

Her mouth fell open again. Her mind was so busy processing what he said, she couldn't find muscles to close the gaping hole. Her dad had aged. Peppery gray hair covered both sides of his head, and the kitchen light shone off the top. More than the deep crevices etched across his face, she saw a man whose heart had been shattered. She'd read his letters. He'd lost the love of his life, and only sorrow remained.

"I read the letters, Dad. For most of my life, I was convinced you didn't come home because you didn't want me."

"Ash." He took a step, then stopped when she waved him off. The emotions in his eyes kept coming after her, pummeling her defenses.

"I get it now. You should know there's nothing to forgive. Your letters helped me understand, but I wish you and Mom would have talked to me. I made some assumptions. Wrong assumptions. But I've corrected them now."

A flicker of relief crossed his face. "Your mother made me promise not to swoop in and help, but I can't help it. I love you. You're all I have left."

He held out his large, callused hand. She

reached out, accepting his as a peace offering, unwilling to allow the past to dictate the future.

"Dance with me, Ashtray?"

"You don't like this music."

"We can make our type of music, as long as you're willing to dance with me." His voice still had that gruff tone, but his intentions blasted away at the stone hardening her heart.

"Do I still get to stand on your toes?"

A small, glistening ray of hope poked through the layer of formality on his face, and his shoulders eased. It had been a long time since she'd seen the softer side of her daddy, and the expression filled her with wonder. "Why are you here? I mean…"

"My Ashtray, always so curious."

Her heart squeezed. She'd waited so long. She leaned in and rested her cheek on his pressed pocket while he moved to a beat he created. They circled around and around, and she listed to the beat of his heart, waiting like she always had.

"Why are you wearing a formal uniform?"

"When you called, I got the impression you needed me. Arranging my schedule and flights home took several days, but I came as soon as I could, which happened to be straight from an important meeting."

She arched back in his arms. "But I didn't call."

He reached into his pocket and pulled out his cell phone. His thumb moved over the pad in a practiced manner, then he turned the phone.

Her distant voice floated out of the speaker. "Oh, Daddy. What am I supposed to do now? I'm so lost."

She dropped her head to his solid chest.

Her dad cleared his throat. "Answer a question for me." Ashley tilted her chin up to listen. "What are your plans? I need to figure out what to do with this house."

Her stomach clenched into a giant bundle of disappointment. *Of course.* He wasn't here for her. He'd come to close the house. Her head fell forward, and she worked to shove the tender childhood memories she'd been reliving back into the discarded toy box where they belonged. He hadn't come home to her. She stepped out of his arms.

"Wait." His voice implored in the way a father asked, not a Marine. "Maybe I didn't ask the right question. If you could map out your future, what would it look like?"

Ashley's ire softened. "What difference does it make? Since the house is being foreclosed and I haven't been able to work for the past three years, my choices are limited. I need to get a job, and I have student loans to pay."

"We can discuss your loans later. You might decide to go back to school."

"How do you know I didn't graduate?"

"I'm your dad. It's my job to know." His arms released from around her back. "Don't tell me what you think I want to hear. Tell me what's in your heart."

If he'd asked her the question a month ago, she might not have been able to answer him, she'd been so fixated on making it to a temporary destination. So many things had changed recently. She knew at least one thing for sure. Elkridge was her home.

"Mom wanted me to be more like you. Get a degree. Travel the world. Take risks. Experience new things. She didn't want me to stay here—like she did—waiting. It's weird how your lives were polar opposites. I land somewhere in the middle. I like to travel. In fact, I have a whole list of places I'd like to see, but Elkridge is my home. No matter where I go, I'll always come back here. I never thought we'd lose this house. I assumed I'd always have a place to call home."

Unable to stand the tension, she moved to the sink and started putting dishes in the dishwasher and wiping down the counter. Her father let her work while he settled silently onto a stool at the kitchen island. His head lowered in contemplation.

Concern grew to a boiling point, and she couldn't stand it anymore. "Why didn't you help us?"

His pain-filled eyes looked at her. "Your mother…well, you see, your mother…"

"Just say it, Dad."

Her dad propped an elbow on his knee and rotated toward her. "Your mother refused my help, and she made me promise not to help you after she was gone. She wanted you to learn what it was like to be on your own—to learn how to support yourself. I didn't question her, ever, when it came to raising you, Ashley. I didn't feel I had a right. But if you want the house, it's yours. I've paid the back mortgage payments to stop the foreclosure proceedings, and I've paid the electric, water, and telephone bills."

Really? "Why are you telling me this now? Why couldn't you have said something before I sold or packed everything?"

"You did a damn fine job figuring out how to execute your plans, get your life on track. But after I got your call, I just couldn't continue to let you struggle. I haven't been much of a father. I've wanted to come home. No, I want to come home, to help, but I won't if it's too much, too soon. I know I have a lot to make up for. Is it too late for us?"

Finally. The truth. She moved around the counter to stand by his side. "Dad, how can you not know? You're my hero. My Superman. The person who made the world safe for me to sleep at night. I love you. In the midst of all my anger, I somehow forgot it. I won't forget again. But you have to know, some days I didn't like you. In fact, I hated you for a long time. I needed you, and you weren't there. That kind of trust is going to take time to rebuild."

His head was bowed and his fist clenched. He said nothing. When he looked up, his jaw pulsed, but the rest of his features remained stoic. Her papa-soldier had a heart somewhere in his broad, steely chest, and maybe she'd made a little dent, the beginning of a crevice he'd let her carve out for herself.

"Is everything all right?" Chase stood in the doorway, swaying on his crutches, his expression watchful, ready to defend her if needed.

Her dad stiffened, but Ashley placed her hand on top of her father's fist. "Dad, I'd like to introduce Gunnery Sergeant Marine Chase Daniels of the Second Battalion. He's recently returned stateside."

Her father stood, and Chase tried to salute, but shifting his weight, balancing, and saluting didn't work so well.

"At ease, son." Her father moved several steps closer. "I heard you busted up my snowmobile pretty bad."

Chase's yellowing, bruised face turned a pasty white. "If you're here to bust my balls, sir, have at it. I can take it."

Ashley physically placed herself between the two men. They were glaring at each other, but her father's face cracked first, and he threw his head back. The wheezing, half-gasping sound caught her off guard, and she wondered if he might be having a stroke until he lowered his head with a semi-circle grin. The expression looked so odd, she had to look twice.

He wrapped a guiding arm around her shoulders. "Equipment is expendable. A Marine is not." The remaining tightness in his lips evaporated. "From what I hear, you're lucky to be alive, and I'm damn glad to see you're healing."

Ashley shifted to see his face. "Have you been spying on me?"

"No. Gathering intelligence, but never spying."

So he really did care. A warm, hot-chocolate comfort filled her belly. "Who's your source?" She crossed her arms over her chest.

"Top-secret and classified, young lady." His lips tightened in a will-not-tell type of way. "I might not have been here. Sometimes I've been on the other side of the globe, but where you're concerned, I've never, ever, been that far away. You only needed to call and I would have moved armies to get home. In fact, I did this past week."

She placed her hand on Chase's arm for support. "Will you be here long, Dad?"

"For as long as you need me."

"So the bank won't be foreclosing on the house?"

"Stay or sell, your choice."

Ashley released a pent-up breath. "Then you better figure on staying in this house for a good, long time, because I've only now discovered you have a sense of humor I knew nothing about."

Her father's eyebrow quirked into an arc. "Is that right?"

"Yep. And you should meet your granddog. His name's Lucky." Hearing his name mentioned, the mutt appeared at the back sliding glass door, ready to be let in.

Her dad's eyebrows arched in that fatherly way. "Looks like you haven't broken the habit of bringing strays home."

Her protective gazed traveled to Chase. "Yeah, but this time, there's no one to tell me to get rid of them."

"The way you're looking at that young

man reminds me of the way your mother looked at me once upon a time. I think maybe I should shower and call it an early night. It's been a tough day. I assume there's still a bed upstairs I can use."

"I didn't sell Mom's bed in the master suite."

Her dad moved to the hall, but before he started up the stairs, he paused. "Ashley?"

"Yes, Dad?"

"I know I have no right to say this, but thank you. Thank you for being the kind of daughter who makes a father proud."

She wanted to respond, but an emotional wad got stuck in her throat and she could only nod in acknowledgment, hoping he didn't notice she was also blinking hard against a swell of tears.

After he disappeared, Chase shifted and wrapped a protective arm around her shoulder. "Forgiving him must have been tough."

Ashley ran a finger under her damp eyelashes. "You have no idea."

CHAPTER TWENTY-FIVE

*D*riving through the gates of the Air Force base, Ashley's stomach tightened, a pending dread making her nauseous. During the night, she'd recommitted to her decision to wait one year for Chase. The decision hadn't been easy, but every cell in her body believed it was the right one.

The truck doors opened. She and her dad managed to get Chase out of the truck and standing. Chase had refused the wheelchair, preferring crutches. He'd be sorry. He'd have to manage the length of an airstrip to get to his military hop, but knowing the stubborn-ass Marine, he wouldn't complain, just grit his teeth and manage the pain.

She waited while Chase was checked in. Her dad oversaw the whole operation to ensure Chase received the care he needed. After all, being a general, he was allowed a few perks.

The stopwatch was counting down, with only a few minutes left.

"Chase, I need to talk to you." A bit of pride filled Ashley's heart for keeping her tone level, without a hint of her jittery panic.

He appeared just as miserable. He shrugged on his backpack and moved away to a private corner.

The nerves in her entire body went on high alert. "I want you to know I've made a decision."

His lips tightened as if bracing for bad news. He lifted a loose strand of her hair and secured it behind her ear. "It's going to be okay."

"I know. That's why I wanted to tell you I'll be here waiting."

His shoulders dropped several centimeters. "Waiting?"

"Yep, waiting. All these years, I believed my mom was insane for hanging out, waiting for a guy, but I understand now. I'm going to live my life. Go back to school. Start a support care business. And I will be here, waiting. You have one year, so you'd better figure things out. I love you. Simple as that. I can't imagine loving anyone else as much as I love you."

He swayed on his crutches, his mouth opening and closing, but no sound emerged.

"Aren't you going to say anything?" Her impatience came out as a shrill whine.

The emotion started slowly, then gained momentum, spreading across his face, finally bursting into an enormous grin. "I'm glad you've changed your mind because I've made a decision as well. Your dad and I had a discussion about my future. And he likes my plan."

"Does your plan include me?"

"As a matter of fact, it does. I asked your dad if he would allow me to ask you to marry me."

Her breath caught and her heart pounded in her ears. "You asked my dad before asking me?"

"Since you don't like Marines, I thought I'd wait until I got out, but I wanted to be sure when the time comes there wouldn't be any more barriers between us."

"Wait, you're getting out?"

"That's part two of the plan. Your dad told me if you agree to a ring on your finger, then he'd loan me tools and enough money to start a handyman business."

Her dad stood off to the side, talking to a few officers who'd guessed they had a top-ranking officer in their midst. He must have felt her looking at him because he met her gaze, his approval clearly written on his face. He'd mentioned something about making up for lost time to her over a piece of toast and orange juice, but she hadn't been quite sure what he'd meant.

"Well, then, get your face down here so I can kiss your lips silly and not hurt you."

Her wish was his command because his lips captured hers in the gentlest, most promising kiss they'd ever exchanged. She sighed and pressed in, sliding her hand lightly down his face.

"I only ask that you communicate. Happy. Sad. Frustrated. Whatever. You're not alone. I want you to know I'm here. You need to talk to someone about your visions and nightmares."

"I will."

Someone in uniform called the flight, and a handful of soldiers picked up their belongings and headed for the plane waiting for them on the tarmac.

Chase hopped over to the group of men to shake her father's hand. Before her dad clasped Chase's, he looked at her for permission. This powerful, resilient man wanted her approval as much as she wanted his. The two women in his life had always guided him in matters of the heart. She hadn't understood that nuance until the past twenty-four hours. Feeling cherished, she also felt a healing had begun. It was even possible she might be able to superglue her heart back together after all.

Chase took a couple of swinging strides and halted inches away. "I will be back. You have my word. I left you something on the back seat of the truck."

With no more time left, he hobbled away. She lifted her chin and plastered a smile on her face in case he turned back. He would see no tears. He would only see a strong, determined woman who'd be waiting for him when he decided to return.

"You did good," her dad said when he came to stand beside her.

She folded her fingers around his stiff hand. She waited...one, two, three, four... and then his fingers slowly enclosed hers, and another ice fragment splintered off of her heart. She tilted her head back. "Let's go home."

They walked out into the warm afternoon sun. The sound from the jet vibrated the air before she caught sight of the massive plane. The burden of finally making a decision lifted from her shoulders.

"I feel like celebrating." She tugged on her dad's arm. "How about a big, juicy hamburger and fries?"

"What, no strawberry shake?"

"If I'm going to fit into Mom's wedding dress, I think we'd better share one."

He paused. She could see he had trouble swallowing, and then he opened the truck door for her. "You'll make the prettiest bride ever. Well, I mean, after your mom, of course."

Ashley squeezed his hand, then became distracted. Sure enough, on the back seat, wrapped in brown paper, sat a package and card.

She dislodged the card from the

envelope. *Ashley, I wanted to give you a part of me to keep until I return.*

She tore open the brown paper gift wrap to find a worn leather binder. His journal. She opened the book to find pages and pages of poems and introspection written over the years. The sting behind her eyes she'd felt most of the day overwhelmed her stubbornness and tears began to fall.

"That must be a pretty darn good book if it's making you cry."

"It's not a simply a book. It's Chase's heart. Like your letters to Mom. He gave me a direct line into his soul."

Her dad gave her shoulder a squeeze. "How did you grow up so fast and get so smart?"

She leaned her head against his strong, sturdy chest. "You forget, Marine. I'm your daughter."

EPILOGUE

The July heat bit down like a mean bulldog and wouldn't let go. She removed the lemonade pitcher from the refrigerator and placed it on a silver platter lined with an intricate, hand-stitched doily before adding glasses and Jenna's sugar cookies to the tray. With her elbow, she slid the patio door open, and Lucky ran out in front of her.

"Break time," she called.

Her dad looked up with two nails sticking out of his mouth, giving him a rather vampire-ish appearance. He rubbed his forehead and gave her the finger—the index finger—meaning he'd be available shortly. Lucky trotted back around the corner with Chase following on his heels.

Sweat glistened on his body and he looked rather sweet, like the sugar cookie she'd just eaten. He walked to the waterspout, filled a plastic bucket, and dumped it over his head and shoulders. The drops of water sparkled off his skin, and her jaw froze in mid-crunch.

"You keep standing there with your jaw open and you're liable to get flies in your mouth," her dad said before collapsing on the deck chair in the shade.

Ashley stuck her sugarcoated tongue out at him.

He pointed toward Chase. "He's a hard worker."

"Did you expect anything less?"

Chase took his time, but made his way up the three porch steps. "Did you look over the financials I put on your desk?"

Her dad raised his eyebrows with a faint

grimace. "I told you, I'm retired. You're the one who wants to run a handyman business, so that's your job."

"Since you put up the capital for my fix-it business, I figured you might want to know what I was up to."

"I know what a good business looks like. Don't need to be doing an inspection every five minutes." He leaned forward and snatched a cookie from the tray. "Never ate sweets until I came home."

Ashley's arms encompassed Chase's waist and gave him a squeeze. "All grandbabies like grandpas with pudgy bellies."

The priceless look on her father's face made them both laugh. Ashley leaned over, topped a glass full of lemonade, and handed it to him.

"I keep telling you I'm too young to be a grandfather," he grumbled, but the smile on his face said different.

She put a protective hand over her belly. "Fido's—I mean, Jimmy's wife Katie is pregnant, too."

"Wasn't that the wedding you attended only a few weeks ago?" Her dad's old-fashioned values added a disapproving scowl.

"Yep," Chase said. "What can I say? Marines are efficient."

Her dad rolled his eyes and scoffed. "Don't you have some repairs to do or something?"

Chase smiled and leaned down to whisper in her ear, "I want to show you what I'm working on," he whispered.

She followed him around the corner by the shed and took two steps, then squealed when he pulled her into his arms. He stifled the sound with his lips. His salty flavor blended with her sweet cookie to make a perfect combination. He pinned her back against the wall and deepened the kiss. When he lifted his head, she sucked on his bottom lip, reluctant to let him go.

"You taste awesome." He dove back in for another nibble on her lip.

She gave him a gentle push. "You were going to show me something."

He leaned his left arm against the wall behind her head while his right hand dug into his pocket, pulling out a worn, yellowing piece of paper. She accepted the little square and unfolded it, scanning the rhyming lines.

"You wrote me a poem."

He tapped the paper. "I just now found it tucked away in my stuff. I wrote it the night after we found Lucky. It's not Pulitzer or anything, but I thought I'd share."

The love we share is bright.
It grows both day and night.
Do you believe in fate?
I believe you're my forever mate.
I see you in my dreams.

I remember snow in your hair.
And skin of porcelain so fair.
The way you felt in my arms.

Shielding you from harm.
I see you in my dreams.

Your love warms me when cold.
A refreshing touch to my soul.
You're the reason my heart beats.
The smile I hold when we meet.
I see you in my dreams.

It's time to close my eyes in sleep.
Come to me, my soul you keep.
Kiss my lips, tender my sweet.
Remove the ache from my heart.
I see you in my dreams.

SHE READ THE WORDS, the sentiment. "You wrote this after we found Lucky. But you didn't know me. We'd just met."

"I think I fell in love with you the day I walked into the antique store. I might have been too stubborn to recognize it for what it was then, and I might not say it enough, but I love you, Mrs. Daniels."

Their July 4th wedding had been perfect. Quiet, small, among the aspen trees, celebrating with family and friends. Her mother's wedding dress fit, and even her hardened dad had shed a tear.

She couldn't have been happier. "I love you too."

"But remember, I loved you first."

Ashley pushed at his chest. "But I love you more, Mr. Daniels."

"Prove it."

She drew his hand down and placed it on her stomach, her hand over his, then lifted her gaze to his.

"I don't have to. Our love grows inside me each and every day."

I'm so glad you could join Ashley and Chase on their journey to their happily

ever after.

THOSE OF YOU who have read my books or been part of my newsletter have heard my explanation for why Authors never see their Star Ratings requested by Amazon, so thank you for allowing me to share the information once again.

When Amazon asks a reader to "Rate this book" on their Kindle, Amazon is the only one to see these ratings.

I'm left clueless about how you feel about this book. Your input matters.

Book reviews help me decide what kind of books I write. Plus, the more people who leave a review, the more likely Amazon is to move a book up in the rankings? Written reviews help other readers find and love a series.

Please continue to rate the book on your Kindle or reader as this helps Amazon, but take an extra moment to pop over to the review section and leave a few words!

Seriously, a few words like, "great story," is enough.

If you have not read my Elkridge Series or the Lonely Ridge Collection, and have no idea why authors keep asking you as a reader to take a few minutes to leave even a couple of word reviews, here's the break down of how reviews work in this crazy business.

Reviews (not ratings) help authors qualify for advertising opportunities. Without triple digit reviews, an author may miss out on these valuable opportunities. And with only a "star rating" the author has little chance of participating in specific promotions, which means authors continue to struggle, and many talented writers give up writing altogether.

Readers aren't the only ones who use reviews to help make purchasing decisions. Producers and directors use your reviews when looking for new projects.

This is why I'm asking for your help.

A few kind words make such a massive difference to me. Your words give me the encouragement I need to continue writing because honestly, I write my books for you, and I'd like to keep delivering the types of stories you want to read.

And, yes, every book in a series needs reviews, not just the first book. Even if a book has been out for awhile, a fresh review can breathe new life into a book.

So, please take a few minutes to leave a short review. Even a couple of words will brighten my day.

Lastly. Thank you for reading this book. I hope to see you again soon. Cheers!

I wish you all the best the day offers, and I hope you enjoy reading the next book in the Elkridge Series.

DEDICATION

For Jen, George, and Jeannine for your sacrifice, and for being brave enough to wait and watch your loved ones' essence drift into the silence.

AUTHOR NOTES

Dear Readers,

For several years, I worked in a health care system. I witnessed doctors, nurses, and technicians extend empathy and care to virtual strangers. Health care professionals are generally made of steel, but there are times, in the quietness, when the tears can no longer be dammed.

My brother worked at the Nations Naval Medical Center (NNMC) in Bethesda, Maryland. As a nurse, he worked with burn victims, some burned over eighty-percent of their bodies. Armed with a great sense of humor, he helped his patients manage the excruciating pain and mental trauma of forever being changed. At night, he found solace in the hospital's nursery. For him, the babies reminded him that life was a never-ending cycle, that with death, there comes life.

Now, every time I see a person in scrubs in the coffee shop or grocery line, I offer them thanks for doing an emotionally hard and sometimes thankless job.

I hope you enjoyed Ashley's and Chase's journey as they struggle to reconcile that life is a never-ending cycle.

~Lyz

More Books By
Lyz Kelley

SILVER FOX RESORT
SILVER SPOON
SILVER DOLLAR
SILVER BELLS

SECRETS
BILLIONAIRE'S SECRET
DOCTOR'S SECRET

THE ELKRIDGE SERIES
BLINDED
ABANDONED
ORPHANED
RESCUED
UNMISTAKEN
ATONEMENT
BITTERSWEET

ACKNOWLEDGMENTS

FOR ABANDONED

To make this story as strong and rewarding as possible, I did a vast amount of research, and asked my hospital colleagues for advice.

While I visited the nursing home every day to see my great-grandmother, I came to realize those brief visits were nothing like spending the entire day being a sole caregiver to a loved one. My sincere thanks goes to Jeannine and the hospice care workers interviewed for this book. To Sue and Lori, my gracious beta readers, who were brave enough to provide constructive suggestions for improvement. To Aimee, who pushed me to dig deeper. To Faith Freewoman, my amazing editor, who demanded I put the emotion on the page and worked tirelessly to make the best book possible. For Shelby Reed and Carol Agnew who crossed every T and dotted every I.

Also, to Fred Doucette, the author of, *Better Off Dead,* a book about post-traumatic stress disorder (PTSD), who allowed me to ask some tough questions. Thank you.

And to my husband, who didn't ask why I was crying or so exhausted when I stopped writing to eat the dinners he prepared.

You all have my sincere gratitude.

~Lyz

THANK YOU FOR READING:
ABANDONED

Award-winning author Lyz Kelley mixes a little bit of heart, healing, humanity, happiness, honor, hope, and honor in all her books that are written especially for you.

She's is a total disaster in the kitchen, a compulsive neat freak, a tea snob, and adores writing about and falling in love with everyday heroes.

Please also consider leaving a review on Amazon Goodreads and/or BookBub. Reviews help readers find new books to read, and authors find their footing.

You can also find Lyz on Facebook and Instagram for news, contests, giveaways, and more exciting stuff!

Cover Art by Lyz Kelley

❋ Created with Vellum